I0603327

TIME TOURIST OUTFITTERS, LTD.

Book One in Toronto Time Agents

C. N. Jackson

Green Dragon Publishing

Published 2022
First Edition published 2019.
Second edition 2022.

Publisher: Green Dragon Publishing
Beacon Falls, CT
www.GreenDragonArtist.com

Dedication

For those that overcome personal disasters to find joy in the little beauties in life, and push above and beyond the everyday to strife for the fantastic.

Acknowledgments

As always, I want to thank my husband, Jason, for all his support. I also want to thank my critique group and my beta readers, especially Ian Morris, Mattea Orr, and Anna Hoyler, for all their help.

Pronunciation Guide and Glossary

People

Fionnuala – Fin-OO-lah
Gizos Igasho - GEE-zoes ee-GASH-oh
Ibn Khalutta – Ib-en ka-LOO-tah
Konaté – koe-NAH-tay
Malinké – mah-LEEN-kay
Mayyada Nouri – mah-YAH-dah NOO-ree
Mekwi – MECH-wee
Mi'kmaw – MICK-maw
Nokemes Di'dias – noe-KOE-mis DEE-dee-as
Pa'nawampske'wiak – pah-NAW-wampsk-eh-WEE-ahk
Quiripi – kee-REE-pee
Rögnvaldr – rog-ne-VALL-der
Skraelings – SKRAY-lings (strangers/supernatural beings)
Tema'kwe – the-MAH-quay
Widad Farooq – wee-DAD fah-ROOK
Wôbigo – WOE-bee-go
Wolastoqiyik – wo-LAST-i-kee-yuke
Wula'mbes – woo-LAH-mbeys
Xanthippe – zan-THEEP

Places

Birgisherað – (beer-GEE-share-athe) Birsay
K'taden – (keh-TAH-din) Mount Katahdin
Pana'wapskik – (pen-a-WOP-ah-skeek) Penobscot
Tomboctou - Timbuktu

Other

Aglebe'mu – (ag-LEM-beh-moo) A monster frog in native legend
As-salāmu ʿalaykunna – (ays-SAY-lam-oo ayl-lay-KOO-nah) Peace
be upon you

Beda'gwigan –(bed-a-KWEE-ken) A large native living structure
Egusi – (eg-goo-see) -- seeds of certain plants
Gæðingar – (GAY-thing-ar) A minor lord
Goði – (GO-thee) A minor lord
Kelewele – (KELL-ee-WELL-ee) fried plantain dish
Kʷsiwa'mbe – (KH-see-WAM-bay) a 'pure man,' an honorary title
Mandé – (man-DAY) A culture in western Africa
Oware – (oh-WAR-ay) an ancient game, now commonly known as Mancala
Pesida'men – (pes-ee-DAH-men) raccoon fat
Pestomuhkati – (PES-teh-moo-KAH-tee) A group of the Wabanaki, the
Passamaquoddy
Thjorsá – (THYOR-sah) Thurso, a town in what is now
northern Scotland
Vǫlva – (VOLE-va) a prophetess
Wa ʿalayka s-salā – (way ayl-AYK-yas sal-AH) And peace
be upon you, too
Wi'gwom – (WI-IG-wam) a small native living structure

Part I
Chapter One

Mattea's voice cut through my afternoon fog. "Hey Wilda! We got a VIP coming in, stat!"

Fan-fricken-tastic. Just what I needed today. After spilling my coffee that morning on the streetcar and ripping my skirt in a flurry of cruel irony, now I had to kit out some over-privileged, tea-sipping time scion. I could take odds she needs full courtier Elizabethan garb. Or Middle Kingdom Egyptian noble.

Throughout my three decades at the Toronto office of Time Tourist Outfitters, Ltd., my motto has been: Things can always get worse. My experience had yet to prove me wrong.

I heard the VIP in question long before I saw her. Her shrill voice cut through the thin clapboard walls like a hot knife through truffle butter. She harangued the receptionist, demanding to see the manager immediately, if not sooner. I took a drink of my coffee, trusting Tarren to handle the cow with aplomb.

Tarren's stolid resistance to her hidden charms and obvious class didn't please the VIP. I took one more sip of coffee. My essential elixir would be too cold to drink soon. I continued ripping the seam on the garb I had been tailoring—an embroidered chemise for a sixteenth century

French merchant woman—glanced at Mattea, my research assistant, and sighed. She responded by sticking out her tongue and blowing a raspberry.

The noise had no chance of being overheard above the relentless complaints from reception. I chugged the last of my coffee and stood, placing my project carefully on the 'in progress' section of my cluttered worktable. Seven other projects lay in wait, a backlog I feared I'd never clear.

Especially when people like Lady Prissy-Pants took inordinate amounts of my precious time.

Mattea waggled her eyebrows, to which I rolled my eyes. This problem wouldn't go away on its own, and to leave Tarren to deal with it any longer would be cruel.

With a final glance down the long, narrow, cluttered workshop, filled with finished travelling garb from all eras and walks of life, I put my hand on the door. The brass knob had been a delightful gift from a grateful customer. I assumed my new client wouldn't be so kind. As I emerged, I nodded my head in a polite greeting. "And how may I help you today?"

The woman, dressed in a modern tea gown festooned with ruffles in vivid shades of pink and purple, spun, her face a lovely shade of scarlet. The enormous purple feather in her hat, large enough to tickle an elephant, twitched as she spoke.

"Help me? Help me? You can start by sacking your servant here. She refused to call you immediately, an affront to my rank! Do I need to remind you who I am?"

Tarren's nose wrinkled, and the reason hit me hard enough to make me blink. The delightful aroma of overripe cheese, a mix between Limburger, petrol, and dirty socks, hit me. I coughed delicately. "Oh, I assure you, while your odour is ripe, I'd never call it rank."

She blinked several times with her perfectly painted mouth hanging open, apparently uncertain if she'd heard me correctly. Before she could process exactly how I'd insulted her, I smiled again. "Did you have a trip to plan, Miss…?"

"*Lady* Xanthippe Thundergrast-Hickenbotham, if you please. And no, you may not shorten the name or the title. I should care to embark upon a journey. I was informed *you* were the best outfitters around." Her disdainful survey of the small reception area, cluttered with costuming samples and gear from myriad times and places, belied her words. To be fair, the front office didn't look precisely luxurious. The fashion district of Toronto offered reasonable rates, but very small shops. The store frontage was barely twenty feet though it stretched back over three hundred. In addition, we had two stories above for storage and a basement for equipment.

"We are honoured to have someone with such an august reputation amongst the elite. May I enquire as to your desired destination and time? Have you already set your itinerary at the Agency next door?"

With pursed lips, she regarded me for a moment before she spoke. "I was told my costuming should be arranged first. My desired destination and time is the French Court of Louis the XV."

Of course. Visions of panniers and miles of ruffles swam in my head. I knew the answer, but I had to ask. "And of which class would you prefer to be perceived?"

She flipped out a fan—a fan! In the twenty-first century, for my ancestor's sake!—and cleared her throat with precise derision. "Noblewoman, of course! I could never be merchant class."

Months as an indentured servant would do her a world of good, but I nodded. At least she hadn't insisted upon being a queen. I wish she'd arranged her itinerary first, but she was here now. "Very well. I'll need to get your measurements first. Please follow me into the workroom."

When she swept in, her gaze lingered on several things. The art nouveau silver frame on my desk, the enormous, complex sewing machine in the back, and the worktable filled with half-complete projects. Finally, she sneered at the FormFitter 3000, which looked out of place next to the modern sewing machine. Instead of gleaming chrome and lasers, the FormFitter sported brass fittings and looked more like an ancient bathysphere.

"You wish me to enter *that*? Surely, this is some sort of poor jest. I am not amused."

"No, ma'am. This is our machine that measures all parts of your body. It takes a full foam mould so we can create your garb precisely to your body's size and conformation. This prevents hours with a measuring tape."

Her nose wrinkled, and she glanced around twice before placing a hand on the nautical-style wheel on the door.

Hesitating, she eyed the tarnished brass. "Is this abominable 'contraption' safe?"

"I assure you, the FormFitter 3000 is in the best repair. You must completely disrobe when you enter. There are cubicles for your clothing. Please ensure to seal the door to the cubicle before you press the button, indicating your readiness. Then you will need to place your feet on each of the plates where marked and grasp the brass handles on either side of the chamber."

Her eyebrows tried to find her scalp. "Disrobe? Is all that absolutely necessary?"

"Yes, ma'am. Even a small bit of clothing can cause an imprecise fit, which means chaffing and unsightly wear. Gathered wrinkles are most unfashionable."

"But I can wear my own underthings. I don't require you to create them."

I shook my head, hiding my smile. "We cannot allow modern clothing to travel back in time. It's against the temporal maxims."

With a delicate *hmph* and a curled lip, she stepped in sideways to accommodate her substantial backside and bosom. I closed and latched the door.

After at least twenty minutes, the green light blinked, indicating the occupant had disrobed. I pulled the brass lever on the outside and said, "Commence measurements."

Within two minutes, startled exclamations filtered from the FormFitter 3000, and I no longer hid my amusement. In fact, I turned to Mattea and Tarren, who had peeked into the workshop, and we shared our smile.

Tarren wrinkled her nose again. "Wow. I'm glad she took her perfume in with her. Why the Hell did she stink so bad?"

I shrugged. "I have no idea, but I have a feeling a raccoon would love her aroma. Or a dog would roll in it."

Finally, the angry imprecations faded, and the buzzer indicated the session had finished. Another twenty minutes passed before the knocking started. I pressed the blue button and when the door clicked ajar, I swung it open.

"That's it? That's all?"

"Indeed. The FormFitter 3000 is efficient. Now, for the timing of your trip…" I turned to the wall and pulled down the SmartGlass calendar board, sweeping my fingers across the surface until I found an open day. I double-tapped to expand the information. I'm certain she'd take the entire day, if not several. "I could have your first fitting…seven weeks from today. Will that suit?"

"Seven weeks? It will most certainly not suit. That is patently ridiculous. I must travel today."

I wanted to laugh in her face. Instead, I blinked several times in feigned confusion. "I am so sorry, Lady Xanthippe Thundergrass-Hickeybottom. Seven weeks is the first open appointment I have. We've been extremely busy this summer. The heat wave and the latest locust infestation have made most people eager to travel to cooler times. If you wished to travel today, you should have made a reservation at least two months prior."

"That's Lady Xanthippe *Thundergrast-Hickenbotham*, if you please. Our family has a long and noble past. Therefore, I am certainly not *most people*. You will simply have to push someone else's appointment aside. I care not how you arrange it. I shall wait in what passes for your reception area while you make the arrangements. I expect a resolution shortly."

I smiled as sweetly as I could manage as I led her out, making certain Tarren had escaped to the workroom. "Then you might wish to fetch a snack. You may get peckish after the first week or so."

When I shut the door, her squawks almost rattled the hinges loose. The grin on my face made Mattea giggle though she covered her mouth to muffle the sound.

Tarren said, "Thank you for not making me stay in the same room with her stench. I'm pretty sure I would have vomited on her elegant heels. At least, if I aimed right."

This one wouldn't have any weapons, at least. Such a *peasant* solution would be beneath her. While true aristocracy in Canada only existed in the colonial memories of the British elite, power remained in the hands of the politically influential.

Only an hour passed before the day should have been over, but I still had my backlog to deal with. I let Mattea and Tarren go home but suggested they go out the back door as Lady Prissy-Pants still lurked in reception.

Just as the back door swung shut, it opened again. I glanced up to see a thirty-something man with brown hair and a goatee. My neighbour, Devin, raised a single eyebrow while another angry, abusive tirade filtered through the wall. "You need any backup? The screeching made it into the restaurant. Reuben, Nami, and I would be happy to put on our scariest hipster duds and scare the hoi polloi back to Sunnybrook."

With a deep chuckle, I waved him off. "No need. She'll get tired of being ignored soon enough. That sort needs a constant diet of attention, or they wither. Could you prep my usual? I'll be done here in ten."

He gave me a thumbs-up and ducked back out of the doorway.

Words sifted through the wall, threatening to complain to the Time Tourist Board, the Temporal Agents, and the Prime Minister. However, the phone in the front desk remained a mystery to anyone but Tarren, and I would lay long odds she wouldn't be able to use it. She might have a private cell phone, but that would be less dignified. She'd have to actually look up a number.

I shut down my laptop and switched off the lights. I listened at the workroom door, but only silence came from the other side. I cracked it open and when I saw no trace of Lady Prissy-Pants, I locked the front door. I turned off the lights and the FormFitter 3000.

After locking the back door, I picked up my Poké Bowl. Ahi tuna, brown rice, scallions, sesame seeds, and kelp salad. I narrowed my eyes at Reuben, but he just nodded. He kept trying to slip in some of his healthier ingredients, like quinoa, but I detest the stuff. The husks got caught in my gums, so I stick with the brown rice. I didn't see Nami, but a loud crash in the kitchen followed by a stream of creative cursing sufficed.

Devin flicked his head to my shop. "Herself still carrying on?"

I shook my head. "She must have eventually realised no one remained for her to yell at. Put this on my tab?"

"Always."

Chapter Two

While balancing my dinner in one hand, I stuck my other hand into the depths of my purse, fishing around for my flat keys. A swaggering young man walked toward me, and I grasped them between my fingers as I pulled them out in case he decided to mug a lone, older woman, but my glare must have dissuaded him.

Once inside my Cabbagetown flat, which took up the entire second floor of a Victorian house, I dropped my dinner on the table and collapsed in my easy chair. I caressed the silver frame next to my chair, the one with a picture of me, my husband, and my son. My Maine Coon cat, Dinah, apparated on my lap, demanding her evening attention.

I flicked the ancient answering machine to play. Only one message remained, the only reason I still kept the thing. Paolo's voice admonished me to be safe coming home, as the icy roads looked treacherous. Over the decades, listening to this last vestige of his mortal self had become a nightly habit; the only recording I had of his voice.

After brushing Dinah's coat for several minutes and removing an entire cat's worth of hair from her brush, I shooed her from my lap and retrieved my food. Next, I plonked my stocking feet on the hassock, and I flicked on the telly streaming, choosing one of the older detective shows. These had become my shameful addiction. Lewis, Morse, Frost, Cracker, whichever British detective I felt in the mood for. While I didn't disdain new offerings, the reruns remained sweet comfort after rough days. Their constant pessimism in the face of naïve, optimistic partners warmed the cockles of my heart.

Today had been rough due to Lady Prissy-Pants. As an anodyne, I found my favourite episode of Morse and opened my dinner bowl. Dinah insisted on her portion, so I flicked a few cubes of Ahi into her bowl to shut her up.

I must have dozed off, for a bang from the telly woke me from my slumber. I spilled the remnants of my brown rice when I jumped.

"Bloody, bloody Hell on a biscuit!" Dinah came to investigate the spilled food, but I shooed her away. I found my whisk and cleaned my mess. Only a bit of rice had spilled. Another *bang* made me glance with resentment at the telly, but the gent who had slammed his garage door glared at Morse rather than at me.

I poured a bit of Canadian Mist to calm my nerves and gulped it down. Savouring the sweet, smoky flavour, I closed my eyes. After a deep breath, I repeated the prescription. By the time I sank into my chair again, my mood had mellowed.

The phone buzzed just as Dinah had jumped in my lap again. Indignant at the interruption, she growled as I glanced at the number.

I took in a deep breath and answered. Not answering my boss wouldn't be an option, even this late at night.

"Wilda here."

My boss' silky voice oozed over the line. The echo proved she had me on speaker phone, so I schooled my reactions. "Wilda! I do hope I haven't called too late? I've a special favour to ask, and you're the only one I can turn to."

I took a deep breath, dreading a directive to cater to Lady Prissy-Pants. "Of course not, Fionnuala. What can I help with?"

"I've a cousin coming into your shop tomorrow, and I need you to show her the red carpet."

"Tomorrow? Not today?"

"No, she landed in town this evening. Her name is Bryonie, and I'm afraid she's a bit of a talker."

Lovely. Nepotism was such a delightful thing. "Leave it to me, Fionnuala. My team will take good care of her."

"Brilliant! I knew I could count on you. Have a lovely evening, now. Ta!"

As my phone dimmed, I considered flinging it at the wall, but that would only result in needing yet another new phone. Bloody things cost too much. Two more fingers of Canadian Mist unruffled my feathers sufficiently for another episode of Morse.

Would I receive a second phone call tonight? Lady Prissy-Pants likely had the ear of some high muckity-muck. A junior minister or commissioner subject to either elite bullying or blackmail could apply pressure to PENDULUM, and thus to Fionnuala.

Dinah curled up into my lap and ratcheted up her purr until it rolled over Morse's voice. When another boom startled her awake, though, it hadn't been the telly. A flash of lightning heralded a storm and, after calming my heartbeat, I hastened to dislodge the cat and close the window. While the summer evening had been pleasant, I didn't need rain blowing sideways into my flat and soaking my sofa.

Not that anyone ever sat on the sofa anymore.

After shoving away a painful attack of nostalgia, I needed something more upbeat than Morse's eternal cynicism and laid-back style. I searched my British streaming selections and settled on the Vicar of Dibley. A bit of brilliant irreverent silliness would be just the thing.

More Canadian Mist wouldn't be wise, not with a difficult new assignment in the morning. Instead, I brewed a chamomile tea. I still added just a splash of the whiskey. For flavour.

Since I hated cooking, I'd rented a flat with a tiny kitchenette. A range I used as a shelf, a small fridge, and a sink. Lots of canned soups, teas, and far more condiments than I'd ever use constituted most of my culinary stock. I always kept sandwich fixings on regular rotation, though, and gave the Toronto take-away shops excellent business. I stashed the sugar back into the cupboard and collapsed into my chair.

The thunder outside rumbled in a constant counterpoint to the laugh track, even after I raised the volume. Dinah had disappeared, as she became even more disconcerted by thunderstorms than I did. Maybe a raucous concert would be a better antidote.

Intellectually, I knew thunder would never hurt me. Unless I rode a bicycle or something when it startled me into an oncoming car. Lightning wouldn't fry me within my wooden flat. However, my reptilian brain still panicked whenever a clap hit.

With a resentful glance at the sky, I increased the volume just as Ewan made a joke about putting his arm up a sheep's arse. Classic.

Once I finished my tea, I glanced at the old-fashioned clock on the wall. Still only nine. I may be over fifty, but I'd be damned if I would fall into the stereotypical 'early bird' crowd and be abed by nine. The storm outside forbade me from wandering the streets of Cabbagetown, but that didn't mean I couldn't do some research.

I fired up my personal laptop and searched for Fionnuala's cousin, Bryonie. I hoped I spelled her name right. Still, as a public figure, Fionnuala's family might be listed somewhere. The name seemed unusual enough to stand out even without a surname to go by.

She's flying in, so she wouldn't be local. I'll start with Canada, though, and only expand the search if needed.

Fionnuala had a meticulous resume. As the head of Time Tourist Outfitters, Ltd., she had power over me. As a member of the Board of Directors of PENDULUM, the Precinct of Enforcement and Nexus of Discipline, Uniformity, and Legislation Under maxim law, she had political aspirations. Aspirations I never shared, despite her constant urging to climb the bureaucracy.

As per the ubiquitous tourism advertisements, small changes in the time stream correct themselves, given enough time. It becomes more difficult to correct an error made fifty years ago than one made five thousand years ago. Certain places, people, and events, the time stream must be left alone. The rules around Time travel, including this list of points, are the temporal maxims. Some maxims stemmed from caution against depleting the ancient period of its source. Just one rare plant, for instance, or small animal, taken from the past, might negate thousands if not millions of descendants.

Sometimes the maxims prohibited a substance from crossing Time because of the dangerous nature of the item. For instance, some rare food item or animal infested with a previously eradicated disease. Once, a disgruntled agent tried exactly that, bringing back a rat infested with bubonic plague. The government regulated portals now had fail-safes programmed with proscribed substances and life forms. A klaxon warned of any contraband of this nature.

Occasionally, a traveller tried to avoid a proscription by travelling to a permitted destination and then physically walking to the proscribed place. Usually, the Agent on guard catches them before they commit any mischief. Occasionally, though, the Temporal Agents have to come in and clean up a right mess.

Fionnuala began as an Agent, as had I. She moved up through the organisation, while I decided I loved the garb creation more than the travelling itself. Therefore, now I outfit the tourists while she makes the policy. She can have that job; I wouldn't touch it with a ten-foot pole covered in dark chocolate.

Aha! A family tree listed for Fionnuala, and a Bryonie Trafalgar as her sister-in-law's child. Not a blood cousin, but that doesn't mean much. Sometimes married kin are closer than blood kin.

Bryonie Trafalgar. I hoped the woman herself wouldn't prove cumbersome as her name. After pulling up a picture, I found a woman with intense blue eyes and a cloud of frizzy blonde hair, a mix between a gypsy fortune-teller and a frazzled Q-tip. Her profile mentioned holistic healing, crystals, and Reiki. Delightful. I took a deep breath and closed my eyes. Tomorrow would likely be wasted baby-sitting this new-age hippie-dippie chippie.

As if I didn't have plenty of real work to do.

Chapter Three

The thunderstorm kept me awake most of the night, but copious infusions of coffee at least got me showered and dressed. The old stairs creaked as I descended to the ground floor and an annoyingly bright ray of sunshine blasted my face when I stepped outside.

Blinking furiously, I shaded my eyes and locked my door. I took two streetcars to get to work and I already ran late. I didn't precisely jog to the streetcar stop—that would have been undignified, besides a likely fall—but I did quickstep it, arriving just in time to catch the 8:10.

As I sat into the only empty seat, next to an odiferous young woman, wearing second-hand fatigues and a grimy jean jacket, I considered my approach to the hippie-dippie chippie. Perhaps she'd turn out to be less flaky than her online persona suggested. Perhaps she'd even be reasonable.

I wouldn't hold my breath. Or maybe I would. My neighbour's aroma had grown particularly putrid.

I escaped the cloud of funk at my stop and waited for the next streetcar, which came by seven minutes later. I saw it in the distance, stuck behind a school bus. When it arrived, no seats remained. I glared at an oblivious young man in the front row, but he declined to be chivalrous. The other folks in my immediate vicinity looked older or more infirm than I, so I took a firm grip on the balance bars.

The streetcar clicked along King Street, and I took a deep breath, thankful those around me seemed to have at least bathed within the last week. Everyone stared at their phone screens except for one older man who rustled a newspaper in obvious censure of the modern generation.

As we crossed Spadina, I prepared to disembark, stumbling as the vehicle came to a sudden brake. The bicyclist who cut in front of the streetcar waved an apology and sped away while the driver cursed. When I stepped off, my legs shook. I disliked taking public transport, but I disliked driving in Toronto far more. Besides, it would have taken just as long to find parking as it did to take two streetcars.

I'd once taken a road trip down to New York, the part of Canada that had been part of the United States before the collapse ten years earlier. It may have once been a lovely city, but now it looked like a war zone, filled with abandoned buildings, crumbling infrastructure, and lost souls.

Cities along the prior Canadian border, such as Toronto, Victoria, Quebec, and Ottowa, swelled in size after the Second Civil War in the states. States along the west coast and much of the northeast had seceded into Canada. A lack of integrated government in the remaining southern states resulted in their general failure as going concerns. The Canadian government offered incentives for locals to stay and rebuild and for Canadian citizens to relocate. I preferred my home city to any former American den of iniquity.

As expected, neither Tarren nor Mattea had arrived yet. I went through my comfortable routine, switching on the air conditioning, flicking on several overhead lights, the computer, and the FormFitter 3000. I pulled down the calendar to check on any appointments today. So far, nothing showed on the horizon, except for Fionnuala's cousin. Today would have been a fantastic day for catching up on my backlog, if she hadn't lobbed that particular wrench into the works. At least I could start on the pile until she arrived.

I settled down to iron out the battered jabot on a men's frock coat from eighteenth-century Colonial America. While I couldn't tell what this traveller had done to wrinkle it so horribly, I'd add a high damage surcharge on his exit billing. Each traveller must care for the garb we provided them. We billed damage, whether repairable or permanent, on a sliding scale. The more often they destroyed or damaged their kit, the higher such a surcharge became until they might consider it a disincentive for further trips.

So far, such a strategy had worked. Soon, the trips became too expensive, even for the idiotic, idle scions who frequented my shop. Most of those only mildly well off took better care of their kit, being on a stricter budget.

A jingle at the door made me glance up through the cracked workshop door, but Mattea's cheerful, "Good morning!" meant I could continue ironing.

"What's good about it?"

With a chuckle, Mattea came in with two cups of coffee from the gourmet coffee place down the street. She handed me one and I softened my sharp tone with a smile. I took a sip and closed my eyes. Mattea knew full well my tastes ran to strong coffee, the darker roast the better. Black as sin and just as sweet.

My assistant also knew not to raise any controversial subjects until I consumed my first coffee, so I continued with my repairs while she grabbed her own project. We worked in silence for a full hour before Tarren came in, just as I drank the dregs. Perfect timing.

"Good morning! Did you see the sunrise today? Glorious shades of peach!"

I specifically never scheduled Tarren to arrive until after I had a chance to drink my first cup of coffee.

"I recall it shining in my face, yes. Just so you know, Fionnuala called last night. She's got her cousin, Bryonie, coming in sometime today, but she didn't say when. She seems the new-agey, crystal-loving type."

"Oh! Roger, roger. Will she go next door first?"

"No, Fionnuala said she wanted to come here first to see the possibilities before planning her itinerary."

"I'm really getting tired of customers skipping that step. I'll break out the herbal tea vault."

Mattea pulled three pins from her mouth. "Is she going on a trip? Or is this a tour?"

I shrugged. "Your guess is as good as mine. I'm just hoping she isn't a twin to Lady Prissy-Pants."

With a half-smile, Mattea pinned more trim to her Mongolian tunic. "I wonder if she'll return or if she wrote us off after our shenanigans yesterday?"

"That is the question today, is it not?"

As my question didn't require an answer, Mattea returned her concentration to her tunic. Tarren took my empty mug and replaced it with a full one. I grinned in thanks. "Where do you think your new VIP will want to go?"

"No idea. Everyone's got a different ideal."

Tarren sipped her own coffee. "Where's your ideal? Where would you go if you could go anywhere, anywhen?"

I didn't hesitate with my answer. "My great-great-grandfather had always fascinated me. He'd invented one of the first sewing machines. He never made it a commercial success, not like Elias Howe had, but he'd made one, used it, and worked as a tailor all his life. I would like to have met him and get his story firsthand." I looked up at my receptionist. "What about you?"

She took a deep breath. "Mine isn't as personal. I want to meet Mother Teresa. She did so much in this world. And Princess Diana."

Both women had angelic reputations combined with darker personal sides, but I didn't want to burst Tarren's ideals, so I let well enough alone. Instead, I climbed upstairs to store the colonial garb and surveyed my to-do piles to decide the next project.

I didn't really want to tackle the leather and fur construction for the Neolithic garb. Besides, I still waited on a shipment from our leather suppliers. Good reindeer pelts had become difficult to procure as the

Canadian sub-breed looked noticeably different from the ancient options. Our usual Norwegian supplier had run afoul of some PETA protesters.

The next pile required a great deal of fine embroidery to repair a tenth century Italian noblewoman's garb, and I absolutely knew Bryonie would arrive just as I got into the groove. Such embroidery required a focused mindset, and I didn't have that in me today, not with my lack of sleep.

The ninth century Icelandic apron dress should be easy enough for my blunted senses. Green and cream tablet-woven trim decorated the edges, but it had a simple cut. I picked up the mustard-yellow linen and settled to my worktable. Spools of sinew, flax thread, leather cord, and silk thread lined the edge of my table, on affixed spindles. Since this wasn't a noblewoman's dress, I reached for the flax rather than the silk and stitched along the hem.

The jingling bell woke me from my doze. I startled enough to knock over the empty cup of coffee on my table. Mattea's chuckle made me scowl in her direction. Her smile widened as I stood to peek out the cracked door.

Before I could steady my focus on the riot of colours, the wave of patchouli and sandalwood wafted in and smacked me in the face. *This must be Bryonie.*

"Oh, hello, my dear! Such a bright and beautiful day we have. Would you happen to be Wilda? My cousin told me to ask for her. Oh, your hair is delightful! Such a lovely shade of maroon. Do you do it yourself? The colour really does match your aura. Well, maybe a shade darker, but that's a minor difference."

Through the crack, I watched as Tarren, visibly trying to keep her laughter from exploding, called back in a sing-song voice. "Wilda! Your visitor is here!"

Wishing I had a discreet pair of nose plugs, I took a deep breath of the relatively clear air and marshalled forth into the reception area. I do believe the term is "wreathed with smiles," and I hoped my expression mimicked the ridiculous phrase sufficiently.

"Greetings. Would you be Bryonie?"

Bits of her costume jingled as she rushed toward me, arms open. Her perfumed mass enveloped me before I could stop her. "Indeed, and I am! How perceptive you are. You must be Wilda. Darling Fionnuala said you'd take excellent care of me."

With gentle insistence, I extracted myself from the pink, orange, and purple silk scarves which had evidently adopted me and handed them back to her. Without blinking an eye, she tucked them back into numerous folds and belts. I couldn't tell if she wore a sarong or a sari underneath the myriad colours. Even my trained eye refused to make sense of the mélange.

"Do follow me, Bryonie. Fionnuala didn't mention if you wanted a tour or if I should fit you out for a trip."

Her grin deepened, and she cocked her head to one side, considering me with intent concentration. "Oh, both would be delightful. You know, you look astonishingly familiar. Have we met before?"

I shook my head, faux smile still plastered onto my face. If I kept it in place too much longer, I worried it would freeze that way. "I'm certain I would remember such a meeting."

"Hmm." She put one finger under my chin as if I were a child. I resisted the urge to slap the hand away and punch her. My jaw clenched, I blinked and continued smiling. "If you come this way, I can show you the workroom and our storage facilities."

"I know you from somewhere. Your aura is unmistakable! Perhaps it will come to me."

I turned and swept my hand toward the fitting machine. "This is the FormFitter 3000. It takes precise measurements of your body so we can create perfectly tailored garb suited to your desired location and period. Once your itinerary is finalised, we can create up to three sets of garb, complete with footwear, outerwear, underthings, and accessories. We also provide your translation implant and homing beacon."

"A homing beacon? In case I get lost?"

Or in case she died, but no need to be morose. "Exactly. If you haven't returned by your designated appointment, a Temporal Agent can suss out your location and fetch you back. This is helpful if you run afoul of local customs, which, I must admit, is more likely with first-time travellers." I forbore mentioning that Temporal Agents on mission might have no set return appointment, due to the variable nature of their task. In those cases, a portal would appear in camouflage at a designated time and place once each day. "Now, if you follow me upstairs, I can show you our warehouse of garb."

We climbed the antique spiral staircase as she exclaimed at the banister's woodwork.

"Oh, yes. This building has been in place since the middle of the nineteenth century. They installed the staircase in 1891. While the building caught fire shortly afterward, the stairs survived."

Once upstairs, she gasped as she beheld the musty corridor filled with furs, silks, and brocades.

"We store the garb by period front to back, and by geographic location from left to right. In the far front left will be the most recent, local garb—that from twenty years back here in Toronto. The far back right will be those from the earliest Paleolithic times in Africa."

"Do you carry all sizes and genders?"

"We'd love to, but it isn't practical. We take our stock and adjust to the client's precise measurements. Most of my work is alterations, as opposed to full-on creation of new garb."

"That must be highly satisfying work. Your aura glows bright when you speak of it. Oh! Now I know where I've met you!"

I raised my eyebrows. "About an hour ago, give or take?"

"Let's see, it must have been…in the fourteenth century? Yes, I think that's when. In Mali. Or Scotland? No, definitely Mali. Well, perhaps both. Someplace else, but I can't remember."

"I've never travelled to Mali in any period, and I had been under the impression you'd never travelled at all."

She shook her head. "No, no, this wouldn't have been a Time trip for me. A prior life. However, I think this must have been your current incarnation, because you look familiar, not just your aura. Perhaps you have yet to travel there."

I pursed my lips. "I no longer travel."

"Oh, dear. Your aura just dimmed, almost to darkness. Whatever did I say?"

I turned to the rack nearest me. "Here we have several examples of tenth century First Nations garb from the Northwestern Territories. We have weapons to go along with the garb, but often authentic materials are more difficult to come by. We don't wish to diminish historical resources for an animal that has been extinct or on the endangered list. Harvesting supplies in the past would diminish current resources, as it deprives the current population of essential ancestors."

Bryonie continued to stare at me as I resolutely remained on a different subject. "Down here we have eleventh century Viking garb, starting in the Vinlandic, Greenlandic, and then Icelandic territories. As we move farther down this aisle, you can see the homeland Scandinavian items, morphing into the Anglo-Saxons. If we move an aisle over, into the thirteenth century—"

"My dear, you must let me do a Reiki massage to slough away the despair. Please, it will only take a moment." She reached for my forehead. I pulled my head back out of reflex.

"I'm certain I don't need a Reiki massage."

"But you do! It's patently clear to anyone who can see."

The wave of sandalwood and patchouli hit me again and warred with my lack of sleep and only one cup of caffeine. My stomach rebelled and I retreated to the stairwell. "You must excuse me for just a moment. I need to use the washroom. Will you wait up here, or shall my assistant keep you company? Mattea is down in the workroom."

I fled down the stairs without waiting for her answer and just slammed the washroom door before getting sick in the toilet. I heaved a few times to make certain no more illness remained, washed my face, and flushed. Still, I loathed returning to Bryonie's overwhelming and annoying presence. So much for the hope she'd be easier to deal with. Over-helpful busy bodies became almost as annoying as self-important spoiled scions.

When I emerged from the washroom, Mattea and Bryonie giggled. I headed straight for the coffeemaker and poured myself some calming fuel before turning to face our visitor.

"Do accept my apologies, Wilda. I didn't mean to make you uncomfortable. But I can help, you see. I'm a certified holistic healer and can heal your aura with just a few sessions. Would you allow me to try?"

I took a sip of coffee, despite its still-scalding temperature and considered my answer. I detested being touched and she'd already done so once. How could I politely refuse?

Mattea touched Bryonie's arm. "Can you explain what you would do? How do you heal an aura?"

"It's quite simple, really. I massage the upper chakra and allow the negative energy to flow back down into the earth, away from the aura. In this way, it drains from the person and allows the positive energy from our Mother Gaia to flow within. This regenerates the soul and revives the aura. Really, each of you should have this maintenance regularly. It must have been quite a while since Wilda has done it."

I've never done such a stupid, airy-fairy thing in my life, and I wasn't about to start now. I needed to get rid of this interfering hippie-dippie chippie. I glanced at Mattea, who nodded.

She turned to Bryonie and, in her sweetest voice, asked, "Would you join me for a cup of tea? There's a wonderful place just down the block. They have delightful Turkish tea, boba tea, anything you can think of."

Once the room had cleared of occupants, I switched on the little metal fan and opened the back door, wafting away the lingering perfumes. My headache eased as soon as I breathed in the fresh smog of Toronto.

A blessed hour later, I'd quite returned to myself as Mattea and Bryonie entered, full of giggles and several cups. Mattea handed me one, and I peered inside suspiciously. However, rather than hipster tea, it contained beautifully black coffee.

I wouldn't survive without Mattea.

Now armed with caffeine, I turned my attention back to Bryonie, who examined me once again. I patted the FormFitter 3000, hoping to stave off another Reiki attack. "Would you like to try out the measuring chamber? Once we have your specs, we can outfit you in whatever you require for your trip. Have you decided where you'd like to visit?"

She didn't even glance at the machine. "We've definitely met in several lifetimes. Let's see. Perhaps a Native tribe? I have a few lives amongst the Hopi and the Wabenaki."

I turned the nautical wheel to open the chamber door. "All you do is go inside, remove all your clothing, place your hands and feet where marked and the chamber does the rest. It's quite painless."

"Hmm. Yes, I recall your insistence upon having things your way. You haven't changed much."

I took in a deep breath. "I haven't travelled to either place you've mentioned, Bryonie. You must have confused me with someone else."

"Oh, no, your aura is unmistakable. A fascinating pattern of red and orange with just a hint of puce in the core. I'd know it anywhere, anywhen." In a mercurial shift, she caressed the FormFitter in an almost sensual affection. "Where would you suggest I visit for my first trip?"

Anywhere but here. I blinked a few times. In all my years of running Time Tourist Outfitters, no one had ever asked my opinion on a trip. The vast majority of my clients had been spoiled, rich dilettantes, stuffed with their own sense of self-importance, and would never consult the opinion of a lowly servant. The few middle-class customers who scraped up enough for their *holiday of a lifetime* planned every aspect of their trip out with fanatical precision.

I took another sip of coffee to order my thoughts. She'd be best hanging out with Lord Byron and his ilk, or some Bohemian enclave of the 1960s. However, such modern options likely didn't hold much appeal. Most first-timers wanted a famous period, something with notorious people or spectacular wealth, like Cleopatra's Egypt or Genghis Khan's court. A few hardy souls opted for important wars or historically significant events, like Napoleon's victories or Julius Caesar's Triumphs. Very, very few preferred to interact with history's fascinating personalities, such as Eleanor of Aquitaine Sun Tzu, or Galileo.

For the first time, I studied her without pre-judgement. She had a kind heart, true, despite her overbearing tendency to meddle. I wouldn't want to send her to a time where she could get summarily executed for wanting to help. That crossed out most of mankind's history.

"Have you any areas of interest? Do you prefer to see great events unfolding, or speak to learned people? Do you crave sumptuous settings or prefer to rough it?"

She considered, staring up at the ceiling as if noticing it for the first time. "I do believe…I would like to experience how my ancestors lived. Most came over to America from Ireland in the nineteenth century, from County Cork. Can you send me there?"

She'd surprised me again. This request had been surprisingly humble and touching. Unfortunately, it ran too close to the current day according to the temporal maxims.

I shook my head. "We discourage interacting with known direct ancestors within the last three hundred years. This sort of trip is against the rules and generally forbidden. While many travellers interact with unknown ancestors, as we are all descended from countless people in history, the fact you know these people as your ancestors affects your actions. We have these rules in place to prevent sullying your personal history. You've heard of the Grandfather Paradox, have you not?"

Bryonie furrowed her brow and shook her head. She must have bells hidden under her hair scarves, as they jingled merrily. "No, what's that?"

"Imagine you travel to the past and, wittingly or not, murder your own grandfather before he conceives your father. This creates a paradox, preventing your own existence, which would have prevented your travel… and thus prevented the murder. This sort of paradox is nullified the farther back one travels. The time stream can fix itself from such rips, given enough years to do so, as there are more options available to 'fill the rip.' However, if there is a rip too recent, it has no chance to repair the hole, and the Temporal Agents get involved. They go back to before the murder and arrest you."

She placed a ring-laden hand over her mouth, her eyes wide. "But I'm not planning on murdering my grandfather!"

"Few people plan such atrocities. Oedipus never planned to murder his father. Consider this; what if you meet your grandfather, and he falls in love with you, rather than your grandmother? This is nothing you've done on purpose, but you've now possibly negated your own existence just as handily."

She swallowed and stared at the floor, considering the implications. "Then I cannot travel to the nineteenth century?"

"You can, but it is standard policy for all travellers to submit immediate family histories to preclude any issues. By immediate, I mean the last three hundred years. Then you may be cleared for travel in areas where your family was *not* living. However, we encourage you to travel farther back, to avoid any problems at all. One area travelling has helped with enormously is genealogical research, so this information is rather well detailed."

This earned me a giggle. "Quite true."

"We also discourage romantic or violent interactions with the locals. This helps avoid the domino effect of such relationships, no matter what time you travel into."

She nodded slowly, again jingling. "This makes sense. With that in mind, perhaps I should choose the place my family lived, but perhaps around the twelfth century? Or should I go farther back?"

"The twelfth century would be fine. What class would you prefer to be? In twelfth century Ireland, there are several options." I pulled down the glass screen and typed in some parameters on the virtual keyboard. "Let's see…you could be farming class, of course, or warrior. That might require some physical training before your trip. Noblewomen usually became either wives or nuns, though a few enclaves of Druids remained hidden in the hills. Norse women had a presence in Limerick and Wexford, but not so many in the Cork area. Nobles usually receive up to three sets of full garb while farmers and peasants receive one."

"What about the language? Customs?"

"We provide a translation implant with up to three languages pre-programmed. You can learn others while travelling, if you wish, and some of the more obscure languages aren't as robust. The customs are why there is a seven-week delay on travel. You receive training in ceremonies, beliefs, hierarchal structure, and laws." While I didn't say it out loud, I ached to scream that she would have gotten all this information if she'd first gone to planning instead of insisting on coming to my shop first. Instead, I kept my smile plastered to my face and blinked several times.

"This is all a great deal more complex than the advertisements portrayed."

I gave her a half-smile. "That is very true. The marketing department refuses to give all these details, worried it will frighten off most clients. However, those who wish to travel must be certified by our Agents, despite any rank or wealth they possess. Our Temporal Agents are sticklers for the proprieties."

She caressed the FormFitter 3000 again. "So, this is where I begin?"

"Indeed. Are you ready?"

As an answer, she climbed into the machine and with a nod, I closed the door and turned the wheel. Within ten minutes, her green light came on and I pulled the brass lever.

Mattea glanced up from her sewing. "She's not so bad once you get to know her."

"Hmm." I didn't wish to admit her answer had surprised and intrigued me. She seemed much less shallow than our normal client.

"Do you want me to pull the twelfth century Irish stuff?"

I nodded absently, waiting for the FormFitter 3000 to finish. The buzzer sounded and Bryonie's gasp filtered out. At least she'd had the decency not to harangue me from inside the machine as Lady Prissy-Pants had.

By the time Mattea descended the stairs with her arms full of garb options, Bryonie had re-draped her sarong and tonne of scarves and emerged. "Well! I feel much cleansed. There must be a spiritual aspect to this contraption you've not told me of."

There went the small bit of respect amassed for Bryonie. Still, she had become less annoying.

As we sorted through the selections, I held up the noblewoman's outfit with a critical eye. "See this headpiece, Mattea? What do you notice?"

My assistant peered at the white linen head covering, touching the embroidery design. She examined the other accessories and the garb itself. "Most of the costume dates from the eleventh century, but this winged cat design," she traced the blackwork along the bottom hem, "is from Sicily. While it's conceivable such an item came available through trade, it would be unusual. We try to discourage travellers from possessing unusual items that require explanation."

I smiled, my heart beaming with pride. "Well done! Do take that back upstairs and store it in the Sicily section."

Chapter Four

The front bell jingled. I spared a glance through the cracked workroom door in case Lady Prissy-Pants had returned. However, the visitors were male and official looking. One appeared in his mid-thirties, fit and trim with light hair, while the other was sixty-ish with a slight paunch and a full beard. The younger man spoke to Tarren with an imperious tone and a Texan accent. I cursed under my breath. "Bryonie, can you work with Mattea when she returns to choose your garb? I have a new client to attend."

"Certainly. Oh, haven't you some brighter colours? I detest dullness."

"Most of the colours should be muted, but we can find you some strong jewel-toned greens and blues. Bide a bit until Mattea returns."

With that assurance, I escaped to assess the clients. The younger man stood, glaring at Tarren, as she tried to hand him an electronic pad. The older man fairly faded into the background, though a few eccentric details, such as a pocket watch fob and a waxed mustache, caught my attention. "Please, sirs, since you didn't make an appointment, I must insist you fill this out. This is a standard information form, required for any new client. It shouldn't take long."

With a nasty grin, the blond pulled out his wallet and flashed an official-looking identification card. I reached from behind him and plucked it out of his hand to examine the card. "Mr. Thompson, is it? My, the badge *does* look authentic. One moment, please, while I run your data through my system. Protocols are so important, don't you think?" Absconding with his entire wallet, I disappeared into the workroom and settled at my laptop while he spluttered in the front room. Tarren offered them a cup of tea while I verified his Temporal Agent credentials. Did the older man have a badge as well? He didn't look the sort, to be honest.

As the confirmation came through, I clenched my teeth. Damnit all to Hell, he looked legit. I returned to the lobby and handed his wallet back. "Here you go, Mr. Thompson. All appears to be in order. How can we help you today?" I glanced at the older man, hoping he would answer instead.

Luckily, he answered the glance. His words, much less imperious than his companions, declared him British and posh. "It is quite urgent that we travel to Sydney, Australia in the fourteenth century today. We'll need you to move quickly, girls."

Not only did I detest when men called grown women 'girls,' what he asked was impossible. The latter pleased me. "That is most certainly out of the question. I am sorry, I'm afraid I didn't catch your name?"

"You may address me as Sir Algernon St. Clair of the Metropolitan Police of London."

I may, indeed. I glowered at him, certain he would produce a valid badge just as readily as Mr. Thompson had. "Well, Sir Algernon St. Clair of the Metropolitan Police of London, a trip today is quite out of the question."

The older man's eyes widened at my firm tone. "I must not have made myself clear, my dear girl. We have a matter of international security. I *do* have the authority, and time is of the essence." He tapped his waistcoat.

"You can have all the authority you want, and you have all the time you need on this end of history. Regardless of all that, it's impossible to send a pompous British aristocrat and a blond farm boy with manure between his toes to pre-European Australia."

Sir Algernon didn't answer but had a small coughing fit into an embroidered handkerchief. Mr. Thompson crossed his arms and glared down at me. "If it's a matter of money…"

"Mr. Thompson, this is most certainly *not* a matter of money. While I'm quite happy to take all the money your Ministry has to offer, along with a hefty surcharge for wasting my time and being rude, under no circumstances will the Time Tourist Outfitters, or the Time Tourist Board at large, send Caucasians to pre-European Australia. Perhaps if you know a darker-skinned colleague you'd like to send in your place, we can talk scheduling and fees. Until that time, I must bid you both a good day."

Tarren and I stared at each other until the door slammed behind them. We burst into laughter. She sat back at her chair. "Someday I'll gain enough confidence to deal with those sorts the way you do."

"Such skill takes many years of being an intractable shrew. It helps to consider all men idiots by default and only change your mind with a mountain of evidence. You'll learn."

She giggled. "I bow to your masterful example."

When I returned to the workroom, I found both Bryonie and Mattea giggling into their teacups.

Mattea rolled her eyes. "No, my last boyfriend turned out to be a complete arse. Dating him felt more like having a teenage son. He played video games, drank beer, and made messes quicker than I could clean them. I'm better off single."

Bryonie's eyes twinkled. "Partners aren't like old cars. You don't buy a broken one, hoping you can fix it. You buy a gently used one, hoping it can carry you as far as you want to go. That may be until next month; it may be for years. Your choice. Still, sometimes you just know the right person as soon as you meet."

Mattea took another sip of her tea. "I've never just *known*. I've often only imagined. My imagination always outstrips reality."

I gave a half-smile of my own and shut the door behind me. Tarren could handle the idiot if he returned. He had his answer. I didn't doubt I'd get a second visit, this time from some walnut-skinned rookie from Jamaica who had neither the desire nor training to go on a mission. Until such a visit, though, we might laugh a bit at the ridiculous Agent's naïve expectations.

Bryonie gestured toward the closed door. "Do you get those often?"

"More often than I like. The Agency usually prepares better than that but, occasionally, you get an up-and-coming Agent, who wants to make a name for themselves and hare off on an investigation without going through the proper channels." I grinned at the door. "That must have been Mr. Thompson's issue. If his superintendent had truly sent him, he would have had his authorisation paperwork and would have been much more physically acceptable. Maybe the posh Brit git is trying to game the system. The Metropolitan Police of London should really know better. Or we'll get a letter arguing racism. But refusing to send a Caucasian Agent to aboriginal Australia isn't racism, any more sending a blond to pre-European China, or an Asian to tenth century Iceland would be. The Agency won't break the temporal maxims lightly."

"I can see that." She picked up a biscuit from a dish Mattea had materialised while I dealt with the Agent. I helped myself to one. Mattea knew ginger biscuits were my favourite.

When she'd brushed the crumbs from her sarong, Bryonie said, "Well, Mattea knows my choice of garb, and tells me I must report for my training and translation implant next door. To the left, is that correct?"

I nodded. "If you want a good lunch, the Poké Bowl place on the other side is fantastic."

Bryonie grinned. "Maybe afterwards. The ginger biscuits tasted delicious. Thank you, Mattea. May I stop back in when I'm finished?"

Mattea nodded, as did I. She really wasn't so bad once the flittering and fluttering calmed down. Her swirl of vibrant colours exited and we both sighed deeply in relief.

"Didn't you go to China once, Wilda?"

I glanced at the photo on my desk, the one with Paolo and Alessandro. I swallowed against the inevitable lump in my throat and glanced away. "Yes, I did. Many years ago. My last mission."

I could think of few things on this earth I wanted to talk about less than that last trip to China. The Agency had sent us to investigate the truth behind some mysteries with the Second Opium War in the nineteenth century, but we'd been unprepared for what else we found.

Yet another visitor interrupted my memories. Today looked like it would be a red letter day all around. With my luck, Lady Prissy-Pants had returned.

The male voice outside reassured me, but the distress of his tone had me out in the lobby in an instant. Tarren had already leapt up to help him. His dark skin looked like ashen mahogany but covered with lesions. Sweat glistened in the harsh lobby light and his clothing felt soaked.

His voice croaked out a hoarse whisper as he collapsed in our arms. "Help…I need…hospital…"

Mattea grabbed the phone and dialed 911 while Tarren and I eased the man to the floor. His garb looked like rags, which might be from any era and any place in the world. I searched for his wallet, but found none, so he probably travelled from some time before the nineteenth century.

Dammit, I needed more data. He still breathed but had passed out. I could do little until the paramedics came, so I examined his rags. No telltale trim, no buttons, only wrapped cloth. It felt like wool, which didn't help me narrow anything down, but the weave looked fine and may have once been blue. At least post-Neolithic.

"Mattea, what can you discern from his clothing? Any clues? I can't find much, but I may have missed something."

She pointed to his feet. "His sandals? They're birch."

"Northern clime, at least. But then again, it could just be a high altitude. *Damn and tarnation!* His panoculation should have been more than a match for any disease in the past. This sort of thing hasn't happened for decades!"

He convulsed once, startling all of us, as the paramedics pounded on the door. Tarren jumped up and let them in. They took the distressed visitor away in very short order.

With sudden decision, I grabbed my purse. "I need to know what he just exposed us to. I've been panoculated in the past, but I may need a booster. Mattea, Tarren, I need you next door, stat. Get your panoculations. If they argue, tell them I said *now*."

Chapter Five

This one street of Toronto had more than its fair share of hospitals. Tucked in behind world-class research hospitals, children's hospitals, and faith-based hospitals, the small facility dedicated to those who travelled in time lay hidden behind the larger buildings. The ambulance threaded the downtown traffic until it pulled up to the nondescript emergency entrance, almost invisible amongst its brown brick and concrete neighbours.

As the medics rushed the traveller through the double doors, I followed. No one challenged my presence, probably assuming me to be a relative. I strode with purpose and few even glanced my way, much less stopped me. Throughout my lifetime, I'd long since discovered a confident manner more than made up for what I lacked in stature.

This armour failed once they wheeled the traveller into a room, however.

A tall, blocky nurse barred my entrance. In a firm voice, he asked, "Are you a relative?"

"The patient came to me when he experienced distress."

"But you aren't related."

I shook my head, trying to peer beyond his bulk into the room. "I run Time Tourist Outfitters, and he's obviously just returned from a Trip. I need to discover what he's exposed my assistants and me to. They've never travelled, so have no panoculations."

"I'm sorry, but only relatives allowed inside. You may sit in the waiting room." He nodded in the direction I'd come. I grimaced and considered pushing past him, but that would solve nothing. He looked capable of picking me up and carrying me out over his shoulder.

With a narrowed glare at the nurse who, to be fair, only did his job, I retreated to the check-in desk.

The nurse's aide glanced up as I approached, but as I didn't appear to be covered in blood or missing a limb, she returned to her computer screen.

With my most ingratiating smile, I asked, "May I please speak to the charge nurse on duty?"

The nurse continued typing several moments before glancing up again. "What can I help you with?"

"Are you the charge nurse?"

"No, but I *am* the nurse you must convince of your need to speak to her."

My grin became more genuine. I appreciated straight forward, honest folk. "Fair enough. I run the garbing department at Time Tourist Outfitters, down on King Street. The gentleman they just brought in arrived at my shop in obvious distress. I need to discover what he's exposed me to and, more importantly, what he's exposed my staff to. While my panoculations had been decades ago, they should still be effective. My staff, however, has never travelled. They are vulnerable to whatever virulent disease this traveller has returned with."

As soon as I'd finished, the nurse punched a call button on her desk. "She's with a patient, but Aminata should be with you shortly. I'll appraise her of your details."

"Thank you."

She nodded, and I shuffled off to the uncomfortable, institutional plastic waiting room seats. Without the impetus of an immediate goal, the exhaustion washed over me. Between troubled sleep from the storm last night, dealing with Bryonie this morning, and the emergency of the ill traveller, I'd used every reserve of strength I possessed. I couldn't remember the last time I ate. Perhaps the ginger biscuits Mattea had given me? In the corner sat an antique, squat coffee vending machine, which might have been new in the last millennium. Although I realised the coffee would be horrible, this option looked more feasible the longer I waited.

My drooping eyelids and growling stomach had just about convinced me caffeine would be more important than taste when the ward door opened and a dark, lanky woman almost twice my height emerged. She walked straight to me, offering her hand. "I am the charge nurse, Aminata Konaté. Will you be pleased to follow me?"

Her lovely accent and velvet voice had me mesmerised as I trailed after her. Instant trust remained incredibly rare for me, but I could see how she would be a successful nurse. Her manner and voice exuded intense peace and comfort. I wanted to curl up on a cushion like a cat and just listen to her read a story.

While I shook off the obvious signs of fatigue, I followed her down several antiseptic halls to a small office. Despite the awful lime-green walls, a few homey touches of décor with bright, West African colours made the space more intimate. I sat on the visitor's chair as she settled into her own, her long fingers steepled.

"Your name is Wilda Firestone, is that correct?"

I thought back over the last several hours but felt certain I'd told no one my name. She must have done her research before calling me. I approved of her competence and nodded.

She glanced at her screen, but it faced away from me. She let out a deep sigh and looked back. "I'm afraid we do not yet understand what Josephus suffers from."

"*Suffers,* present tense? He's still alive, then?"

"For the moment, but his continued life is not certain, by any means. I see no reason to mince words, Ms. Firestone. You have been an Agent in the past, so you understand the consequences of breaking the rules. It appears Josephus did not observe such respect for the maxims."

I raised my eyebrows. She wouldn't have mentioned that fact unless she planned to explain.

"Indeed. It appears there is a rogue portal in town."

"Bloody Hell."

She grinned, but her eyes remained grim. "Just so."

I thought back to the early days of travelling. At first, everyone who could afford the investment threw up portals, unheeding of any safety warnings or tests. Only much later did they discover a basic flaw in the technology. Cellular degeneration became unavoidable after several trips in the early portals. Three, perhaps four trips could be taken safely. After that, major organs began failing. PENDULUM discovered a way to remove this flaw, but in order to regulate travel, didn't share that technology. Therefore, the only safe portals were official portals.

I wondered how much experience Aminata had with identifying the issues with the original portals. "His lesions appear in line with cellular degeneration documentation I've studied, but I don't remember fever being part of it."

She nodded, playing with a small wooden figurine on her desk, carved as a camel. "That is true. The fever is asymptomatic. However, he may have a fever in addition to the degeneration. We haven't yet determined that."

"Did you verify the portal is in Toronto?"

"You just assisted in that proof. Josephus arrived at your office in obvious distress. We believe he would not have left his Time unless he needed modern healing. He wouldn't have travelled far in his condition. Therefore, the authorities are certain the portal must be local. In fact, it may even be close to your shop."

The authorities. I wondered which Agents conducted the investigation. Hopefully, it would be someone I remembered. This had gotten out of hand.

I took a deep breath. "What can I do to help?"

Aminata's smile deepened. "You're helping by doing your job, which you have done. Investigating Agents will come by this afternoon with some questions, I'm certain. I shall keep you apprised of Josephus' condition, as much as I'm permitted. He is, unfortunately, not the first ill traveller we've heard of in the last few weeks."

"What is Josephus' last name, if I may ask? Can we tell where he last travelled? Where are the other ill travellers?"

Her jaw clenched, but she answered after a moment. "His last name is Konaté. We haven't yet determined from when he travelled, as he hadn't registered with any known Agency. As for the other travellers…we got a report yesterday of a rogue portal located in Edinburgh, and another in Lima. There may be others. We're trying to trace anyone who has shown signs of the illness, and where they travelled from."

"Konaté?"

"Josephus is my cousin."

"Bloody Hell again."

"Just so. Therefore, you will believe me when I say I shall do whatever is necessary to find out what has happened and to prevent it from happening again."

Chapter Six

I'd given up trying to figure a streetcar schedule from the hospital and splurged on an Uber. I regretted it the instant I stepped into the dingy vehicle. The raucous gangster rap music assaulted my headache and the heavy cologne the driver had bathed in didn't help in the slightest. By the time my shop came in sight, I practically leapt out of the moving car, flinging cash in the cabbie's direction.

I found the shop locked and empty. I flicked on a few lights and glanced at the clock, cursing at the late hour. I must have been at the hospital longer than I realised. After a quick but thorough shower in the small bathroom in the back of the shop, I felt much refreshed. Also, hopefully, much less contagious.

I ducked next door to the Agency. I don't visit them often, but sometimes we need to coordinate a particular traveller's itinerary or equipment needs. While they kept normal daytime hours, they stayed open late when dealing with a backlog. The antique bell on the door jingled cheerfully as I peered in the dim reception area.

No one sat at the desk, so I walked into the interview room. When a first-time traveller set up their itinerary, this is where they completed their trip details. A SmartScreen filled one wall to project realistic footage of whatever time or place they wanted to visit, so the traveller could have an honest vision of their destination.

Many travellers cancelled their trip then and there. One might be surprised at how many think a trip into history should be antiseptic and safe. This wasn't Disneyworld.

This room also being empty, I walked to the next one, where travellers who made it this far filled out paperwork and liability releases. I still found no one, but I heard voices in the next room.

The medical labs seemed less depressing than the hospital had been, but still stank of industrial cleaner.

I let out my breath when I saw Tarren and Mattea chatting amiably with the medics. They looked up from the chairs when I came in, their arms hooked up to the panoculation apparatus. Their hair looked flat, suggesting they, too, had showered. I smiled in approval.

Mattea grinned. "You survived! At least you gave us plenty of time to make bets. I'm happy to say I lost this one."

I glared at her in mock resentment.

"Did they explain to you what they're doing, and how it works? And what it won't protect from?"

Tarren nodded. "Jamie here explained how the first additive to our blood creates a kind of molecular coating over the bacteria and viruses within our system, so even if we pass them on to someone in the past, they'll be inert. The second additive isolates any foreign bacteria or viruses and coat them, isolating them within our bloodstream. The additives work to retard viral replication, so even if one escapes the coating, it should do little to no harm."

I nodded. "Keep in mind they can't do a full spectrum of every disease in the history of mankind. However, like our translation software, they target the area and time you are travelling to. They have a broad spectrum panoculation, which you're getting now, but if you travelled to, say, Ming China, you'd get a specific booster."

Tarren clapped her hands. "We're almost done here, and I'm starving. I called Ray to let him know I'd be out for the evening. We've almost finished our fourth hour on this thing. Want to grab dinner?"

After my stomach roared in agreement to her words, I placed my hand over it. "That has got to be the best suggestion I've heard all day."

Once the medics completed their treatment, with instructions on steering clear of heavy exertion activities for the next several days, we went to the Poké Bowl. The open sign still blinked, if only just. I glanced at the menu, though I shouldn't have bothered. I always ordered the same thing. Still, sometimes new intriguing things showed up. Another type of quinoa; like anyone needed another. What in the name of my ancestors was farro? Wasn't that a card game? I noticed a new mushroom, one I'd read about recently, but I detested fungus. White tuna might be a tasty addition to my normal meal. Despite my good intentions, I ordered my usual.

I felt bad making them stay open, but Nami sat down with us. "Business stayed slow tonight. I'm glad to let Reuben and Devin clean up for once. Did you send the new age queen to us earlier?"

I nodded as I chewed a chunk of Ahi. "Sorry. I figured she had more money than sense. She's my boss' cousin, but I needed to get her out of my hair."

Nami waved her hand, showing off a new spiderweb tattoo. "She was fine. Mind you, I couldn't taste anything for hours after the waves of patchouli. Fun fact. Patchouli is believed to be a prophylactic in China, Japan, and some Middle Eastern countries."

"My nose is numb from her patchouli. I'm not certain I will ever smell anything again."

Nami laughed. "You'll mend, eventually. First, she chatted with Reuben during the lunch rush, but she offered to help out, too. Then she discussed some of our ingredients, classifying each one as sustainable or organic. She didn't even like the new gourmet spices or mushrooms, calling them 'forbidden.' I searched the list of items not allowed from New America, but none popped up. An odd duck, that one."

In my driest voice, I replied, "I can't argue with that assessment in the slightest. Wait, you didn't put any of those mushrooms in my food, did you? You know my rules. No kale, no fungi, no quinoa."

Nami chuckled, shook her head. "I wouldn't dare. I know better, and so do they." She sucked down a couple bobas from her bubble tea. "Now, what has you at work so late? Anything fun and interesting?"

I glanced at Mattea. While a man on death's door certainly sounded interesting, the maxims forbade us speaking of an open investigation. My assistant gave the slightest of nods. "I'm afraid nothing fun. A few fires to put out, that's all."

"Damn! I'd hoped for an entertaining tale. Devin and Reuben have both been in a foul mood today, and I need a little cheer. We had a customer in today who got sick all over the counter. We had to close right in the middle of the lunch rush, and they took them to A&E."

"Lovely. Were they sick after they ate your food?"

Nami snorted. "Not hardly. As soon as they entered, they spewed across everything. It smelled horrible. So, cheer me up, please?"

"I did have a rather remarkable spoiled woman in the other day. We've deemed her 'Lady Prissy-Pants,' but I believe her real name was Lady Xanthippe."

Nami's eyes grew wide. "Xanthippe? Are you fucking kidding me?" Howls of laughter echoed through the small café until both Nami's husbands came around to discover the joke.

In my most exaggerated posh accent, I repeated, "Lady Xanthippe Thundergrast-Hickenbotham, if you please. And no, you may *not* shorten it." Dropping the accent, I continued, "She wanted to travel that day, if you can believe it."

Nami gave me a half-smile. "Let me guess. Did she wish to be Queen Elizabeth's sister?"

"Nope. Guess again. Reuben?"

The dark-skinned young man raised one eyebrow. "Roman Senate?"

I shook my head again, taking a bite of my dinner. "Devin?"

He narrowed his eyes. "Manchurian China."

"Boom! Our dinner is free."

Mattea, Tarren, and I all raised our drinks for a toast.

Nami rolled her eyes. "Yeah, yeah. So tell us, where was her desired destination?"

Mattea grinned. "Think high heels and outrageous wigs."

Rueben snapped his fingers. "Of course! Louis XV's court! I should have guessed, insisting on a name like that. Bloody pretentious git."

A loud knock startled me, but not at the restaurant. Someone pounded the door to my shop. I didn't need to glance at the clock to realise it was way past time I should be open for business. We exchanged glances before I pushed back from the table. "I need to see who it is. It might have something to do with our…last client today."

Mattea and Tarren's smiles turned to grim lines as I walked out the front door to find a troop of Temporal Agents. "Agent Wilda Permelia Firestone?"

"You've identified me, gentlemen. Please return the favour."

"If you are Agent Firestone, you are well familiar with our uniforms."

"That's Mrs. Firestone, as I've long since retired. However, as a professional garber, I'm also well familiar with the fact that uniforms don't make the Agent."

Time Tourist Outfitters, Ltd.

Chapter Seven

Several hours later, I regretted my testiness. If I'd been less waspish, we might have been done long ago.

Mattea and Tarren sat in separate interview rooms at the Temporal Agents Canadian Headquarters near the Distillery District, while I remained ensconced with what had to be the greenest rookie Temporal Agent I'd ever encountered in my long career.

He swallowed and blinked several times, staring at his chicken-scratched notes. Paper notes, no less, not even on a computer. He had a slight peach fuzz on his chin, but other than that, offered no clues to him being out of primary school, much less academy.

The lime-green walls intensified my headache, and I just wanted to go home, away from the antiseptic stench.

"Tell me the sequence of events once again, Mrs. Firestone."

I sighed. I'd had enough of this and worried how Tarren and Mattea handled this farce of an investigation. "The sequence of events has not changed since the last three times I told you, Agent Cote. I'm tired, I'm aching, I haven't eaten for hours, and I need a pee. I retain rights as a former Agent and an employee of the Time Tourist Board. Once you supply my basic needs and those of my staff, I am far more likely to answer your questions in a pleasant manner. Until that time, I assure you, I shall intensify my ornery nature. I possess fifty-five years of learning how not to answer uppity, self-important people, young man, and I am more than willing to bring that wealth of experience to bear upon you."

The poor child looked about ready to cry and for an instant, I regretted my heavy-handedness. However, he swallowed again, highlighting the outrageous size of his Adam's apple, and rose with a nervous nod.

Three minutes later, a clerk entered with a cheese sandwich, coffee, and water. "I assure you, Mrs. Firestone, your staff are being similarly cared for."

He left before I could thank him. A different Agent entered before the door shut. This one's grizzled sideburns and portly figure suggested he would be more difficult to intimidate.

He sat silently as I ate my sandwich and sipped my coffee. I didn't hurry, nor did he urge me to. He didn't engage in silly idle chatter, which I appreciated.

When I finished my repast, he asked, "Mrs. Firestone, I am Agent Pembley. Will you need a loo break before we proceed?"

"I would welcome a break. Are you to escort me?"

He nodded, and we took care of that detail before we sat again. He steepled his fingers on the desk and frowned at the illegible notes his predecessor had left. "Since young Jonas never seemed to learn how to write, would you please repeat your sequence of events? I assure you, this will be the last time we ask."

It would do no good to be stubborn, as they'd granted all my requests. I closed my eyes.

"The traveller came into my shop, where my receptionist, Tarren, greeted him. She called for help as he appeared to be in physical distress. My assistant, Mattea, and I rushed to the front room to help him. Sweat drenched his skin and his breath appeared laboured. He spoke several words. To the best of my recollection, he said, 'Help…I need…hospital…' and then collapsed into unconsciousness. Tarren called emergency services while this happened. Before the paramedics arrived, I did my best to assess his origin through clues in his garb. He had on nondescript linen and wool rags, no patterns I could discern, worn birchbark shoes, and no identification of any sort."

"And you didn't recognise him?"

"Correct, I didn't. Which is surprising, as I outfit every traveller in North America, as far as I know. However, occasionally we get travellers that begin on another continent and through an emergency, need to travel back through our portal. Did the staff next door not notice him when he returned? I'm sure he caused quite a stir."

Agent Pembley frowned before answering. "I'm sure you realise we can only disclose certain details of our investigation."

My urge to obstinacy returned, but I repressed it. For now.

"You're certain you've never seen him?"

"Never? I don't know. I see thousands of people on the street every day. I take public transport. But no, I don't recall interacting with him. He had a remarkably dark skin tone. I would have remembered someone so unusual, even if the shade changed with illness."

The Agent frowned again and typed on his computer. He paused occasionally, searching the ceiling for words. When he finally stopped, he asked, "Why were you in the shop so late?"

"It wasn't too late. I'd just finished sending a client next door. Wait, maybe she saw him emerge! Did you speak to Bryonie Trafalgar?"

His eyes widened. "You didn't mention this person before. Did she witness the traveller's arrival?"

I shook my head impatiently. "No, no. I told you, I'd just sent her to get her itinerary settled. After she left, the traveller showed up. But if he came through the portal, she must have crossed paths with him at some point. Would you like a full list of my customers that day? Earlier, two officials showed up trying to travel that day, a Mr. Thompson and a Sir Algernon St. Clair of the Metropolitan Police of London. However, they'd cleared off before well the sick man showed up."

He turned off his tablet and studied me for several seconds. My jaw clenched, wanting to spit out something sarcastic, but my wisdom, such as it was, kept my mouth shut. Still, keeping silent pained me.

"We don't think he came through an official portal, Mrs. Firestone."

I blinked. "Then where did he come from? Hell itself?"

With a rueful chuckle, he unsuccessfully hid a half-smile. "No, Mrs. Firestone. We think he came through a bootleg portal."

As Aminata had surmised at the hospital, a rogue portal could create countless disasters. She'd indicated several across the world. One was a problem. Three could be a disaster.

"Have you spoken to the charge nurse at the hospital? Aminata Konaté?"

He steepled his fingers. "Indeed I have. I was unaware that you had."

"She spoke to you about the other sick travellers? And portals?"

He nodded, his eyes narrowing. We shared a sigh of knowing horror.

Back when the technology had been discovered about forty years before, several 'entrepreneurs' set up their own portals, to keep the government from a monopoly. At first, it looked like the free market would rule. Dozens of operators set up portals, taking cash from all comers.

Then the cellular degeneration became apparent.

At first, people simply seemed tired. The first theory was that travelling created a heavy fatigue upon the musculoskeletal system. Travellers subsequently spaced out their trips to allow the body to recover. This didn't work.

After several unexpected, horrific deaths, scientists realised something within the technology of the portal didn't stem cellular degeneration from occurring after several trips. One trip back and forth might do no harm, but more than three resulted in weakened bones, tendons, or worse, blood vessel interruption.

It's difficult to get to a hospital in time when your aorta re-materialises in a different place than your heart.

The Department of Health ordered all portals closed. The government took over and conducted studies. A method for avoiding the problem eventually came clear, but that secret remains in the hands of PENDULUM. Proprietary information to keep rogue portals from setting up shop.

This detriment hadn't been enough. Even the worst horrors can be forgotten in just a few decades.

The Agent tapped his pen, recalling me from my thoughts. "Can anyone verify your whereabouts the night before this, Mrs. Firestone?"

I narrowed my eyes at him. "Me? You can't imagine I've got anything to do with a rogue portal? I work for the Agency, for my ancestor's sake."

"We're well aware of your employment, Mrs. Firestone. We're also well aware of your husband's employment background. Did he not work on the team that developed the original portals?"

I laughed at his idiocy. "Of course, he did. But he worked as a clerk at the lab, not a scientist. He didn't get his degree until years later. And, in case you don't have it in your copious notes, my husband died over thirty years ago. Do you imagine he's setting up rogue portals from beyond the grave? Do you want to check my purse for my Ouija board? Or maybe I found his long-lost diary of diabolical secrets?"

He didn't laugh. Instead, he scowled and crossed his arms. "You aren't taking this inquiry as seriously as you should, Mrs. Firestone. Please answer my questions."

Still chuckling, I wagged my finger at him. "You are barking in the wrong forest entirely, Agent Pembley, if you'll pardon me saying so. I created no rogue portal, I wouldn't know how to set one up, and I would never do such an irresponsible thing. Anyone who has worked with me in the past can attest to this."

"And they can attest to your whereabouts last night, as well?"

After taking a deep sigh, I said, "The only being who can attest to my whereabouts last night is my cat, Dinah. She's rather short on English. I've lived alone for many years, Agent Pembley."

He stared at me for several moments while I stared back, just as hard. I refused to allow a Temporal Agent to intimidate me, having been one myself for many years. Of course, I worked in the Investigative branch, not the Compliance branch. However, I knew the rules and my rights.

"Very well. You are free to go, for now. However, we may wish to ask you and your staff more questions later. Don't leave this time or country, please."

I snorted at him. "I no longer travel and my staff are not wealthy. You have no fear on that account."

He stood and held the door open for me. I nodded thanks and with great relief, found both Mattea and Tarren waiting for me outside. They looked worse for wear, but I'm sure I was no spring rose, either.

Together we exited the premises with alacrity. Tarren had a car, and she dropped each of us off. None of us wished to discuss the evening's events or the implications.

Chapter Eight

More than a week passed before any of us heard about the patient again. Our custom had fallen considerably, though, and I felt certain Lady Prissy-Pants had put out the word our establishment should be shunned. I laughed at the conceit. Only one sanctioned portal operated on this continent. Paris, Buenos Aires, Kiev, Shanghai, and Johannesburg had portals. However, the organisations in each location maintained prejudice against travellers from other locales. To be fair, we did as well. Call it professional territorialism. Call it politics. Call it sheer stubbornness. Whatever it was, most offices would only allow their own through.

I'd had time to catch up on my backlog of repairs, and I'd become heartily bored with waiting. To combat the boredom, both Mattea and I created new garb for fun. All perfectly accurate, of course. I sent back one bolt of wool fabric as the red had been dyed too bright to be the deep scarlet of a proper eighteenth-century British officer uniform. When they finally delivered the proper colour, the weight was wrong, and much too thin to guard against freezing Scottish winters.

After a nasty curse at incompetent suppliers, I rose, intending to march down the street to confront them when the jingling door made my heart leap in anticipation of a new client.

It sank again when I recognised the second Agent who had questioned me. He spoke a few words to Tarren before she buzzed me.

With a sigh and a last sip of my coffee, I said, "I'll be right there."

"Mrs. Firestone, I wanted to apprise you of our investigation and extend to you an invitation."

I glanced at Tarren, who zipped out of the reception area, closing the workroom door behind her. This gave us a vestige of privacy, though I knew both women would be likely listening at the thin door. I sat down on one chintz chesterfield in the waiting area and gestured to Agent Pembley to sit in the other.

I glared and gritted my teeth. "And?"

He clutched onto his clipboard. "The patient you brought in is still alive. However, he remains gravely ill, and we have yet to determine the cause of his illness. The patient they discovered in Edinburgh, one Emory McKenzie, has worsened. I have no word yet on the patient in Lima. His name is Mario del Socorro."

"I thought it was cellular degeneration of a possible rogue portal?"

My suggestion must have interrupted his rehearsed delivery, for he coughed and cleared his throat. "We considered that and continue to investigate the possibility. However, the symptoms don't match the prior data on such effect."

This took me aback. I'd been so certain Josephus' condition had been due to a counterfeit portal. I searched my mind for other possibilities for the man's distress, but I had no background in biological pathogens. My areas of expertise had been political intrigue and fashion.

Pembley continued. "We've determined the disease is organic in nature, and while the original contagion is unknown, the disease must have mutated into a contagious vector. We need an Agent to go back to investigate any possible contagions Patient Zero came into contact with. Agencies in Peru and Scotland are doing the same."

My eyes narrowed in suspicion. "We know his name, Agent Pembley. Please call him Josephus. And while I appreciate the update, isn't it against procedure to disseminate such information until your investigation is complete?"

He refused to become ruffled, despite my grimmest scowl. "You are correct, Mrs. Firestone. However, we have encountered unusual circumstances."

I cocked my head and waited, putting on my best displeased schoolmarm glare.

Pembley cleared his throat and placed his clipboard next to him on the chesterfield. "From what we can tell, anyone who has come into contact with Patient...with Josephus and travelled within the last ten years has become ill. The incubation period seems to be four to six days. During that time, those people are also contagious. Many more Agents and travellers have contracted this illness, as we failed to contain the contagion at once. The entire active Agency is either in hospital or under quarantine. Other Agencies have reported the same."

A lump of dread formed in my throat, but it didn't feel scratchy. "Go on."

"Therefore, we need someone both familiar with Temporal Investigation procedures and someone who hasn't travelled in several years. In addition, since you appear to be in perfect health—"

I snorted at that idea, but he continued.

"—you seem to be immune."

I clenched my jaws and refused to rise to the bait. I meant to make him ask.

He wiped his hands on his trousers and clenched them. "Mrs. Firestone, the department would like to request your assistance in this matter. Will you go on this mission?"

"You want me to become an Agent again and travel back in time to wherever Josephus came from to find this contagion."

"Where Josephus travelled, yes, but also to where the other two patients travelled. Each one must have contracted this illness from a common vector. I need someone with a keen analytic mind and experience as an Agent." He picked up his clipboard again and fiddled with his pen clipped to the top.

I stared at him. When he looked about to burst from anticipation, I let loose. "Certainly not. If you cannot tell by the surrounding shop, I retired from travelling many years ago. My reasons for such retirement are final and not subject to discussion. If that is all?"

"Mrs. Firestone, you must..."

I stood, coming close to his face, mustering all the rage I'd pent up. "I must do absolutely nothing! Which part of 'no' did you not understand? The N or the O? If you like, I can say no in several languages. You're certain to recognise one. *Nyet. Nein. Non. Nej. Ní hea. Bú shì. Neyn.*"

"You're still listed as an Agent."

I flung my hands up as I paced. "So are plenty of others, far more able to conduct such an investigation. It's patently ridiculous for you to ask me. For my ancestor's sake, I'm fifty-five years old. I retired from active duty thirty years ago. My bones ache and my joints pop. I have no business going on a mission!"

"I'm afraid I haven't made myself clear. The illness has affected many Agents, Mrs. Firestone. The ward in our hospital is bursting. There's no one else we can send."

I stopped pacing and stared at him. "No one? You can't be serious. I realise none of the Agencies have been robust, but you must have a dozen able-bodied Agents. What about Thomas Gagnon?"

"In the hospital ward."

"Hamish Fraser?"

"Practically blind."

"Uhm…Antoinette Ouellet?"

"Disappeared while travelling. We presume she married a local and went off the grid."

I mentally cheered her bravery while digging up more ancient memories. "Tamara Michaud?"

"In the hospital ward. Please, trust me, Mrs. Firestone, we've investigated every Agent we could before we came to you, both here and abroad. Your reputation precedes you."

I laughed out loud with a snort of incredulity.

"No, I mean that. I've read your past reports. You were one of the best."

I sat back on the chesterfield and clasped my hands.

"What about Agents from the other offices? Paris? Kiev?"

He shook his head. "Their ranks are similarly deprecated. Their Boards refused to help. Politics."

I snorted. "Folly, you mean. If this is as serious as all that, damn the politics."

The fact he had these names, and their status, so readily to mind, rocked me. They *had* tried other Agents. I picked at the skin on the edge of my nail, trying to sort through the myriad thoughts screaming through my mind. Part of me gibbered in fear at travelling again. Another part, long since locked away, threatened to creak open. I slammed it shut and twisted the key in the lock. A third part of me jumped up, excited at the prospect of going on another mission. I slapped that part of me down with a stern look.

"I'm in no shape to go on an extended trip, Agent Pembley. A single, older woman in any time of history is vulnerable. Why don't you travel to the last decade and snag an Agent from that time?"

"You know better than that, Mrs. Firestone. Not only is it against temporal maxims, it could unravel the time stream. We can't even go back to retrieve an Agent who dies on mission for the same reason. Besides, I understand your assistant would like to travel but cannot afford such a trip. You may take your assistant with you."

I stood again. "This isn't a fun holiday! This is dangerous investigative work! Agents die doing things like this. You can't ask me to take a young, untrained seamstress on such a mission!"

His voice remained quiet and even, almost a whisper. "We can ask, because we must, Mrs. Firestone. We truly have no one else to send."

The precise calm of his words sucked the wind out of my angry sails. When I sat this time, I let out a sigh of resignation. "I must insist on at least the basic investigative training course for Mattea. Have you been able to determine Josephus' itinerary?"

Chapter Nine

After studying the changes in investigative procedures, I remembered one reason I quit being an active Agent. The red tape each Agent must tie around every report grew epic. With electronic communication, why should I create four different reports for four different branches of PENDULUM? One report should be more than sufficient for all departments.

I glanced at Mattea, who had furrowed her brow in concentration. I considered crumpling my paper and throwing it at her to lighten the mood but talked myself out of such a childish prank. The sense of urgency kept me going. With more and more Agents contracting whatever disease affected the travellers, time truly was of the essence, for once.

Mattea sat beside me, trying to absorb a full three years' worth of training in as many days. She needed that much time for her panoculations to settle, and we needed to create our own garb for the trip. Most of our pre-made garb fit people of normal height. My five-foot nothing frame made things problematic. While most people in the past, depending on the location, stood shorter, the travellers from this time averaged much taller.

When I'd received the itinerary, I shook my head. "Fourteenth century Mali? Twelfth century Orkney? Tenth century Maine? What in the name of seven Hells did Josephus search for?"

Pembley shook his head. "Only one of those is Josephus', remember. He went to Mali. Orkney was where the traveller from Edinburgh came from. Maine was the Lima traveller. We don't know why any of them travelled. They may have been smuggling people or proscribed substances, or searching for some ancient artifact, but that's just a guess. We found traces of organic matter on their clothing. That's how we determined the locations and times. Why they chose those places and times remains unclear."

"Will we be able to return between each trip?"

He nodded. "We must test the samples you bring back. Anything they came in contact with, gifts they received, foods they ate, the people they touched. You'll have one of the new collection bags to preserve each sample as they're placed inside. Still, the capacity isn't infinite."

"Bloody Hell. I'll be picking up everything! Does this collection bag offset the sheer mass I'll be carrying? And you know I can't actually shove people into that bag, right?"

Again nodding, Pembley handed me a sheet with the specifications. "Panoculation isn't the only thing we've improved since you Agented. The collection bags have a small-scale gyroscope to help cancel higher mass effects. However, it makes the bag much more dangerous to take into the past. While the workings are solid state, you don't want to allow locals access to the technology. And yes, I realise we cannot collect people or animals as samples. But you can collect hair and other substances from them."

I raised my eyebrows and glanced at Mattea. "Other substances? Exactly what substances do you expect us to collect from people?"

Pembley's blush spread quickly across his face, and I laughed, having achieved the desired effect. I waved away his stammer and frowned at the specs, adding them to the growing list of things I hated about this assignment. My bones protested the fact I'd been sitting in a classroom chair for two days with no regard to comfort or ergonomics. Mattea didn't seem to mind as much, as she busily devoured every tidbit of information they fed her. I compared each datum to that I'd learned thirty years ago, searching for equivalents and differences. Such a change might make a huge difference in the success of my mission. I couldn't rely on years of honed instincts this trip.

Every time I considered the trip itself, I remembered my first step into the Temporal Shifter, with its brass and copper nautical fittings and its antique steam-powered engine. When I first travelled, the necessity for steam power seemed quaint and charming. The process of travel didn't work well with internal combustion or traditional electricity, so steam remained the power vector of choice. While designers might (and in some countries, did) use modern fittings, the conceit and romanticism in the Toronto office insisted on this Verne-like construction.

I took that first step over thirty years ago, with my husband, Paolo. He'd insisted that I go first. "You'll never forgive me for being a chauvinist bastard if I don't allow you first boarding, my dear. You know as well as I do."

He'd been right. Paolo had always been well aware my adventurous nature outstripped his, but he'd been good about encouraging me to shine. I swallowed down the lump in my throat and pushed the memory away. As active as his ghost grew the last few days, I couldn't afford a full-on breakdown. I had too much crap to deal with at the moment.

Nevertheless, his ghost persisted. We'd met while training for the Agency. I'd barely been out of university, while he had worldly experience under his belt. We almost qualified as the perfect age for a bride and groom, according to Jane Austen, and soon we refused missions unless we could go together. Fraternisation grew commonplace between both Agents and people in the past back then.

When had the Agency instituted this rule on fraternisation? Agents getting involved with locals had never been encouraged, but if a traveller enjoyed a fling, as long as they kept their infertility treatment current, no one cared. Now the Agency classed such activity a level three infraction. Still, not as bad as killing someone at level ten.

When the instructor, a reedy man who might blow over if I sneezed, addressed the infractions, Mattea asked, "What happens if someone tries to commit a level ten infraction?"

The instructor sniffed, annoyed at the interruption in his monotone delivery. "A traveller working toward killing someone in the past resulted in them growing horribly ill before completing their task. I never witnessed the effect personally, but I've seen simulation vids. The man bent over with intense pain, as if someone had stabbed him in the gut."

"But couldn't he push through the pain?"

I shook my head. "This is worse than childbirth pain, from all accounts. No one is pushing through that level of pain."

The built-in 'repair' function of the traveller had been the stickiest part of approving travel for public consumption. The possibility of traveller changing the past indelibly, either by mistake or intent, kept it to trained Agents for decades. The option only became public when they'd been able to add on an algorithm in the Temporal Shifter. This algorithm made a traveller ill if they might change time in a major way. Minor changes corrected themselves if they travelled over three hundred years in the past. However, affecting history significantly held inherent danger, became forbidden, and now came with a built-in deterrent.

Every few years, some intrepid soul tried to assassinate Hitler, Julius Caesar, or Attila the Hun before they committed their atrocities. Every time, the Meddling Deterrent, as travellers dubbed it, kicked in.

I never understood the science behind such deterrents, but Paolo had. He tried to explain it many times, but I usually shut him up with some obscure costume detail from prehistoric India until we both laughed.

I wondered if the illness Josephus contracted might be related to the Meddling Deterrent. The hallmark symptoms seemed different. Extreme nausea and diarrhoea combined with severe migraines should be enough to deter anyone from planned mayhem. The Agency must have investigated that as the first option. No, Josephus and his compatriots must have contracted a different malady.

Were the three working together for some misguided grand purpose? Or an organized band of Time criminals? Or were they all simply unlucky at the same time? I distrusted coincidences.

What if there were more rogue travellers we never found?

All travellers received a broad spectrum panoculation, but got boosters tailored to their itinerary. If they travelled to eighteenth century Panama, for instance, the Agency added malaria. However, if he'd used a rogue portal, Josephus may not have gotten panoculated for a specific time, if at all.

Such a possibility made me more than angry. How dare they? How dare these rogue operators endanger everyone in the past and the present? Our current environment carried super-germs, things that could destroy a small population in, say, eighth century Poland or twelfth century Indonesia. Look at the disease devastation that killed ninety percent of the eastern native population after the Spanish came to the Americas. This ignorance reminded me of the anti-vaccination trolls, convinced the science was a conspiracy to make more money for the doctors and drug manufacturers. I never understood how dying children weren't a strong enough argument for vaccinations.

I shoved aside my subsidiary anger and concentrated on the primary source. If Josephus travelled through a knock-off portal, he may not be panoculated, hadn't gone through any other protocols of training, and likely got hit with a dose of cellular degeneration. That technology remained a guarded secret, designed to stop this type of chaos. I'm betting whoever set up their portals didn't tell their *clients* about the dangers. I felt more sorry than angry for Josephus. He seemed like an innocent mule now.

Still, the media brimmed with adverts for the official trips. Most had the usual disclaimers ad nauseam about panoculations, liability clauses, etc. Even if no one reads the fine print, they must be aware it exists.

Shaking my head at the idiocy of humanity, I concentrated on memorising the newest spate of directives on official travelling. This section dealt with fitting into local customs and religious beliefs, even if your own didn't mesh. This included extremes like sacrificing animals if required to do so in your persona. If such acts flew against your conscience, you simply didn't travel to that time or place or didn't put yourself in such a situation. Posing as a noble or a priestly caste would likely to get you into such a jam.

While being a peasant was unpleasant through most of history, it also came with few real responsibilities, other than hard work.

When Paolo and I travelled, we tried to choose either merchant or peasant class. Such a stature in society allowed for the greatest mobility. True peasants didn't travel because they lacked resources to make a move from a more miserable place to a less miserable place. As a Temporal Agent, one had more resources than most.

Mattea nudged me and pointed at her paper. "Wilda? What does this phrase mean?"

I peered at the words. "*Transversal time dilation.* Why are you trying to figure out the quantum mechanics of the trip? All we need to do is go, behave ourselves, find what Josephus found, and return. We don't need to understand how the bloody thing works."

She frowned down at the paper. "I want to understand what they're doing to me."

"Do you have a degree in quantum physics? Time Theory? Tipler Cylinders? Have you studied String Theory?"

Mattea shook her head, drooping. "I guess I'm not cut out for this."

"Nonsense! You don't need to understand the science to travel. In fact, I think it's better if you don't. An Agent isn't a physicist. An Agent is an investigator, and you have a keen eye for detail and an analytic mind. You get along well with people without trying, and you're eager to learn. That's all you need in basic skills. Learn the rest of the rules and you'll be brilliant. Didn't you always want to travel?"

Staring out the window, she sighed. "I *have* always wanted to travel, either here in this time or in history. To absorb the realities of other people, cultures, and mores. To be someone else, even for a little bit. That's always been my dream."

"Then do it! You have the talent. Make it a reality. I have faith in you."

After the basic skills, we took a crash course in the history and politics for our first trip. The others would come afterwards.

Our first visit would be to fourteenth century Mali, at the height of Mansa Musa's rule. Mattea evidently had never heard of the richest man in the world.

She furrowed her brow and interrupted the instructor. "He did what in Egypt?"

The instructor blinked a few times before answering. "He gave away so much gold it depressed the local economy for decades. His generosity screwed up the gold trade for years. In fact, he gave all his gold away and then needed to borrow more gold just to pay for the trip back to Mali."

"Sounds like he needed a financial advisor."

I turned to her. "And you think he'd listen to a woman in that regard? Besides, we're travelling to the time after he returned, so any advice you may offer would be too late. He passed a law that all gold nuggets belonged to him, but gold dust could be used as currency. They also used pieces of iron, red copper, spices, and cowrie shells."

"Cowrie shells? Doesn't that seem rather…primitive?"

Primitive. A dangerous word. People didn't like being called primitive. They tended to react poorly to such criticism. It evoked sudden visions of Mattea as the centrepiece of a ritual. Her long, wavy gold-brown hair tumbled over her shoulders, her tall, slender body lain out and decked in flowers. Perhaps tribal facial paint on her delicate, refined face. I scowled at her. "Get rid of that word. Excise it from your vocabulary now before it gets you executed, Mattea. I'm serious. Never judge another culture or their customs. Never speak such judgement. We have less protection than male Agents, and even less than locals of status and reputation. We're female strangers, and thus must walk a tight line of respect and humility. If you cannot keep that in mind at every moment of every day, you will get us both killed. Do you understand?"

Only once did I make the mistake of allowing my modern sensibilities to colour my actions in the past and almost paid for such insolence with my life. Other cultures were as complex as our own and much less tolerant. If Mattea couldn't grasp that, she had no business being an Agent or travelling even as a tourist.

Mattea hung her head. "I understand, I do! Maybe I didn't think, but I will. I promise."

I hoped she did. "Other things you can get executed for in Mansa Musa's court include sneezing in his presence, wearing sandals in his presence, speaking directly to him, refusing his bed—"

She bolted straight up in her chair. "What? I might have to sleep with him?"

I laughed, now enjoying her surprise. "Likely not. After his hajj to Mecca, his priest informed him that Muslim law forbade even kings the right to bed any woman they wished. From all reports, he avoided such things afterward. However, he may ask you to be one of his wives. I don't know the penalty for refusing that, but if you've already got a husband somewhere, you may escape such a fate."

"Will they ostracize me for being white?"

I shrugged. "I shouldn't think so. They'd met Venetian traders. I might pass for a Middle Eastern woman, even if my darker skin comes from First Nations heritage rather than Egyptian. You would pass for Sicilian or even Portuguese. Both traded heavily with western Africa at this point."

"Must I create a persona for each trip, as well? Complete with a history and family?"

"The Agency takes care of that. We should get our personas tonight, so we have time to study them before the trip. They're pretty good about finding names similar to our own. Now, shall we learn more about fourteenth century Mali?"

We concentrated on the instructor's presentation on trade practises, court traditions, common languages, and the roles of women in society. Secretly, I looked forward to this trip. Mansa Musa and his legendary court fascinated me, but such a trip never came up on our radar in the past. Any man who crossed a desert with his chief wife and five hundred maids-in-waiting—and survived the trip—deserved respect and wonder.

Besides, I'd always wanted to peruse his magnificent library at Tombouctou. I once explored the Library at Alexandria and still dreamt of that mystical visit. Tombouctou held a similar wealth of knowledge.

I wished the translator implant extended to reading as well as hearing and speaking the languages programmed within, but alas, it wasn't so. Since illiteracy remained the default for most people throughout history, this rarely became an issue for either Agents or tourists. The technology involved hadn't kept pace with that of the audial translator. Still, it would be nice.

Which three languages should we choose? Each translator only held three, and the more obscure the language became, the more uncertain the translator became. Pictish, for example, or Uruk, remained ambiguous on many words and concepts, reducing the implant's efficacy.

The Agency implanted devices behind each Agent's ear and loaded them with appropriate languages for the trip. Our first choice must be Arabic. Mandé became a strong second language, and I chose the more common Bambara as a third. I suggested to Mattea that her third language be different so we'd have a greater coverage, so she chose Soninke. Luckily, I'd studied written Arabic in my youth, so could puzzle out a few scripts. The beauty and artistry of Arabic calligraphy had always fascinated me.

With our fill of information on the Mali Empire, we took a break before our next class. I grinned as Mattea dropped into the lounge chesterfield and flung her arms over her head. "Tired yet?"

"My brain wants to explode. We have two more cultures to cram for? Christ on a piece of toast. I'm exhausted."

With a ruthless chuckle, I patted her on the shoulder. "We'll soon be done with Mali, for now. Native culture is next."

"Which area are we visiting on the second trip?"

"Northern Maine about five hundred years before Columbus showed up. The tribal family is Wabenaki, and forensics believes Josephus visited the Pa'nawampske'wiak people, the Penobscot, around Oldtown."

Mattea seemed pensive, but I guessed at what troubled her. "My own obvious tribal blood will help. Natives saw Caucasians when the Norse settled L'Anse aux Meadows. Sure, Newfoundland lay a thousand miles north, but tales and legends stay strong in oral traditions."

By her pensive look, I hadn't convinced her.

"Don't worry. The tables will turn when we visit Orkney. Pictish tribes mixed with Norse invaders? That's the whitest of the white. I'll stick out like a sore thumb and get showed around as a novelty item. You'll end up having the chief eating out of your hand."

She gave me a weak smile. "If I survive all the training. Native culture is next?"

I nodded with another laugh. "Which languages will you choose for that leg of the journey?"

"The local tribal language, Wolastoqiyik, and Mi'kmaw. I thought a Newfoundland Native language might be helpful if I'm to be related to the Norse settlers. They'd be the people encountered, the so-called Skraelings, wouldn't they?"

"Mostly. Tribes shifted both populations and languages over centuries, and firsthand accounts from travellers to that time and place are scarce. Still, those are decent language choices. I'm loading Pa'nawampske'wiak, Quiripi, in case we must head farther south, and Ojibwe to bolster my background as Ontario First Nations people. Just don't get too friendly with the shamans. They may want to take you on a spirit quest. From what I understand, that involves some hallucinogens."

Her eyes widened as the buzzer sounded, signalling the end of our break and we shuffled into the classroom. I gripped my jumbo cup of coffee and honey bun while Mattea grabbed chips and a pop. My intention was to drink every ounce of coffee I could get my hands on in the next three days. It could be days, or even weeks, without the life-giving elixir. I suspected Mattea felt the same about her pop addiction.

Hot baths, plumbing, reading glasses—these were all wonderful modern conveniences. I cared more about the lack of scientific health care and coffee. What can I say, I had my priorities straight.

Part II
Chapter Ten

As I lay in my bed the night before our trip, I stared at the ceiling and tried hard not to think of my husband.

It didn't work. His voice from the message machine ran in an endless loop within my memory.

Twisted, swirling images of Paolo swam in my mind, some coloured like old sepia photographs or mid-twentieth century movies. Dressed in Manchurian garb, or a Jacobite kilt, as a plague-era doctor, or a Neolithic hunter. Each persona my husband played in the past rushed to haunt me as I contemplated stepping once more into the abyss of time. One by one, a parade of garbed spouses marched across my mind's eye. Some gave me a jaunty wink. Others tipped their hats or blew a kiss. Not one stopped for me, though I ached as each version of my husband passed, only to fade into the dream distance, lost forever.

What if I couldn't do this? I'd given Mattea countless reassurances she'd be up to the task, but what about me? I'd quit travelling for an excellent reason, a reason which hadn't changed.

Frustrated, I flung the covers off my sweating body, eliciting an angry complaint from Dinah.

"Oh, relax, cat, this is nothing. You'll be pampered at the pet hotel while I'm gone and won't even miss me."

With a glance full of indignant reproach, she proceeded to groom herself. I stood and went into the kitchenette to make myself a cup of tea. Perhaps a soothing chamomile brew would help me sleep, but I doubted it. Too much of my past hammered on the walls of my memory like barbarians at the gate. Eventually, they'd break through. Where would I be when that happened? *When* would I be? Would I breakdown and abandon Mattea in a strange land?

The cup rattled in my hand, and I placed it on the table before I dropped it. I gripped the sides of the marble countertop and closed my eyes, begging the panic to subside. The fear burst inside me, making my heart pound and my ears ring. Sweat dripped down my face, and I struggled to sit before I passed out, my back to the sink cabinet.

Deep breaths. Count to five. Concentrate on five things I could see. The tile. The table leg. The chair. The door jamb. The cat.

The last thing I wanted now was contact, but Dinah had other ideas. She jumped into my lap and curled up, purring until the vibration drowned my tremors. I concentrated on petting her from head all the way down her spine to the end of her tail, repeating the soothing motion. As I petted, my breathing slowed to a normal rhythm. Ten more pets and my sweat stopped dripping.

I took a deep breath and glanced above me. The lip of the tea saucer peeked over the edge. I wanted to retrieve my tea, but I remained loath to move Dinah, especially after she'd helped me control my panic attack. I settled on more petting.

I glanced at the window, but night still ruled the sky. The one good thing about a panic attack, I usually slept afterward. They exhausted me beyond belief. Carefully, I removed Dinah from my lap, pulled myself to my feet, gulped the tepid tea, and shambled into the bedroom. I must have reached the bed because when my alarm woke me, I had to untangle myself from the quilted duvet.

When I washed my face, I scrubbed hard, trying to scrape away long-buried painful memories. The hot water of the shower did little to erase my nightmares, but as I went through the mechanical motions of getting ready for work, they sloughed away like dew fairies in the sunrise.

I spent no effort deciding on today's clothing, as we'd only be changing into our Malinké garb as soon as we arrived. I didn't look forward to the task, as getting used to foreign clothing always took time. Malinké women favoured draped tunic-like cloth with little tailoring or decoration, unless in a high ceremony, secured by a belt, with a mantle around the shoulders and a sheer veil over their nose and mouth. Even then, the law forbade certain colours, such as red or green. Only prostitutes wore red, as per Maliki Law, and angels or the family of Muhammed wore green, depending on the ruler's beliefs.

The journey to the office blurred in my mind. No one was in the garb shop, so I changed, finishing up just as Mattea came in.

Once I had donned my garb and helped Mattea arrange her own, she looked in the mirror. She fussed with her long, curly hair under her veil, wiggling and shifting until she felt more comfortable. "I love the varying shades of blue and gold, and all the stripes. However, this feels like everything will fall off if I move an inch the wrong way. What's keeping it in place?"

"Tucked fabrics and folds. I have a few discreet pins here and there if we need them. However, they'd be imported items, so we shouldn't bring attention to them. They'd encourage questions we might find difficult to answer."

"I suspect that's going to be a common theme. How do you answer nosy questions about your past, your family, your life?"

"The trick is to say the truth but change the salient details. For instance, I'm a widow from a land far across the water. They'll assume I'm from Europe, or perhaps the Arabian Peninsula."

"My persona history says I just arrived in Mali from Sicily. Sicily? Do I look Italian?" She spread her hands in question.

I laughed as I hid my Temporal Tracker under my clothing. The device detected other travellers by glowing when I pressed a hidden button.

While it looked like a simple carved wooden pendant, keeping it from sight made my trip safer. I pulled out the several loops of brightly coloured glass beads and cowrie shells serving as currency. Gold nuggets all belonged to the king, so merchants used gold dust as payment for goods. We included no gold beads in our jewellery.

"Don't you remember the blurb we got on medieval Sicily? So many cultures invaded that little island over the centuries, you might be descended from any culture in the western world. It's the Agency's favourite origin location. Greeks colonised it first, then the Romans, Vandals, Byzantines, Vikings, Muslims, and many minor settlements amongst them. Even if you encounter another Sicilian, the island is big enough that he likely never visited your village. If pressed by someone who lived on Sicily all his life, you just shrug and say your husband brought you there as a bride from somewhere else, perhaps the British Isles."

"That's right, the Americas hadn't been discovered yet. I hope I can make it convincing."

"Discovered and remembered by the Europeans, no. Natives lived here for thousands of years, and the Norse found the Americas long before Columbus convinced Queen Isabella to hock her jewels. Being a foreigner is a blessing, because any misunderstandings can be waved away as a lack of expertise in the nuances of the language."

Mattea rubbed the edge of her linen where the hand-stitched hem formed a design with the silk thread. "We're going as upper-class. What if I make a horrible mistake in protocol?"

"It depends on the mistake. We can wave off most minor ones as the innocent mistake of a stranger. Some are more serious and a few have deadly consequences. You received a list of the worst offences as part of our training, remember?"

She nodded, still looking pensive. "I'm just getting nervous."

With a grin and a fierce hug, I assured her, "We all do, especially the first time. We'll be fine. Now, are you ready for your first trip into the past?"

With a deep breath, Mattea nodded, and we walked next door to the Temporal Shifter. We had our panoculations, our translator implants, and our training. The Agency had facilitated our paperwork so we only needed to show up. The director showed us to the Shifter's entrance.

The Shifter, covered in the quaint brass and copper fittings, looked like something out of a Jules Verne tale. The enormous steam whistle had been a silly conceit, but I had to admit, it engendered a burst of nostalgia. I swallowed my nerves and took Mattea's hand as the door opened. We stepped inside and sat on the benches, strapped in with antique seat belts from some 1980s automobile, and waited.

This part always made me the most nervous. When the Temporal Shifter snatched our bodies from the current time stream, I'd never grown sanguine about reappearing whole on the other side. I'd seen too many horror stories from the days before, when the Shifter didn't have that life-saving algorithm to avoid cellular degeneration. What if this Shifter miscalculated? What if the algorithm had short-circuited? What if we never re-entered the time stream? Would we be lost forever, adrift between worlds?

As I mused upon the nothingness of time, the Shifter did its work and with a boom, several hisses, and a pop, we arrived.

The door blew open and my lungs filled with sand and dust. Both Mattea and I coughed fitfully as we emerged, gazing upon the dry desert sands of the Sahara. The portal dropped us outside the city of Tombouctou, along the Niger River, but the northern edge of the city bordered the desert. Once we exited, it popped out of existence, to reappear every two days until we returned.

"Get used to the colour of sand, Mattea. And the taste of grit in your mouth. Despite all the wonders of this city, we can't avoid certain inconveniences."

After spitting and coughing orange sputum, Mattea glared at me. "So I noticed." She glanced around at the abandoned farmland. "Couldn't the portal drop us closer to the city?"

"So, we can be caught and executed as sorcerers?"

"Oh. Right. So, which direction is Timbuktu?"

"Tombouctou is the better pronunciation in this time. Though a few intentional mistakes make the unintentional ones easier to forgive. We head south. See the plume of dust there? That's likely a caravan. We should only have to walk a few miles. You have your waterskin? All your other supplies?"

She patted the various things strapped to her girdles and nodded. "I'm the White Knight. I have every single thing under the sun, save the kitchen sink. I feel like a hippopotamus."

"At least you'll be a hydrated hippopotamus. Let's go."

I clicked a hidden button on my pendant so we could find the portal again, and we set off toward the dust.

Walking in the desert may seem romantic and exciting, but the reality fell short of the dream. The heat grew oppressive, the sand got in every bit of mucus membrane one possesses despite the veils, and while I ached to chug my waterskin and relieve my dry, cracked lips, I knew better than to indulge. We had enough supplies to last a few days and the city lay only a few miles away, but anything could happen in the desert, even if we only marched near the edge of the deadly Sahara. The climate didn't forgive the slightest error.

As we passed the few poor farms on the outskirts, we received guarded nods of acknowledgment from the residents. Strangers were a common occurrence in this metropolitan trade centre, but that didn't mean strangers were safe or friendly. While the cut of our outfits showed we were females of an upper class, clothing can be faked. Those residents outside the city walls might have fallen prey to raiders pretending to be something they weren't.

Soon, we found a packed-earth road and fell in behind a small trading caravan of camels, heavy slabs of salt on each side of their pannikins.

I'd hoped never to smell the stink of camels again in my lifetime, but still, safety came in numbers. If something happened, guards armed with swords intent on defending their caravan might protect us. To combat the stench, I concentrated on their garb.

By their clothing, they came from Mossi States to the southwest. I covertly studied the trim designs on their garb, making mental notes for later use. I realised I'd be doing that a lot these trips and resolved to write the details as soon as I might safely do so. No need to waste these missions when I could gather relevant data for my shop.

By the time we arrived in Tombouctou proper, everything looked that same, red-gold colour, the shade of sand that permeated everything. Sun-baked mud bricks formed all the buildings, the clothing became inundated with it, as did skin, human or animal. This monochromatic vista, nonetheless, impressed both Mattea and me. The soaring majesty of the Sankoré Madrasah, a sacred centre of learning for the Muslim faith, rose from the dust clouds in a rough pyramid, with structural beams poking out in exotic relief.

The smooth surface of the central building, the mihrab, had been constructed of sunbaked earth bricks. It looked like the world's biggest sandcastle. I ached to explore the literature housed within, speak to each of the imams, and soak in their knowledge.

Beyond the Madrasah, the tall peaks of Mansa Musa's palace came into view, rising from the red-gold dust. While this building had straight sides rather than a pyramid shape, it also had structural palm beams in dark, contrasting brown and housed a larger area. Rising at least three stories and surrounded by a defensive wall, the palace couldn't fail to impress traders and visiting nobles.

The press of people amplified as we approached the city centre. Now we stood, shoulder to shoulder, as the crowd shifted in unpredictable ways. My head spun with the attempt to study every person's outfit until I forced myself to stop. I had more urgent things to deal with at the moment.

I held tight to Mattea's hand and edged toward the palace. My aching feet screamed, just as my skin ached for humidity. As I shoved past a pair of Egyptian traders, their camel sneezed on my back. I glanced over my shoulder to see if Mattea had gotten hit, and from the disgusted expression on her face, I gathered she had. "Don't worry, the dust will cover it soon enough."

She glared at me, but I couldn't tell if her eyes held mock rage or true anger. At this point, it didn't matter. I just wanted to escape the press of the crowd. At least in modern, downtown Toronto, people respected personal space. Mediaeval Islamic culture did not. If you stood in the best place to see a person walk by in Canada, the next person would stake a position far enough away from you to be polite. In this culture, the next person would stand directly next to you, close enough to touch shoulders, as that is the second-best place to see someone walk past. The lack of personal space was almost as bad as driving a car in London.

Drums, horns, and cheers drifted across the cacophony of people, traders, and arguments. I craned my neck, trying to see what the kerfuffle was about, and then cursed my short stature. "Mattea, can you see what's happening?"

Taller than me by over half a foot, she could just about see through the shoulders of those in front of us. "Some sort of procession. Camels, elephants. Is that a giraffe? Seriously?"

"Why not? The richest man in the world can afford to import all sorts of animals, and at least the giraffe is native to this continent. They usually live much farther west and south, though."

Bells jingled in rhythmic patterns as the crowd quieted, watching the procession pass by. I gritted my teeth and waited for someone to shift before I glimpsed the parade. Vivid shades of blue and gold swarmed in the few slivers of vision, but I never focused on one figure.

More horns sounded as another section of the procession went by. Now a matched pair of lions passed, according to the gasping spectators. I'd seen lions, of course, but I'm certain Mattea had never seen any outside the Toronto Zoo. She had a huge smile on her face, and I thought this moment may have just been worth the long, dusty trek from the drop site.

I tugged on Mattea's arm. "Come on! Let's get in the back end of that parade."

"What? Why?"

"How better to gain quick access to the palace?"

Chapter Eleven

After the punishing din of the Tombouctou streets, the interior of the palace was eerily peaceful. A buzz still filtered through the adobe walls, but the cool shade and the open spaces became a welcome relief. Noise still surrounded us, but not the pummeling cacophony outside. While we stood in the courtyard in the company of a multitude of animals and people, the chaos of so many creatures became far from silent. Still, the chaos remained controlled and controllable. Mattea and I peeled ourselves from the main body and walked down a hallway.

The trick to not being caught is to act as if you belong there. I'd learned this technique many years ago, from Paolo, who'd been an expert. We strode down to the kitchens, greeting those we passed with gracious nods or keeping our eyes to the floor, as dictated by the apparent status of each passerby. My surreptitious glances at their backs gave me more information for my growing mental list of garb minutiae.

Mattea whispered while we passed a group of slaves wearing only loincloths. "Where are we going?"

"The kitchen."

"Not to the musa?"

I snorted, drawing attention from a young man carrying several scrolls. I beamed at him, and he scuttled away. "Not the king, unless we must. Kings rarely understand what's going on in their court. What I want is the equivalent of the head housekeeper or butler. They know every single person who visits, those who work here, those who meet in the night and shouldn't be here. Those administrative people will have the real information."

Following my nose, I found the kitchen and pulled out my pendant. If another traveller had been near, it would glow green. Mattea and I had already been programmed within the device as red and blue. If I pressed the right combination of carved details on the side, it would glow for us as well. Best to leave the glowing to a minimum in a pre-electronic culture, though.

Several workers glanced up as we walked in, but one straightened and brushed her hands on her apron. The large woman approached us with a polite smile and a slight bow of her head. She'd tied her utilitarian, undyed robes with several lengths of plain cord to keep them out of bowls and cauldrons. "*As-salāmu ʿalaykunna.* How may I help you today?"

I returned the precise level of bow. "*Wa ʿalayka s-salā.* I'm looking for my relative. He visited here some time ago, but I'm unsure when. Who might best help us find him?"

She frowned, glancing over her shoulder. The entire kitchen staff, who had been listening intently, busied themselves with their tasks. They banged pots, slammed wood into the oven, and bent with a will to the quieter tasks of chopping and cleaning.

"Do you know for certain he visited the palace?"

The forensic reports had indicated exotic foodstuffs, uncommon to this area. While Josephus might have purchased them in the marketplace, the higher end items must have been from a palace feast. I nodded as I pulled the strings of beads out from the folds of my clothing. "Mostly certain."

She studied me for several moments as the sounds of the kitchen grew quiet again. The beads proved my wealth and status and gave her some framework in which to judge my request and her reaction to it. She cleared her throat and the industry resumed with renewed vigour. "Very well, then. I shall put you in touch with the chamber master. He houses all our visitors and will know of whom you seek. If he doesn't, he can direct you to another who can."

Vestiges of baobab flour puffed as she clapped her hands twice, filing the air with the tangy, sweet odours of vanilla and grapefruit. Long, wooden tables covered in bowls of fruit, vegetables, nuts, spices, and other supplies lined the walls. Meat and root vegetables hung from hooks around the ceiling.

A small boy scurried to her side, dressed in sandals and a long tunic. "Yes, mistress?"

"Find Ibn Khalutta. Quickly, now! Tell him we shall meet him in the Palm Room."

The child scuttled away, weaving through the kitchen, narrowly ducking under a cook as he removed a wooden paddle of bread from the stone oven.

"Now, please follow me." Obviously the headwoman, she led us through three sand-brown hallways and up two flights of stairs into a pleasant room with wide windows and palm trees. The view of the mosque and the city below seemed clearer of the ever-present desert sand, and the hum of city life muted.

"I have water for your feet here and for your mouth there. Dates and figs are for your sampling. Ibn Khalutta should be here soon. I must return to my kitchen."

She bowed more deeply than when she first greeted us. I returned the same bow as before, as she must have judged us to be higher status than she. In reality, the beads around my neck would be more than she'd make in several years, even as a valued headwoman.

We washed our feet in the warm water by the door and drank the cool water by the window. The stickiness of the candied fruit tasted too cloying for my palate. However, Mattea devoured the sweets while I smiled at her delight.

Only about ten minutes passed before the man arrived, his skin almost blue-black in the murky shadow of the corridor. His elaborate robes of saffron silk burned bright in the dim light. I stood as he came in and Mattea hastened to do the same.

His voice, a rich, velvet baritone, caressed me. "*As-salāmu ʿalaykunna.* I am Ibn Khalutta, the master of guests for our most beloved musa. Sekou informs me you search for a relative. Can you describe him?"

I bowed, lower than for Sekou. "*Wa ʿalaykum s-salā.* I can do better than describe him." After pulling out a miniature painting of Josephus in an ornate silver frame, I handed it to him. "This is my cousin, Josephus. Might you remember him in the last season?"

He took the image with raised eyebrows but walked to the window to study it in strong sunlight. After a moment, he nodded. "Yes. Yes, I recall this man. He stayed for several weeks, in conference with the musa. I did not hear what they discussed, but they had many meetings. He also met with one of musa's minor wives. I suspected he helped her with some project, but I am uncertain what. The musa is too busy now, but I will inquire if you may meet Baheera." He looked up, studying both of us. "May I have your names, so I may present you properly? She is not at the palace now but should return in a few days. In the meantime, I am happy to house you as guests of the musa."

After gritting my teeth at the delay, I nodded as graciously as I could. "We are honoured to be guests. I am called Widad Farooq, and my companion is Mayyada Nouri."

"Please come with me, and I shall show you to your quarters."

Once he showed us the sumptuous rooms, complete with washing room and sweet-scented flowers, he left, and I collapsed on the bed. "God, I forgot how much effort it took to be forever polite. I miss Toronto, where I could sass someone off with little fear of reprisal."

Mattea laughed at me. "When we get back, I feel sorry for the first person you meet. All that pent up sarcasm could kill someone when released!"

"Careful, or I'll use you as a relief valve."

She placed one hand on her forehead with dramatic flourish. "If I must sacrifice myself for the good of humanity, so be it."

I rewarded her with a half-smile for her efforts. "You might not survive a full onslaught."

"You forget, I've survived five deadbeat boyfriends in as many years."

I looked at the *welcome tray* of kelewele, bread, pickled mushrooms, and egusi seeds in palm oil. The aroma was strong and pungent, but not unpleasant. The peppers tickled my nose and made me sneeze even as stomach growled. While I had disdained the candied dates, this looked inviting. I made myself a plate and munched with relish. Mattea sniffed the kelewele. "What's that?"

"Try it." I put samples of each foodstuff into my collection bag. I'd already sampled the sand, the water, the dirt of the palm, and the palm leaf. I even pinched some baobab flour from Sekou's table.

She tentatively put a little dab on a piece of bread and chewed. Her eyes lit up and she fixed a bigger piece.

"It starts with plantains, and they add spices like ginger, cloves, peppers, and onions."

Around a full mouth, she mumbled, "I didn't think cloves and onions would go together, but this is delicious."

"Just be cautious. Those peppers can sneak up on you."

Chapter Twelve

We spent several days sampling the delights Sekou brought us. I developed a cautious friendship with the headwoman, and we chatted during some of her few hours of leisure. I discovered she loved playing a game called Oware, which I knew as Mancala. She brought a beautiful board carved from a giant seedpod with two rows of pits for seeds. We played several companionable games as we chatted, and I even taught Mattea how to play.

That morning, Sekou eschewed her utilitarian robes and arrived in a lovely pale blue linen, trimmed with cream embroidery. She set up the board by the window as Mattea and I set down the lunch tray she brought. "Tell me more about your home, Widad. Do you miss it?"

After taking a deep breath, I nodded. "I *do* miss my home. I live north, where snow falls in the winter and trees shade the sky in the summer."

"Across the sands, then?"

"Far across, and then across a sea, and a mighty mountain range. Mountains so high they are ever clad in ice and snow."

Sekou gazed out at the city. "I would like to see snow someday. I know the mountains to the east have snow, but I've never travelled much out of the city. Only to my sister's house in Djenne a few times."

I followed her gaze, noticing a plume of dust in the distance. Perhaps another caravan had arrived. "Snow is beautiful, but it's also painfully cold. You can die in the snow if you don't prepare."

She shifted her gaze to the Oware board and studied it before making her move. As she clicked the dried seeds into each rounded pit, it became a rhythm, soothing and hypnotic. If her final seed landed in a pit with more seeds, she picked those up and started again. When she ran out of seeds, I took my turn.

"The desert kills without mercy, as well. All it takes is one sandstorm and you may be lost forever. Water is scarce. At least with snow, you always have water."

"That's true, but snow can also have avalanches and blizzards, where half a mountain of snow falls upon you, or a storm of snow blinds your way. Either can mean death, sometimes quick, sometimes slow and painful."

She grinned and took a sip of her water. "You can always put more clothing on, but there is only so much you can take off."

We shared a laugh and Mattea rose from her nap, stretching. "Are you two still playing? Do you never get bored of this? Oh, how I wish I read Arabic. At least then I might keep busy." She curled around and stared out the window. Neither of us cared for forced idleness. I'm afraid I'd never make a good king's wife. My hands itched to create, build, or at least write. This indolent lifestyle might be fine for a holiday, but for my entire life? No, thank you. Luxury seemed ponderous laziness when one loved to work.

At least I'd been able to sneak notes about the garb I'd seen, in its rich and lush variety, each day. I tucked the details and scribbled sketches into my bag of holding, to retrieve only when we returned to modern times. Sketches, colours, trim designs, fabric, cuts, and style, along with origins if I recognised them, increased my archival wealth.

The dust cloud came closer, and a spark of hope grew in my heart that the wife might finally have returned. However, I forbore mentioning that possibility. I didn't want to get Mattea's hopes up.

I took my turn and stared at the cloud. A caravan lumbered toward the palace. Mattea sat up to see what caught my attention. "Is that her?"

Sekou looked out now, her brow furrowed. "It's possible. Baheera is due back any day now, and she doesn't like being late."

I had held off asking before for fear of being impolite, but Sekou had just given me the perfect opening. "What is Baheera like? Is she gracious? Demanding?"

Sekou studied me before answering, her jaw clenched. "You understand any criticism I might utter about the musa or the musa's wife might cause my execution, do you not?"

Dammit, I did, and I'd asked anyhow. It had been so long since I'd been an Agent, I had forgotten one of the basic truths. "I apologise and withdraw my question. Instead, I shall ask, what approach might work best with her?"

After a couple more moves on the Oware board, Sekou nodded. "She delights in unusual things. The stranger the better. Show her something interesting from your homeland, or tell her a new story, a tale she's never heard before. Doing so will ingratiate you to her presence, and she will be much more likely to listen to any request or favour."

I smiled and took my turn. "That's a fair exchange. I have tales she may enjoy."

When Sekou left that afternoon, I went through several possible stories in my mind. I could completely steal any modern or medieval tales.

Mattea still lay on the bed, staring out the window.

"What do you think, Mattea? *Romeo and Juliet* or a Sherlock Holmes adventure?"

She groaned and rolled to her back. "My hip hurts. These beds don't hold a candle to modern mattresses. How about the *Princess and the Pea?*"

"That might hit too close to home for a true king's wife. Still, Hans Christian Andersen also wrote *The Little Mermaid.* I might adapt that."

The commotion in the front courtyard drew my attention, and I glanced down to see the caravan had arrived. Several canopies with bright fabrics with golden fringe, more lions and elephants, clustered next to what appeared to be a delegation of Europeans. Venetian traders, judging by the cut of their velvet and pearl doublets.

A tall, dark woman stepped from the largest canopy, glanced around, and held her hand up. A servant rushed up and took several items, running off again. The woman strode toward the wing containing the royal apartments.

I took a long drink of cool water. "Baheera has arrived, unless I miss my guess."

Mattea stood and joined me at the window. "The tall woman with her back to us?"

"Probably. Ibn Khalutta should let us know when she is ready to receive guest petitions. I'm sure she'll want to rest after her journey."

Mattea stared while the woman disappeared into a shadowed archway. "Please let her be the energetic sort who wants to get back to work right away, and not a slothful lap dog satisfied with eating bonbons on her bed all day."

"Fie upon you, reminding me of chocolate. Or coffee. Crap on toast, I would kill for a cup."

"Didn't coffee come from this time in Africa?"

I picked up one of the wooden mugs and peered inside, trying to conjure the magical elixir by sheer will. "Almost. Ethiopia, about a hundred years after us. Which does us no good just now." I threw the empty cup against the wall but softly enough not to damage either cup or wall. To be fair, after almost a week with no coffee, the withdrawal effects had diminished. In another week, I might not even miss it. I hoped not to endure another week in this desert.

I settled back into my seat as the caravan below dispersed. Slaves took animals to the stables and supplies to the storerooms while traders headed to their market stalls along the edge of the courtyard. Increased conversation and renewed haggling drifted up through the window as the market burst forth into new life.

Mattea had laid back down on the bed and closed her eyes. In the mid-afternoon heat, I couldn't blame her. Having been born and raised in Canada, she must be melting. Even in the height of summer in Toronto, most places had air conditioning to relieve oppressive heat. No such luxury helped us here, though I'd learned how to deal with such privations on prior journeys. Not enjoy them, per se, but at least handle them. I thought of chilly days with Vikings exploring Iceland, or amongst the Innuit seal hunters of the Aleutian Islands.

The one place I'd always hoped to visit, in any time, was Antarctica. Since Paolo harboured the same desire, it felt like a betrayal to go without him. Still, thoughts of the windswept, icy wasteland served as a panacea against the heat.

A wave of music drifted up from the street. I tried to find the source, but it became lost in the maelstrom of sights, sounds, and scents below. The tantalising jingling of bells and some woodwind instrument wove through the shouts, laughter, and camel brays.

We didn't get a message from Ibn Khalutta that day, nor the next. However, as the third day dawned, bright and hot, a timid knock at our door proved to be a rather short young man. From his garb and manner, he was a slave. "*As-salāmu ʿalaykunna,* most honoured guests. My master, Ibn Khalutta, bids you to find me to his audience chamber."

With shuffling steps, he led us through three courtyards, along a wide hall, and down a staircase. When we arrived at Ibn Khalutta's chamber, the young man bowed low and ran away.

Inside the cool room, the Master of Guests greeted us and asked us to sit while he spoke. "As you may have heard, the musa's wife has returned from her journey, and, I am pleased to inform you, has agreed to grant you audience. However, there are matters of protocol I must make certain you understand before such an audience can occur." His face seemed pinched and uncomfortable with these words.

I nodded with a genuine smile. "I am certain you will be most effective in such instruction. I would never wish to insult our gracious host unwittingly."

His apprehensive expression cleared as he returned my smile. "Just so. You have my gratitude for your graciousness."

Mattea glanced at the door, and I turned my head as a slave, dressed in a simple linen tunic, came in with a tray of refreshments. He set down a silver pitcher, bread, and chutney on the table. "If it please you, good ladies, is there requiring else? I am smiling to fetch your desires."

Ibn Khalutta smacked the slave's head. "Go on, Nijaz. Shoo. You must forgive his difficulty with our language, please. He is from the outer provinces, and while he has been here many years, he has never mastered the language."

With a clenched jaw, I broke off a piece of the bread and tried the chutney. Tart fruit and spicy pepper mixed with a sweet onion; the taste was delightful. Still, I needed the cool fruit juice to ease the spice burning my tongue.

Despite the many trips I'd taken into the past and into societies which not only own slaves, but celebrate their abuse, I never got used to the practise nor ever condoned it. Still, we daren't jeopardise our mission to make a moral stand with the richest man in the world, and I didn't intend to. That didn't mean I had to like it.

From Mattea's sour expression, I guessed similar thoughts ran through her head. I gave her a warning glance before I spoke to Ibn Khalutta. "When we approach the musa's wife, how should I hold myself?"

I knew the answers to most of the questions I asked in the next hour. We'd educated ourselves to the court customs and protocols before we travelled. However, education can only go so far. Each period and place remains unique. What a king demanded a hundred years ago in a Mali court might earn a death sentence now. We never had enough Agents to research all of history for the minute details.

In addition, I couldn't be certain Mattea had absorbed all the pertinent education before our trip, so this refresher would help her even more than it helped me.

Other than a few details, Ibn Khalutta's information matched the Agency's information. Armed with his refinements, we allowed him to send another slave to help us dress for the event.

With our finest clothing, jewellery, and veils, we processed into Baheera's audience chambers. She had at least a dozen handmaidens lounging around her in all colours of the rainbow, except red or green. Gauzy silk, fine linen, stitches of gold, all vied for attention. Baheera herself wore an outfit of white and lilac stripes, covering her from head to toe, etched in floral patterns of gold thread. I couldn't count the necklaces of beads, shells, gold, and other, less identifiable items.

Slaves stood in each corner, waving their enormous palm fans with quiet dignity. An endless parade of more slaves with food and drink cycled through the room. Several other petitioners stood along one wall, waiting their turn to speak to Baheera.

She listened to a woman with a babe in her arms. We stood too far away to understand her words, but her tear-streaked cheeks proved the petitioner's distress. Baheera paid attention to her request, consulted one of her handmaidens, and then nodded with a wave of her hand. The plaintiff bowed deep several times, thanking Baheera with profuse gratitude as she backed away.

As our turn came closer, I had to decide which tale to relate. I would begin with offering a tale in exchange for a favour, with a caveat she should only consider my favour if my tale delighted her. This should at least intrigue her enough to allow me to continue. Whether she would have me perform here and now, or later after her official audience concluded, I had no idea. Either way, I needed a story.

With a glance at Mattea, I made my decision and stepped into the space before Baheera when signalled.

I bowed deep, as Ibn Khalutta had demonstrated, and kept myself in a bow until Baheera waved her hand. "My most honoured hostess, jewel of the city, I offer you a tale from a far-off land, a story from my home. In exchange, if you are delighted with my story, I would ask you a boon."

She narrowed her dusky eyes and studied both of us. When her eyes flicked over Mattea's pale complexion, Baheera's eyebrow rose, and she glanced to her chief handmaiden. The other woman shrugged.

I held my breath as Baheera motioned another handmaiden to her side. They spoke in low voices, and I understood nothing they said. After several exchanges, the musa's wife nodded. "Very well, honoured guests. I shall hear your tale. I respect the elders amongst us. It is said that when an old person dies, a library burns to the ground, and my husband values learning. You will be the entertainment tonight as we sup."

With a nod, she dismissed us. I bowed low as I backed away, and Mattea did the same, though she stumbled on the uneven floor.

When we were clear of the audience chamber, I released my breath with a huge sigh. "One hurdle down."

As we headed back to our quarters, Mattea stared at me. "Just the one? I'm amazed at the hoops we've had to jump through so far. We don't even know if she'll remember Josephus, where he stayed, what he did, nothing."

"We're making progress. I've been sampling the food, drinks, plants, and other substances. Even some gold dust. Still, her information could be the key to finding his purpose here."

"You think there was a purpose in his itinerary? Or just a holiday?"

"I believe he had a purpose, and I believe we can find out what it is. That might help us find whatever infected him."

She shook her head. "You have far more faith than I do."

Chapter Thirteen

While we waited for Baheera's audience to conclude, we observed her make several judgements upon the petitioners. We couldn't always determine what the petitioner wanted, at least not at first. In some, we figured it out by the time Baheera gave her judgement. Others remained a mystery. It pleased me that most of the petitioners seemed happy with their result, as it proved Baheera had either a generous nature or mood.

After two older women brought in a goat with two kids, and they left with a kid a piece, I glanced at the rest waiting. No petitioners were male, though some waited with their women. Men probably all petitioned the musa directly. I wondered if the musa's other wives held similar audiences. He had four wives, the maximum allowed for a Muslim man, assuming he had the wealth to support that many. As the richest man in the world, even after giving away so much gold in Egypt it depressed the gold market, support wouldn't be an issue.

A clamour at the door interrupted my musings. Five scantily clad petitioners came forward, their skin so dark it looked blue. They wore strange necklaces, and I couldn't figure out what dangled from them until I heard Mattea gasp. Her hands covered her mouth, and her eyes grew wide.

"What?"

She pointed, still keeping her mouth covered with the other hand. "Those are ears."

"Ears? Where?"

"On their necklaces. Human ears."

I peered at the jewellery, not eager to verify the statement. Their silk mantles looked stained with brown on the edges, though the rest of their clothing looked pristine white and gold. As they approached, they bowed low.

Baheera stood, her eyes flicking to the guards at the door of the audience chamber. For the first time since I'd met her, she seemed nervous and unsure of her power.

One woman in the front spoke. "We thank you, honoured Queen. Your hospitality-gift is much appreciated. We would give you a similar gift."

Baheera held up her hand. "I assure you, I require no reciprocal gift. My customs are not the same as yours. If you—"

The woman laughed, a low, rich sound which reverberated on the mud-brick walls. Nervous giggles answered her laugh until the entire chamber filled with nervous mirth laced with a good dose of hysteria.

When the laughter died, the petitioner bowed again. "We are well aware you would not have a good meal if we gifted you a tasty servant. Our customs are our own, and we do not push them unto others. However, I have, in sensibility of your own beliefs, removed a servant from our own pool of sacrifices. She will live a full life in your care, rather than on our table, I am certain. With her, we have also included several exotic foods and delicacies."

With that, several guards brought in a plump, young woman with red-black skin, her hands tied in rope coils. Her gaze remained fixed upon the ground, showing no life and no hope. A guard placed a sack next to her, with more care than they showed for the woman. The dark women drew her forward and bowed as they left her.

Baheera stepped down from her dais and lifted the servant woman's chin with one finger. Whatever passed between them in that gaze fueled the servant with a glimmer of hope and the shadow of a smile. Baheera clapped twice and her slaves took the woman into another small room off the main hall.

I guessed at what the brown stain on their mantles might be and shuddered.

Another slave opened the bag, her eyes growing wide. She ran to Baheera and dropped to her knees, genuflecting before her mistress. "If it please you, honoured Queen, the offering is rich."

Baheera raised one perfectly sculpted eyebrow and strode to the bag. She reached in and pulled out a package wrapped in oily paper. "Candied dates? That is not so unusual."

The slave shook her head. "Please, there is more."

She reached in again, this time pulling out a small burlap sack. When she opened up, the stench of rotten fruit assaulted us, and everyone cringed. "Oh. Oh, I see. Very well. Take this to Sekou immediately." She straightened, and the slave rushed to do her bidding. As the sack disappeared, everyone took a deep breath of sweeter air.

As the last petitioner walked away with a sour expression, the courtiers and handmaidens worked to clear the room. One young lady came to us and gave a shallow bow. "If it please you, can you return at sundown? This is the time for the evening meal."

I nodded and took Mattea's hand. As we left, we spied the slave boy, Nijaz, who must have waited this whole time. "Would you want to me show you room you sleep?"

I imagined the translator crackled with a short circuit, trying to make sense of the young man's mangled words. I placed a hand over the bone behind my ear, in case it popped out in protest.

Mattea must have seen my gesture, as she chuckled behind me. I shushed her as the lad walked us to our quarters. "Can we take off the heavier jewellery? My neck is aching."

I shook my head. "Sunset is only about a half hour away. We'll just have to re-drape it all again."

"Seriously. Even a half hour relief will help."

With a roll of my eyes, I said, "Fine. Come here and I'll take them off."

The bulky necklaces *thunked* as I placed them on the small table. Mattea massaged the back of her neck and then stretched her arms up high, cracking her back. This made her clothing gap and drape in ways she should never show outside of these rooms. It looked both painful and wonderful, so I stretched, too. I must remember my bones and joints had aged more than Mattea's. While it felt luxurious to stretch, my joints popped a great deal more noisily. I let out a groan. My elbow cracked as if it snapped out of place, and I yipped, cradling it in my hand.

"Did you hurt yourself?"

"No, not really. I'm just not used to such gyrations." My necklaces clattered against my face, so I removed them, placing them next to Mattea's.

The sun inched closer to the horizon as we sat, enjoying the relief from the heat as the day died. Flame orange clouds hugged the edge of the town. While I had already become heartily tired of russet colours, with everything covered in desert sand, this nightly display took my breath away.

A knock at the door surprised us both, and we jumped up. I hastily rearranged our jewellery as Nijaz came in to lead us back to Baheera's chambers.

Still adjusting Mattea's last necklace, we hastened back to the audience chamber. Servants had transformed the space with trestle tables and benches. Platters of meat, fruit, and bread stood on each. Spicy aromas greeted us as we stood in the doorway, and I wondered where we should sit. Baheera sat at the head of one table, chatting companionably with one of her handmaidens.

Nijaz led us to one of the other tables, where a few gaps showed between other women. Other than the serving slaves, no men remained in the room.

The women scooted down the bench to make room for us, and we sampled the platters. Spiced goat meat, flatbread, candied dates, palm oil for dipping, and other, less identifiable, morsels gave them plenty of options. The honeyed fruit juice and clear water in silver pitchers glistened with condensation. I wondered how they kept such things cool but then I remembered they had cellars, of a sort. Down deep into the earth, things would remain cool until needed.

While I ate, I once again catalogued the different colours, cuts, and embellishments on the surrounding clothing. Bold geometric shapes and vivid colours drew my eyes to a vastly different ensemble, one which must come from the far west, perhaps from the Benin Empire.

Once we finished our meal, I glanced over at the head table. Baheera still picked at her food, so I figured we had some time. I still hadn't settled on a tale to tell, but I'd best do so without delay. Should I choose a fairy tale, something from the Brothers Grimm? They dealt with universal themes, and they'd based many of their tales on prior stories. Andersen had done the same.

Shakespeare's stories wove a more complex plot and relied on more interesting personalities, but they also relied upon a cultural base. Such cultural differences might be misinterpreted in this Muslim culture. I considered my favourite mysteries, but so many of them relied on knowing English culture. What about one of the Sherlock Holmes tales? *Hound of the Baskervilles* had many thrills. Or *The Five Orange Pips*? Oh, wait! *The Adventure of the Dancing Men*. I should be able to translate most of the elements into a medieval setting. A woman escaping an abusive family life by travelling to a strange land, pursued by an ex-suitor, leaving cryptic messages in a private language. The story should hold up, even in an alien culture. Jealousy and love lost would be a universal theme.

I worked out the details of the converted tale in my mind, giving it a Roman/Greek veneer. That would be familiar enough that Baheera might have a cultural grounding, and yet exotic enough to be new and unusual.

When Baheera stopped conversing with her handmaiden, she clapped her hands three times, and the slaves cleared each dish from the table with amazing quickness. The tables clear, she moved to the single chair they'd set up in the dais in the front of the room. She clapped again and a slave whispered in my ear, "It is your turn."

I almost jumped out of my seat. I hadn't even noticed her standing behind me, but at least I stood quickly. Standing, I walked to the space in front of Baheera and bowed. Then I opened my mouth to begin my tale.

The entire story I'd organised in my head fled. I couldn't even remember which story I had chosen. I glanced at Mattea, who widened her eyes, urging me to get on with it. My mind insisted on staying utterly blank.

Fairy tale. story. Legend. Myth. What in the name of all that's holy had I decided on reciting?

A silly thing popped into my mind. The scene of the Dormouse reciting *Twinkle, twinkle, little bat* to Alice, the March Hare, and the Mad Hatter. This made me smile, an expression that at least gained me a few precious moments.

The Mad Hatter saved me. I connected his hats to the Deerstalker cap worn by Sherlock Holmes, and thus back to my crafted modification of *The Adventure of the Dancing Men*. After clearing my throat, I launched into the story, making the woman the daughter of an Italian house of great corruption and power. Since the original tale had the woman as a daughter of a Chicago mob boss, the change rang true to the original.

While I spoke of the strange notes with dancing men left for her to find, and her violent overreaction to these notes, Baheera's brow furrowed in concern and confusion. Perhaps she didn't read? While Mansa Musa created Tombouctou and the Sankore Madrasah to be a centre of great learning, women may not be included in this bounty, even his wives. Perhaps especially his wives.

Still, the dancing men were pictographs and anyone living in a less-than-fully literate society should be familiar with pictographs. I sallied forth, assuming my tale had meaning.

When I told of the standoff between the husband and the ex-suitor, Baheera and her handmaidens gasped and held their hands over their hearts. I had them.

When I concluded the story, and revealed the truth, Baheera smiled wide and clapped her hands for a slave. The slave brought me a tall glass of cool fruit juice, which I swigged, my mouth having become parched.

"You have pleased me with your tale, honoured guest. Come, sit beside me and ask your boon."

Now came the more difficult part. I wished Mattea could sit with me, but she was still along the edge of the room with the other handmaidens.

"Most honoured hostess, I have come in search of a relative. I believe you might have spoken to him. Might I enquire of him?"

She nodded, her expression guarded. "I speak to many people. True, more women than men, but by the same token, I may not have spoken to this man. Can you describe him?"

I pulled out the painted miniature and handed it to her. She raised her eyebrows, but took it, examining the image. As she squinted, I realised she may not have great eyesight. Her eyes widened after a moment.

"I remember this man. He came in attendance to my husband but spoke to me about some relatives of his own. He searched for a man who had been in his family. I had no information to help him in his quest, so perhaps he sought answers in another court."

A genealogical quest? Josephus had gone searching for his ancestors?

Of all the ridiculous, self-serving quests…but I supposed I'd heard worse. My place was not to judge the idiot, just find out what the idiot did and when and where he did it.

"He also entertained me with fascinating stories. Perhaps this talent runs in your family?"

I swallowed, unsure how to answer such an assumption. "Which stories did he tell you, honoured hostess?"

She laughed, the rich sound caressing the space. "Wondrous stories of future imaginings, truly. He spoke of flying machines and magic. He almost had me convinced if I just came with him, he could show me this world."

I clenched my fists. "Did he say how he would show you such wonders?"

Baheera narrowed her eyes and gave me a sly smile. "In exchange for some precious things, he said he would take me to his paradise, a land of bounty and magic."

"Precious things?"

"Some trade goods which are much sought after. Alas, I had none to trade, and had to turn down his offer."

Her arched eyebrow forbade me from asking which trade goods Josephus sought.

How dare he? How dare he try to smuggle someone to the future? Such an offer went against the temporal maxims for a very good reason. Trying to get a firm hold on my blood and my temper, I bowed to Baheera. "Thank you so very much, my honoured hostess. Your words help me understand his quest, which is of great value."

She smiled, glancing behind me. A handmaid stood there, waiting for me to vacate the coveted spot, so I rose. "I am much fatigued from my performance. Might I have your permission to retire? For me and my companion?"

"You may, but I would ask you a question."

I swallowed and smiled. "Whatever you like, honoured hostess."

"You are familiar, and I would know why."

I furrowed my brow. "I've not been here before, honoured hostess. Perhaps you are reacting to my cousin's likeness? I know his skin is darker than mine, but there may be a family resemblance."

She shook her head and frowned. "No, that is not it. You are familiar. Your energy. Your soul. I have encountered you before this."

Frantically, I recalled my travels to other areas in the medieval Muslim world but came up with no possibilities. I'd been to Egypt, but thousands of years before Baheera had been born. While I'd been to Mecca, that mission had been centuries earlier, in the time of Mohammad. "I cannot think how that would be."

She scrutinised me. "Hmm. As a Muslim, I do not believe we live several lives. One life suffices to find Allah within. However, sometimes I think this might not be the whole story. Regardless, we have met before, and I believe we will meet again."

Bryonie's eyes gazed into mine and a chill danced along my spine. I shivered as I bowed, taking my leave. My knees shook, despite my efforts.

Careful not to turn our backs on Baheera, we left. As soon as we reached the sanctuary of the hallway, my shoulders slumped. Nijaz led us to our quarters once again.

As soon as the door closed, Mattea blurted out, "So? What did she say? Did she remember Josephus?"

I nodded. "He searched for his ancestors. Well, not exactly, but from what she said, it's what he must be doing. He also tried to get some sort of trade goods and asked her to come to the future with him."

"People do that?"

"Which? The genealogy or the coming to the future?"

"Uh…either?"

"The family history…of course. There are worse pursuits, I suppose. Look how many people spend hundreds, if not thousands, searching for the ancestry in genealogical research, even without travelling. However, such searches are proscribed, due to the high probability of derailing your ancestral line. The coming to the future, though, absolutely not. It's forbidden by the maxims."

Mattea sighed. "For his research, would he have had to clear that itinerary with the Agency before going through official channels?"

"Which may be why he risked a rogue portal. Still, what would be so horribly important that he would risk his life with a second-rate Time portal?" I shook my head, not understanding the risk to reward ratio. It made no sense. Then again, my non-Native ancestry had only vaguely interested me.

Part French-Canadian, part Ojibwe First Nation, my ancestors had been in the Toronto area for at least three hundred years. I'd always felt at home in Toronto.

People quested for their ancestors when they didn't feel comfortable in their own skin, or perhaps to search for some greatness in their family line. Some people needed to discover everything about themselves and how they got here. I didn't share that obsession. Perhaps I missed out on something profound. More likely I just saved my cash.

I sighed and took off the heavy jewellery still draped around my neck. Mattea had already removed hers and mostly disrobed. The evening chill had set in, so she curled up in the thick woollen blanket on her bed.

I considered telling Mattea about that final conversation with Baheera, and Bryonie's eyes. However, I still didn't quite believe what I saw, and needn't open my delusions to well-deserved ridicule.

Instead, I scribbled down the aspects I'd observed of all the women's garb that evening, delving into my memory to transcribe what I saw in the greatest detail I could manage. I wish I knew what those mysterious trade goods had been.

Chapter Fourteen

Agent Pembley hadn't lied when he touted the benefits of the sample bag. Each food sample remained sealed in its bag, each rock, lichen, dirt, and drink sample added to the bag, and it still felt empty. I marvelled at the technology, a throwback to my role-playing game days of Dungeons and Dragons. A real-life bag of holding.

Just as we packed our last bit of costume and jewellery, Nijaz knocked on our door. "Today you will leaving be the city? I'm to the road bring you, find guards for you to have."

After rearranging his words, Mattea nodded. "That's correct, Nijaz. We'll be ready momentarily. Would you like some bread? We can't possibly eat this all."

He shook his head, holding up his hands and backing away. "Oh, no, please, no. To accept such would dismiss me."

This took her aback, as she blinked several times. "Oh. I apologise, then. I didn't realise."

"He's right. He isn't our slave, so accepting food from another master would raise questions about his loyalties. It's a rule to discourage bribery and poaching of servants. It works well enough, I think. You can't give this Dobby a sock. Nijaz is well aware of the rules, even if he can't articulate them."

Another knock interrupted our preparations. When I opened the door and Sekou entered, I smiled.

"What is it you've done? The court is abuzz with your story and Baheera's reaction. Something momentous must have happened."

The words chilled my blood. No Agent wanted a momentous effect on the past. Such a thing should be avoided. "I did little. I only told a story."

She shook her head, her grin still wide. "Little indeed. Baheera has been most generous in her dealings since then. She has pardoned three criminals whom she'd previously condemned! One young boy had my own nephew, so I must thank you. If you acted as an agent of change, you are to be congratulated."

My skin crawled with the implications, but nothing I might do now would change things.

Sekou left after several more expressions of gratitude and farewell. Mattea cast a pitying glance at the young slave as we finished our packing. Once we had everything in place, we trekked to the edge of the city.

After the relative cleanliness and pristine air of the palace, the stink and dust of the city streets almost choked me. I coughed and wheezed the entire trip back to the road we arrived on. Nijaz helped us negotiate for an armed escort out of town to where we needed to meet our caravan, as per our cover story.

I frowned at the price, and while I did some expected haggling, we spent almost as much as he first asked. The guard's agent, a little man who reminded me of a used car dealer, negotiated well. We included a necessary clause that the guard would leave us once we arrived at our destination. We paid half the fee now, and half upon completion of the journey.

The burly man who escorted us spoke little. His red-black skin almost glowed in the morning sun, though the red dust may have contributed to that effect. He wore a plain, dark linen robe, tightly bound to his arms and legs with ties. He held a curved sword with menacing silence as he walked behind us. Mattea kept glancing over her shoulder at the guard until I told her to stop.

"He makes me nervous."

"Good. That means he'll be more likely to make brigands nervous."

She took a deep breath, and then coughed at the dust. "Fine. I'll do my best to stop."

"I'm sure he's used to it, but I'm also sure we should trust him to do what he's paid to do."

A small cloud of dust ahead of us caused us to pull over to the side of the road to wait for the oncoming traffic to pass. I had no wish to be run over by a trade caravan uninterested in stopping their camel train for pedestrian women, and outlanders no less. We travelled without our jewellery and fine clothing displayed in the interest of not attracting thieves.

The dust cloud resolved into six turbaned men on camels, their swords drawn. Both Mattea and I scooted behind our single guard, and wished I'd splurged on more. As burly as this one looked, six to one were very poor odds.

It grew difficult to breathe. I tried swallowing to relieve the dust in my throat, but it just got worse. I coughed and pulled out the long, thin knife I'd secreted into the bag of holding. It seemed horribly inadequate to the menace before us, as it might snap before it penetrated skin, but holding it made me stand taller. I glanced at Mattea. She'd held her spikier jewellery, pointed shells, in her fist, poking through her fingers like delicate, pale, brass knuckles.

The six armed men stopped on the road about twenty feet before us, arranged in a line of gleaming steel and angry eyes peeking out from the well-wrapped heads.

Flashes of *Lawrence of Arabia* flickered through my mind, and I searched the horizon for Peter O'Toole to save us both. However, our guard planted his feet and growled. One bandits' camel pawed the ground while a second one spit. No other sound cut the dry air.

The first bandit let out a ululating cry and spurred his camel forward. The creature didn't move like a horse, but he still charged toward them with frightening speed.

Our guard said, "Move!" and shoved us to the side as he danced around the edge of the camel's path, hamstringing the animal as it rode past. It screamed and fell on top of his rider. The red blood mixed with the golden sand into an orange mud.

The guard glanced at our pitiful weapons, and then into my eyes. He must have seen something strong there, for he pulled two knives from his belt and handed one to each of us. They looked sturdier than my thin table knife, and certainly stronger than Mattea's shells. We nodded in thanks and turned to our attackers.

The guard smiled, showing gleaming white teeth against his red-black skin. He stood ready again and beckoned the other bandits to come forward. He didn't even look out of breath. I no longer begrudged one cowrie shell of our guard's fee. We ranged well behind him but also stood ready to defend ourselves against the onslaught.

The other bandits exchanged glances, shrugged, and the rest charged at once. I cursed this for not being a Hollywood movie, where the villains came at the hero one by one, allowing him to dispatch them in a methodical manner. Real life seldom gave such chances.

One bandit barreled toward me. I waited until he'd almost reached me and jumped to one side, slicing blindly with both knives. I might have cut the bandit's leg, or the camel's hide, or neither. No blood stained my blades. I twirled around in a circle, looking for immediate threats. Mattea grappled with one bandit while the guard faced three others. Mine wheeled around and charged toward me again.

This time I crouched low as he came. I jumped in the other direction, but he anticipated the move and shifted his vector. Instead of slashing sideways, though, I stabbed up. The camel bellowed. While I'd bear guilt for the beast later, now I needed to make the bandit dismount.

Blood stained on my blade, but not enough. It hadn't worked. Damn it all to Hell! I used to know how to fight passably well. This is what I get for not training in decades. My body no longer obeyed me.

Once again, my attacker came toward me. Once again, I gripped both knives, wondering what in Hell I'd try this time. A scream behind me distracted me, but I refused to turn. Instead, I clenched my jaw as the camel thundered down on me. I wished I could throw knives, but that skill had never been in my wheelhouse.

I cut at the tendons in the camel's front leg. A scream which cut through my heart rewarded my effort. I hated hurting the animals. I'd much rather slice evil men's throats. When mounted, it remained difficult to reach said throats.

Once the camel fell, though, I could attack my attacker with wild abandon. I just needed him to fall.

Another scream ripped through the air. I turned to find Mattea brandishing a knife, blood up to elbow, grinning in mad glee at the eviscerated bandit at her feet. A glance at our guard showed he'd vanquished two of his bandits, and now grappled with a third. My own attacker fell trapped under his camel, so I could slice his throat at leisure.

I did so, eliciting less satisfaction with the killing than I expected. I then helped Mattea and the guard finish the last bandit. However, the lone survivor thought better of his chances and wheeled around on his camel, loping into the distance. Soon, only a cloud of dust and a bad smell remained.

I glanced at the surrounding carnage, already coated with the ever-present sand. One camel cried out. I examined him and saw his leg sticking out at an odd angle. The guard also saw and nodded. I sliced the animal's throat to end his suffering.

Both Mattea and I retched at the side of the road. Adrenaline can have that effect.

My muscles and joints refused to be ignored further. They complained most bitterly about their abuse. I told them to shut up, but they wouldn't listen. Blood and sand soaked our clothing. I didn't care, and I don't think Mattea did, either. We needed to get back to our rendezvous and the return portal.

For a moment, I couldn't remember the day. The portal would only return on every even day. Would we be able to stand waiting in the middle of the desert for another day, covered in blood and dust? We would have to, regardless. I glanced sidelong at the guard, determined to pay him more than his negotiator had agreed upon. He certainly earned his keep. We only sustained a few bruised ribs and some minor scratches.

My throat had become more parched than ever, and I took a sip of water. I knew better than to chug the precious life-giving liquid. Two more sips, and my throat felt less like sandpaper and more like glue. One more, and I breathed normally.

The guard looted the bandits, and he offered us a share of the bounty. I shook my head. "You take it all. You deserve it. Thank you." He nodded, still silent, and we trudged on down the road.

The dry desert wind whipped us for several hours before we stopped for the afternoon. I searched my pack for some bread, and offered some to the guard, and some to Mattea. While he chewed his food, I asked him his name. We should have done so when we embarked, but I'd been so focused on returning home, all courtesy slipped my mind.

"I take no name when on duty."

Was this some religious belief? Or perhaps a foreign warrior code? Nevertheless, I nodded. If he wished to remain nameless, I would honour his request.

After our break, we walked the road again. The wind had increased, making the walk more difficult. Eddies of swirling dust and sand buffeted us as we struggled through. It eased after a little bit, and we walked faster. I didn't want to be caught out if a true sandstorm came at us. Surviving a sandstorm would be difficult in the open. We had no shelter against such a force.

For several hours we travelled, step after step on the dry, dusty road. We met a few groups going toward Tomboctou, either traders or visitors. None menaced us as the bandits had, though we approached each with due caution. The sight of our guard and the bloodstains on our skin and clothing, must have made them much warier of us than we of them.

The drying blood itched and chafed. I rubbed at my skin, trying to get the flakes to come off. Some blood came away, but most of it lingered in the creases of my skin. I worked at it, neurotically needing to clean my conscience.

I'd killed before, though I'd lay long odds Mattea hadn't. I'd needed to defend myself several times in the past on travels to other times and places. Once to defend my child, three times to defend myself, and once, because I must as part of a cultural norm for a sacrifice. I'd truly landed myself in hot water that time, finding myself in a no-win situation involving a local Sami shaman and a condemned prisoner. I comforted my niggling conscience with the knowledge the man had committed heinous acts himself, against a young girl. He deserved death, and my role demanded I gift it to him. Therefore, I did.

Oddly enough, the temporal maxims could be cloudy on such situations. The rips in Time which result in a traveller being noticed were sometimes greater than those resulting from someone who would have been killed regardless. This man would have been a sacrifice, even if someone else held the blade that slit his throat. I happened to be in the wrong place at the wrong time.

I worked hard to ensure I never came into that situation again. I didn't care for killing, even when it was necessary. Others could do the culling and leave me out of the equation.

I glanced at Mattea, who stewed within her own thoughts. I put a light hand on her shoulder, which earned me a haunted half-smile. She'd need some decompression when we returned, certainly. I wondered how much time they'd allow us after our debriefing. Well, they'd damn well allow her enough time to heal. A first killing is nothing to gloss over and sublimating it would only result in greater problems down the line. I refused to allow Mattea that necessity.

The wind picked up again. I pulled the silk mantle closer around my neck, trying to reduce the amount of dust inside my wrap. It didn't matter. Everything in the world was grit and gale. My legs chafed, my hands chafed, and my teeth grated with sand. Every muscle ached, either from the long day of walking, the battle, or the constant tensing against the wind. What I wouldn't give for a long, relaxing bath in hot water.

I imagined a thermal bath in Iceland, like the ones I'd enjoyed during a trip in the modern day. Each little town had a local hot spring, easy to soak away ancient aches and pains. We might not have the luxury of such a recovery between missions, but it didn't stop me from wanting it.

I took another small sip of water, swishing it around my mouth before swallowing. I took another and savoured it. I put the rest away. The waterskin remained half full.

We came to a tepid watering hole. To call it an oasis would be overselling it, but a small mudhole of water and a sturdy lean-to at least cut down the wind. We huddled beneath, rubbing our feet and refilling our waterskins.

Mattea closed her eyes and pressed the heels of her hands against her eyelids. "How much longer to our rendezvous?"

I'd been making calculations every hour along our trip. "About another five hours' walk, if all goes well."

"Ugh. I never want to see sand again. The next time I suggest we go to the beach, slap me."

I chuckled. "Gladly."

We gathered our supplies and took off again. The wind against our faces grew stronger, and the sting of the sand became painful. I wrapped the silk across my entire face, trusting in my ability to see the path through the thin fabric. Mattea noticed this and did the same, a sigh of relief sounding over the call of the wind.

Not too long later, I wished we had stayed with the lean-to. At least it had offered protection, though it would never stand up to a full sandstorm. So far, this remained merely a strong wind. We wouldn't survive a full one.

We plodded through the burning sand, grateful for our sandals and turbans. I tried not to lick my lips too often, as all I got was sand in my mouth. My lips remained as parched as ever. Still, we marched on.

I glanced at the guard frequently. He must walk these roads every day. If he looked worried, we'd head back. However, he appeared unruffled and plodded on next to us with stoic reserve. I did my best to emulate his quiet strength. I couldn't say I succeeded, but at least I kept up appearances.

Finally, our rendezvous came into view. The small stand of palm trees and another shelter, made with sturdier walls than the lean-to, made me gasp in relief. The amenities weren't any more palatial than the mudhole, but it represented safety. Watching the sun on the horizon, I decided the portal should open in another hour. We had just made it, if today was the correct day.

"Thank you. We will be safe here, as our caravan should be here soon. Please, let me pay you a premium for your fine service." I held out a small bag of gold dust, but he shook his head.

"I cannot take more than we agreed upon. It would be a smirch on my honour. I also cannot leave you alone until I have delivered you into safe care."

"But the contract said to deliver us to this spot and then leave us, which you have done. We will be safe."

He set his jaw in stubborn intransigence. I set mine the same way. He may be muscular and fast, but I'm old and cranky. I couldn't keep the portal from opening simply because I foolishly allowed a witness to stay.

"The contract terms are clear. We are grateful for your services, but I must insist that you leave. It's a matter of privacy and delicacy, you understand. The Musa would be displeased if certain details of his affairs were discovered."

If the wind kept up, no one would witness anything.

The guard clenched his jaw again, but the flicker of caution in his eyes told me he had taken my warning to heart. With a final check of our surroundings, he bowed once and took the other half of his fee.

As he disappeared into the swirling eddies of dust, Mattea said, "Next time, can we come with a little more fire-power? I feel incredibly vulnerable."

"The portal should open soon. The edge of my skin is tingling. Can you sense that? It's an unmistakable sensation. You always know when a portal is about to open. While it appears camouflaged, we will always be able to find it"

She rubbed her forearms and grimaced, likely due to her sandblasted skin. When the portal emerged in the dusty air as an adobe brick doorway to nowhere, we both stepped through.

Chapter Fifteen

I drank in the clear air of downtown Toronto and swore I'd never leave its modern embrace again, though that was a lie. In just a few days, we'd have to travel to our second itinerary stop. At least Mali had been warm, though at some point too warm is definitely a thing. Still, I hoped the Maine destination would be in the summer.

We arrived through the portal without issues and dumped our sample bag into the eagerly awaiting hands of the Agency scientists. They'd take it to their labs, perhaps send samples to the European Temporal Medical Research Institute of Infectious Diseases and Centre for Disease Control. I didn't understand their inner workings nor did I care. At this point, I only wanted to soak in a hot bath and scrub the inches of blood and sand from every crevice of my body. Any Agent returning from a mission deserved such a recovery.

Alas, my luxury must wait. Agent Pembley accosted us…sorry, debriefed us…as we left the Temporal Office.

"I will need detailed statements from each of you and an official report from you, Wilda. Then we must prepare you for the next journey."

"Bloody Hell, Pembley. At least let us wash the grime off? There's a shower in the back of our office we can use. It won't take twenty minutes, I promise. I realise time is of the essence, but Agent protocol 1A-3B-Z means we get at least this."

His sour expression deepened, but he nodded. Mattea and I rushed into the office, stripped without a care, and both jumped into the tiny shower together. I cared far more about being clean than being modest.

Once the worst of the grime had sluiced away and our hair scrubbed, we emerged, fresh and raw from the hot water. We grabbed clean modern clothing and came back into the front room. I believe the phrase is 'wreathed in smiles.'

Pembley cleared his throat. "That's the first time a woman has said twenty minutes and kept on schedule. Perhaps in history."

"Remarks like that will make the debriefing much more difficult, Pembley."

"Noted, Mrs. Firestone."

I grinned at him, in a generous mood after my shower. "Wilda. We'll be working together on this, and Wilda is much shorter. What's your first name, Pembley?"

He coughed a few times and his face turned bright red. "I'd rather not say, uh, Wilda. Truly."

With a sidelong glance at Mattea, I tapped my nose. "Well. That's intriguing. Lead on, MacDuff."

The debriefing became a mind-numbing recitation of the facts of our journey. Mattea finished before I did, but she looked drawn. Her face showed ashen against the harsh office light, as I'm certain mine did.

Pembley had recommended we get sleep. I'm afraid I snapped. "That's what I had planned on doing as soon as we got back! But no, you had to grill us for three hours about our adventures. On a Mission I never wanted to go on to begin with!"

He puffed up with indignation. "We needed your report, Wilda. Right away."

"What couldn't have kept a few hours?"

He handed us each a cup of coffee. I peered in, thankful to see nothing but black. "Josephus expired last night."

This news deflated my anger. "Oh."

"Yes, exactly. We still haven't determined what he brought back with him. Isolation has prevented more Agents from becoming infected and non-Agents are fine. However, anyone who has travelled is susceptible."

I glanced at Mattea, blowing on her creamy coffee. "We've both travelled now. We may no longer be safe."

"Have you noticed anyone else in this office? Have you met one other person?"

"No one but you, and you look healthy enough." I took a sip of my blessed coffee. It scalded my tongue, but I didn't mind. I savoured my third cup since we'd returned three hours ago. I still needed more after a week of deprivation.

"They decontaminated me before I met you, just like the scientists. Also, I've never travelled."

I nodded at my assistant. "Even if I'm immune, she'll be vulnerable if we're lucky enough to find this vector."

Mattea's tired voice cut through our conversation. "Don't I have any choice in this? Or should I sit here and allow my betters to choose my fate?"

Abashed, I relented. "What do you want to do, Mattea?"

"I'm going with you. I'm not hanging around, waiting to get sick." She glared at both of us. I shrugged at Pembley.

"I need a second, Pembley. It's difficult enough to travel into the past as a female. Backup is a necessity. Unless you have another candidate I'm willing to work with?"

My phrasing made him clench his jaw again, the edges popping in and out as if he chewed gum. "The only faint possibility is that officious Metropolitan Police bloke you met."

"Sir Algernon the Pompous? Absolutely not."

Mattea grinned, knowing she'd won.

"I wish you could wait until our scientists comb through your samples, but that will take weeks of testing. You need to go back quickly. Three days."

"Three days! That's the entire education course! There's no time to rest!"

"Do I need to remind you that Josephus is dead, and we don't understand why? Or that two other rogue travellers are waiting on death's door?"

I sighed, knowing the answer.

Despite my exhaustion, tucked in my warm bed with Dinah curled up against my side, I got little rest that night.

*****

The morning dawned bright and got brighter after my third cup of coffee.

First things first. I took my usual streetcar to Time Tourist Outfitters to check in with Tarren. While she seemed relieved to see me, she didn't look happy when I told her we had two more Missions.

"Has Lady Prissy-Pants returned to give you any grief?"

She swirled her pencil in her disgustingly creamy-white coffee. "No, nothing like that. It's just not the same with both you and Mattea gone. My job has morphed into putting off everyone that comes in the door. The temp you hired for alterations barely talks to me. He grunts and waves me off with this condescending buzzing noise."

I stood up straighter. "Does he, now? Well, I'm certain a word or two in his ear can affect a severe attitude adjustment. When does he show up?"

She glanced at the antique clock. "About an hour from now, I should say. Give or take. He sort of drifts in and out as he pleases, despite the backlog."

I ground my teeth. The Agency had insisted Maximilian would be the best fit for our department while we left on mission, but I considered firing him anyway. Tarren had a huge store of patience. To see her so done with this waste of space after only a week spoke volumes.

I waited with Tarren, supplying myself with more black coffee and decompressed. A chat with Tarren always calmed me, one of many reasons I valued her.

I heard him outside the door saying "ta ta" to someone in a stereotypical singsong tone. When he flounced, yes flounced, into the office, he stopped dead cold when he saw me, my arms crossed and blocking his path.

"Oh, dear. Do we have a grumpy customer already, little Miss Tarren?"

I donned my sternest grandmother glare. "We most certainly do not have a grumpy customer, Mr. Perry. What we have is a displeased boss."

I derived considerable pleasure from the apprehension which flickered across his eyes at these words. Nervous fear with several glances toward Tarren.

"Don't even think about blaming her for anything. I've heard of your exploits and your attitude. Why should I keep you employed in my office when you gallivant in here an hour later than your shift? When you sass a potential customer as soon as you enter? When you belittle and condescend to my extremely competent receptionist and dear friend? Well? I'm waiting. Impatiently, I might add."

His hands fluttered to his throat as his skin turned a dusky red. "I...uh...I don't...well..."

I lifted my hand. "Save it, buster. You're out of here."

"But...but you can't fire me like that! The Agency hired my contract."

"I have final say on who works with my clients, Perry. Shoo. Go. Get out. Do you need me to translate that into Arrogant Idiot for you?"

When he spluttered his way out the door, Tarren clapped. "Encore! Encore!"

I smiled at her but then raised my eyebrows. "You realise this means you have to find a replacement, right?"

She nodded, her diminished joy unsullied by her wide grin. "Understood. Do I need to go through the Agency?"

I nodded. "I'm afraid so. However, have them send over three. That way you can pick the best one. If they argue with you, I empower you to invoke the threat of my wrath."

She saluted. "Aye, aye, Cap'n. Anything else you need?"

"No, you've got things in hand. I have to fly, as this idiot has already made me late. Still, I'll make sure to lay all blame on his shoulders."

I rushed into the education facility just in time to start our intense instruction on Wabenaki culture, ceremonies, religion, and art.

I did my best to wipe the facts I'd memorised about Mali from my mind and shift to the new mindspace. The details of the cultures diverged, except for a basic toxic masculinity most cultures seem to embrace throughout history. Still, as patriarchal societies went, this one didn't seem too bad. The ultimate deciding body was the Council of Mothers, which bespoke a respect for older women I admired. I approved heartily, being an older woman myself.

The demonstration on Native culture didn't have as many surprises for me as the Malinké presentation did. I'd travelled to my Ojibwe ancestors before, and while the Wabenaki tribal cultures had differences, the basics remained similar. A reverence for nature spirits, respect for the wisdom of the Council of Elders, with strong clan, family, and trade ties remained the same throughout the northeastern tribes.

I became fascinated by the descriptions of foods common to the area, as they differed from the Ontario region natives. The eastern seaboard tribes ate more fish, shellfish, and seals, along with the more familiar moose, bear, and caribou. I didn't look forward to trying green lichen tea, but red clover heads and sour grass sounded intriguing.

When the instructor taught that some women became leaders in their own right, and not only as a consort leader to their spouse, Mattea bolted up from her tired slump. I might have told her Native tribes weren't as patriarchal as Europeans. Still, the dynamics always depended on the individual tribe and the personalities involved. I'd yet to meet a tribe who didn't respect their Council of Mothers, though, and most reserved final judgement on weighty legislative decisions.

Mattea returned to burying her nose in her book, and I wondered if she snoozed behind her study. While I hoped not, I could sympathise. The First Nations cultures fell into my wheelhouse, as I'd studied my ancestry extensively at one point. I even lived within the Ojibwe lands of four hundred years ago, getting in touch with my own roots. I spent several months amongst them, learning to sow, reap, cook, create, sing, dance, and pray. They taught me the joy of the rain and the sorrow of the dawn. I honoured my ancestors and nurtured the children. I shared the mourning and the celebrations.

Some days I longed for that simpler life, but then I remembered hot showers and coffee, and the romantic notions of my misplaced youth fade away into the realities of the modern day. Convenience is a stronger bribe than any amount of gold or power. And perhaps dark chocolate. But definitely coffee.

The Wabenaki tribes of the northeast coast were Algonquin, like my Ojibwe. However, regional differences could be strong. The particular area we needed to visit lay in what we now called Southern Maine. The tribe of the Wolastoqiyik had been hunters in the region in the summer, retreating to the coast during the winter to live off the ocean's bounty.

While we expected to arrive in the tenth century, they wouldn't be near enough to Newfoundland to meet up with any of the Norse settlers of L'Anse aux Meadows. Disappointment and relief warred within me. I'd met Icelanders before, in modern times, and ancient Northmen in both Ireland and Norway on prior missions. However, meeting the brave souls who ventured to an unknown land for the first time, to settle a whole new continent would be exciting. Also, dangerous. I look more like the skraelings who deviled them than I looked like them. At least we could use the Norse colony as an excuse for Mattea's pale skin.

Mattea would have fit right in and end up betrothed to a Jarl or Goði before the week had finished. Her youth, wit, and beauty would be a huge prize to any Viking. From her relationship history, Mattea preferred female company. Still, a big hairy Norseman might be a thrill for her. Or she might find a big, hairy Norsewoman.

Or not. We would be amongst the First Nations, not the Vinland colony, even if it still existed when we arrived. I set myself to memorising the clan hierarchy, the basic religious beliefs, and some of the finer points of dining etiquette while Mattea frowned at the garb pictures. "These don't cover much. Do I have to go barelegged if it's winter?"

With a chuckle, I shook my head. "Leggings work for both men and women in the winter. Never fear, the Natives weren't stupid. Smarter than most modern idiots walking around in shorts in the winter. But guess what? You get more heavy-ass jewellery to drag down on your neck. Aren't you excited?"

"Oh, joy and rapture. Just what I always wanted." She wrinkled her nose and rubbed the back of her neck in anticipatory ache. "Couldn't we have just gotten all this instruction at the beginning? Rather than before each trip?"

"We could. But studies have proven having an overview and then a reinforcement of the details increases recall."

Her only answer was a sigh.

After the days' classes finished, I took a cab over to the hospital. I tried to talk to Aminata, the charge nurse I'd first spoken to about Josephus. She'd gone into quarantine three days after I spoke to her. While I wanted to push in and speak to her anyhow, even through the door, I chided myself for foolish indulgence. I could communicate via computer, but I decided I shouldn't bother her. Just from our brief conversation, I suspected she worked while sick, trying to help find a cure or a treatment. Interrupting her to satisfy my own morbid curiosity wouldn't be kind.

Kind? When had I become kind? I must have mellowed with age. Hopefully, no one would discover the change. I've a reputation to maintain.

I stopped into Nami's restaurant for a Poké Bowl. The new gourmet mushroom had a line through it on the menu.

"Did you discover they were on the New America proscribed list, after all?"

"Nah, we just ran out. They've become a huge hit, and we can't seem to get our supply any longer. No one in town can get any. A bit of a shame, really. They sold like wildfire."

I snorted. "Fads are like that, I guess. What's so good about them?"

She shrugged. "A slight psychotropic effect, I think. I'm allergic to most mushrooms so I stay well away from them, and they're wicked pungent, throwing some people into sneezing fits. Devin said he liked them well enough, but not like some of these weirdos. We had a fist fight here three days ago, if you can believe it."

I squinted at my bowl. "Reuben didn't sneak any quinoa in here, did he? It crunched."

"That's just the sesame seeds. Stop being paranoid."

I laughed and she realised I'd trolled her. She rolled her eyes and handed me a boba tea.

"I didn't order one."

Nami grinned, her smile lighting up her face. "Yeah, but you want one. I've rarely seen you so knackered. If you want, I'll spike it."

I peered into the taro boba tea and decided a dollop of the sauce would do me fine. I held my cup out and she took it behind the counter. Out of sight, she fussed for a while before returning. The tea looked paler.

Nami handed over the tea. "Fun fact. Boba tea was invented by a bored woman at a meeting who dumped her tapioca into her tea for entertainment. She liked it so much, she added it to her tea house's menu."

I took an experimental sniff, raising my eyebrows at the strong alcoholic odor. I took a sip and coughed. "How much whiskey did you add?"

"Enough, evidently. Drink up."

I took a longer draught and sighed as the whiskey spread warmth down my throat and into my stomach. I closed my eyes in relaxation and pleasure.

"So, when are you going to let me help you, Wilda?"

I cracked one eye and peered at Nami. "Help me with what? You helped me by adding a sweetener to my tea."

"I mean with your husband and son."

The top popped off my boba tea cup when I squeezed it too hard. The cold liquid dripped over my fingers, but Nami handed me a serviette.

"I don't need any help."

"That is so obviously untrue I don't know where to start. You know my work, Wilda. You've seen me help others handle their grief. It's my job as a death priestess. Keeping the grief and anger just simmers inside you until it burns. You need to get a handle on it."

I stood abruptly and the chair clattered behind me. "Thank you for the drink, Nami. I'd better get home now."

Part III
Chapter Sixteen

As we waited to enter the Temporal Shifter, Mattea picked at the moose-hair embroidery on her buckskin overshirt while I slapped her hand down. "Stop fidgeting with it. It's sturdy enough, but if you pick it off, you'll have to repair it yourself."

She scowled at me, but she still seemed tired from the last trip. I couldn't blame her, as I still hadn't caught up on my rest. Still, we had a mission to complete, and we needed to do it now.

I held my emptied collection bag, this time camouflaged with an otter skin, like a medicine bag. Around our necks, we had beaded amulet pouches, and under our buckskin overshirts and mid-calf skirts, we wore warm leggings. The moose hide moccasins had been lined in rabbit fur. With those and the moose hair stockings, my feet grew sweaty.

Mattea fiddled with her embroidery again and then stopped when I glared at her. "Are you certain we must arrive in the winter?"

"It's not winter. April is the end of the snow season."

She rolled her eyes. "Right. I remember it being downright balmy in Toronto in April. Just before the ice storms."

"Hey, now! Don't use up all our allotted sarcasm. Remember, I need a lot to get by."

"If only sarcasm could be crafted into coffee."

I took a deep breath, not relishing yet another week without coffee. "Don't remind me."

In this state of mind, we entered the Temporal Shifter a second time in two weeks. The routine grew familiar, the flickering vestige of a memory so long ago. Mission after mission flashed through my mind, though usually we had sufficient time to rest between each trip. This time, rest was scarce. My muscles hated me already, and we'd barely begun.

The door opened, revealing a shaded oak grove, light frost still dusting the ground in the morning mist. A few pines showed green through the skeletal branches, with glittering water of the river beyond the hill. My knees cracked when I stood, making me wince.

Mattea put a hand on my shoulder as I stepped out. I didn't need her help but smiled at her in gratitude. It took a big heart to offer help despite her own exhaustion.

This portal dropped us off close enough to Pana'wapskik Island to see Mount K'taden looming in the distant mist. This should be the largest settlement of the Pa'nawampske'wiak, a tribe known in modern times as the Penobscot, or People of Where the River Broadens Out. Hopefully, they hadn't yet moved into the hills for their summer hunts. We didn't want to travel too long without supplies.

I'd learned how to hunt, but my hunting expertise was with guns, not snares and traps. I could fish, but I hadn't constructed a fishing pole from scratch for decades. We had taken classes on edible plants and animals before our trip, but little grew this early in the spring. Every creature was skinny from the winter months, eager to eat any green shoot to stave off starvation.

In modern times, a concrete bridge connected the tribal island to the mainland. However, in this pre-Columbian time, we could only traverse the distance with canoes. If we had arrived at the wrong time, we must decide whether to try crossing ourselves or find the tribe elsewhere. I wondered if del Socorro had been here with or without the tribe in residence. If he came during their semi-nomadic journeys, he may have had no interaction at all with the locals, which would make our own task much more difficult. We'd still take samples of everything around us, but we would gain no further knowledge of his journey, his purpose, or his activities. Forensic evidence only worked so far.

The mournful sound of a moose echoed through the trees. Mattea's eyes shifted around with nervous reaction, but I chuckled. "Don't worry. Unless you're threatening her young, a moose won't bother with you much. Just like bears."

"Is that an attempt to reassure me? Because it isn't working."

"Relax. We have much more to worry about from the local hunters than the local wildlife."

"Says you."

We picked our way around the shore, looking for any sign of life on the island. Some movement within the trees caught my attention, but I couldn't discern if it was an owl or a human. We found the remains of a campfire on the mainland, and we built our fire on top. Night would come soon enough and, if we couldn't contact the Pa'nawampske'wiak, we must care for our own comfort and survival.

While Mattea collected firewood and kindling, I scraped out the detritus in the firepit and cleared a ring around it. When she returned with her first armful, I stacked them into a scout-approved cone and took the fire-making implements from one of my many belt bags. I took off my hood, a cap decorated with porcupine quill embroidery with a square bottom edge. I didn't want to chance a stray spark flying up and catching the moose-hair wool.

A strong breeze came through and made me shiver. I bent to my task with determination, hoping to get the cheerful fire going before dusk fell. The day should only be half-over, but we still had a lean-to to craft after we established the fire, and it may take longer to find sufficient pine boughs and birch bark to construct that. April may not be the height of winter, but it remained chilly enough to kill us if we weren't careful.

Mattea returned with more firewood, and a bonus; a handful of green violets. She'd evidently paid close attention during the foraging class.

I took the flowers and leaves from her and grinned. I took the small folded birchbark vessel and placed the flowers in it. Later, once the fire settled, we'd fill it with water and place hot stones inside. Inside, we'd steep tea, boil vegetables into a stew, whatever we wanted to cook.

First, though, I needed to get this blasted fire started. Mattea had collected plenty of fuel, so I sent her in search of pine boughs and birch bark. "Also, any stout bare branches you can find, especially straight ones. We can use those as a frame for the roof."

She rolled her eyes, sighed, and stood again. "I think I prefer being pampered in Mali."

"Would you like me to sprinkle sand on your food, so you can reminisce? Or scrounge up a camel to sneeze in your face? I'm sure moose snot would be just as delightful."

"Don't you dare!"

I chuckled and shooed her away. With a practised but rusty hand, I operated the native fire-drill, marvelling at the spindle and wheel construction. After about twenty minutes, I created a spark with the contraption, and fed first spunk and then kindling into the growing blaze. By the time Mattea returned, towing a huge bundle of boughs, the fire had become a respectable size.

"Well done. I had doubts when I saw that thing. How long did you practise?"

"This time? About an hour. But I'd used a similar device on a prior trip. I just needed to remind my muscles how it worked."

She nodded. "Can I try it next time? It seems like it requires a great deal of stamina and coordination."

"It can be tricky. Here, let me help you with those." As I stood, my knees cracked and popped. I winced but clenched my teeth against the stiffness. Despite the chill, I needed to work the kinks out of my joints. I'd just have to push through the pain.

With a great deal of grunting and giggling, we got four support branches notched and pushed into the earth, the roof frame supports lashed to those and a large pine, and birch bark onto the roof. We leaned the pine boughs along the edge except for the front door, forming a surface for any rain or snow to slide off. I'd packed a couple lengths of deer hide to use as a front flap.

We needed more birch bark, so we both searched for more. Since Mattea had done most of her foraging to the east, I travelled west as she headed north. By the time I returned, she'd already gotten back, placed her bark, and busied herself with chopping some of our provisions into the birchbark cooking vessel. I nodded in approval and placed my own foraged pieces.

By the time I finished, every muscle and joint in my body ached. I needed more time to recover from the desert before travelling to a winter clime. I stretched my arms over my head, ignoring the pops and pulling tendons, and let out a groan. My ungrateful assistant laughed at me.

"Careful, or I'll sic a badger on you."

"I've never seen a badger in real life. They look cute, as if they'd invite you in for tea and a cookie."

I let out an evil laugh. "You, my dear, are thinking of English badgers. The American variety is different. They look more like they're about to tear you apart to feed their meth habit."

She paled and for a moment, I regretted my candour. Then I remembered it would do her no favours to shield her from the realities of our time and place. She needed to learn the dangers before facing them. Therefore, I gave her a sardonic smile and a sombre nod.

"Come on, let's get this stew going. I'm starved."

We added venison pemmican, a few chopped onions, and some wild garlic to the violets and river water. Then, using several green branches, I taught Mattea how to lift a hot stone from the campfire and place it into the birchbark pot. As the water sizzled and frothed, she grinned. We added several more stones until the water boiled.

While I wished we'd brought salt, the stew didn't taste half bad. The violets added a nice bit of spice. We might have done worse on our first primitive meal.

A drop of water hit the top of my head, and I glanced up, only to get another in my eye. No, not water—flakes of snow drifted down upon us. *Wonderful.*

I turned to Mattea, who had also peered up into the dark grey sky. "Okay, you get the supplies and arrange them within the lean-to. Don't forget our packs over there. I'll bank the fire. It's close to the lean-to, and we have enough space inside to place several hot rocks and bank the embers. That will heat the interior throughout the night. If we get a nice layer of snow, that will help."

"Snow will help? Wouldn't that make it colder?"

"Initially, yes, but the insulative properties of snow keeps the warmth in the lean-to. We might even sweat come morning."

"Yeah, right. I'll believe that when I see it. Well, feel it. You know what I mean."

Chapter Seventeen

While I delighted in watching snow fall, especially outside of the city, I had so few energy reserves left, I simply curled up near the hot rocks and passed out. We should have arranged a watch schedule, but my exhaustion kept that thought from bubbling up until the next morning.

When I woke, perfect quiet roared in my ears. I opened the flap of the lean-to and peered out, seeing a thin blanket of white over everything. I smiled, enjoying the beauty of the snow sparkling in the bright morning sun. Enough trees still hadn't gained their spring foliage to interfere with the sunlight, so the snow glittered and shone.

Next to me, Mattea groaned and rolled over. The stones no longer held any heat and my hips shot through with agony. I grunted, closing my eyes against the throbbing pain. Sleeping on the cold ground had never been my idea of a luxurious night, even when I had been young. During my missions as a Temporal Agent, I'd slept rough plenty of times. However, we would have some padding beneath us, despite our circumstances.

I tried to stand, but my legs didn't respond. I used the tree trunk to drag myself to my feet, despite my shaking knees. The helplessness pushed upon my chest, making my heart beat faster. Without being able to move, I wouldn't be able to escape whatever danger might stalk me. My breath grew shorter. I couldn't take in enough air for a full gasp. The snow outside pressed against me, suddenly menacing, dangerous, and eternal.

I touched the lean-to flap, the pole, my sleeping fur. I counted the number of ties along the deer skin, holding it to the frame. My breathing slowed, and I gripped reality once again.

Once I stood, I shoved the incident from my attention. Thinking about panic attacks only made them happen more often. When did standing become such a chore? Oh, yeah, when I decided sleeping on the cold ground would be a fantastic idea. I'm such an idiot.

With creaking steps and much wincing, I walked outside, relieved myself, and found the banked fire. I found the pile of collected wood and scraped it clear. The snow felt soft and fluffy, and the wood didn't seem too wet. I fed the fire until it flickered to life. I then revelled in the delicious warmth, willing it to remove the aches from my bones and my joints.

A twig snapped, and I swivelled, searching for the source. Nothing moved in the white wonderland. I returned to the lean-to and retrieved my antler-bone handled flint knife. I wished I had a good steel blade, but pre-Columbian natives didn't smelt iron. The handle had been carved with a wolf head on the back. I'd been rather proud of that detail, despite the difficulty in carving it. It must have been ten years ago I made this piece? I hefted it and searched the trees again.

Another sound from behind me made me whirl. Still nothing.

I nudged Mattea with my toe, still scanning around us. I whispered to her, "Mattea, wake up. I believe we have company."

She groaned, and I nudged her again. "Shh! Silently."

She sat up when something thudded. "Wha-what?"

"Will you be quiet? Someone is coming. Get ready."

My eyes ached from staring at the bright snow, now, but at least the snow would show any figure. Unless they wore white fur. Movement caught my eye to the left. A blur of movement made me steady my gaze, grateful I'd never needed glasses. The hare sped across the edge of the glade, leaving a line of tracks in the snow.

I let out my breath, and my knees shook again. I leaned against the tree trunk, tired again, despite the night's sleep.

Mattea poked her head out. "What was it?"

"Just a hare. But tomorrow night we need to set a watch schedule. Should have done last night."

She nodded, her expression solemn. She went to relieve herself and joined me at the fire. "What's our plan today?"

I stirred the embers with a stick, eliciting a shower of sparks and a higher flame. "We need to find the local tribe and make our inquiries, just as we did in Tombouctou. Someone here must remember him and can give us some information on his activities. Did you collect samples for your collection bag while you foraged yesterday?"

She smiled. "That much of my training sunk in, at least."

"Good. Get bundled up, and we'll head back to the island. This snow will leave lovely tracks if anyone has come or gone."

We repacked all our belongings but left the lean-to. If we didn't find people today, we'd come back again, rather than rebuild another elsewhere. We'd use this as a base camp while we explored the surrounding area. Then we would have to move to a new one and repeat the process.

Another hare, or perhaps the same one, darted past us as we moved out. His winter coat had become mottled with darker brown, in anticipation of the warmer season. I entertained the notion of setting snares at our camp, but I hoped we found people before we needed to resort to hunting for our food.

While I had hunted, fished, dressed, cleaned, skinned, and cooked more than my fair share of game over the course of our missions, the process remained messy and stinky. I longed for the sweet-smelling soaps of my time.

I gazed up at the sky to gauge the likely weather, but the light cloud cover that had blown in did little to reveal its secrets. The air didn't feel particularly chilly, despite the snow on the ground. White piles of snow already drooped,, and I suspected they'll have melted by noon.

The ground, however, had become mushy and muddy, so we had to tread with care as we made the trek back to the island. The constant drip,

drip, drip of melting snow became a symphony around us. It reminded me of a song from my childhood, one in the movie Bambi. Drip, drip, drip, and something about April showers. Almost a madrigal-singing type of arrangement. Try as I might, I didn't dredge up more than a bare fragment of melody. I cursed my memory's betrayal and plodded on through the mud.

One deep step into the mud, and I almost lost my moccasin. I wished we'd had the foresight to bring mukluks, but I learned long ago one can't think of everything. To travel like the White Knight in *Alice in Wonderland*, carrying everything but the kitchen sink, is to invite disaster. One wouldn't be able to move for the sheer mass of objects.

What if our scientists adjusted the technology for the collection bag into a true bag of holding to bring supplies? With the current configuration, one placed samples inside but had to return to the present to retrieve them. The idea had merit. I'd have to mention it to Pembley when we returned from this part of the mission. He might set the wheels into motion.

I shouldn't be musing on future conveniences. I should pay bloody attention to where I bloody walked and stop bloody stepping in bloody mud holes.

One moccasin squished with every step. I grimaced at both the sound and the disgusting feeling of freezing mud between my toes. We'd not even been here two days, and I already wanted to return.

We reached the edge of the lake again, and ambled around the banks, searching for signs of humans. I scanned the sky for smoke plumes but saw none. That, more than any lack of footprints, convinced me no one camped on the island. Who wouldn't build a hearth fire in the snow?

Mattea stood next to me as we looked out over the water to the pine-clad island. Therefore, the sound behind us couldn't be her. I clutched my knife and whispered, "Don't move. We have company."

I whirled with my knife in my hand and searched for the source of the sound. Nothing stirred in the brown and white landscape. Damn it, if another bloody hare spooked us, I'd have him for stew before the day died.

The trees parted to our left and three native men emerged, spears in hand but not brandished in a threatening manner. Why would three hunters fear of two lone women? Especially when one had white-streaked hair.

Each man wore leather tunics and leggings, decorated with porcupine quill embroidery, feathers, and strips of beadwork. The designs looked floral or curling from here, but I couldn't make out the iconography at this distance. I ached to examine them.

Our two groups stared at each other for several seconds before I lifted my knife and replaced it in the sheaf on my belt. One hunter, a tall young man with tanned buckskin clothing and two feathers pointed down behind his head, nodded. Mattea put her knife away in the same manner. We took two steps forward, and they did the same. We repeated this until we stood close enough to speak.

I spoke in Pa'nawampske'wiak, addressing the clear leader, "We mean no harm. We search for information about a relative who may have walked these lands."

The first man glanced at the hunter on his left, a burly man with lines of age on his face. The short, slender third hunter kept silent, their youthful face stoically still. Their features looked delicate, and their skin seemed paler than the others, and I couldn't figure out if they were male or female. Perhaps neither? Many native societies recognized more than two genders.

The lead hunter nodded and replied, "You speak our language well, yet your clothing is of the Children of the Dawn Country, the Wolastoqiyik. How is this? We call the Wolastoqiyik 'Malicete' because they speak strange, yet your language is precise. We are wary of visitors who make no sense."

After controlling my urge to curse, I nodded with a smile and a small bow. "I mean no disrespect to your tribe or your ways. I have walked from my own lands, far to the west. For many months, I studied your language and customs, but my teacher may have confused your tribe with the Wolastoqiyik. I didn't realise this clothing would be of concern."

I didn't know what else to say. We'd received flawed research. I wondered which Agent had brought back the faulty information. I meant to find out. Offering no information about a culture, their ceremonies, clothing, and language remained acceptable practise for a Temporal Agent. In fact, the Agency encouraged such gaps if the Agent couldn't be certain of their information. To bring back incorrect data and certify it as verified led to the situation we found ourselves in. Instead of an even playing field, we began this mission at a disadvantage of suspicion because we wore the contentious neighbours' clothing style, and not the tribe we hoped to guest with.

The lead hunter stared at me and then Mattea for a few tense moments before he gave a reluctant nod. His gaze lingered on Mattea and my shoulders tensed. His look didn't assess her for threat, but for beauty.

An eternal truth of Temporal Agents remained that any time, any place in history had been dangerous, especially for women. Rape and abuse had always been endemic, and in some times and places, considered normal and acceptable, depending on the class and status of the players in question. As far as I'd learned, rape in native culture only became accepted in cases of slaves. However, I didn't wish to test this theory on Mattea and this bold hunter.

They turned and walked back through the trees. We followed.

Chapter Eighteen

We never would have found the camp on our own. Hidden within a hollow, even their fires wouldn't have given it away. The thick canopy of trees filtered the smoke and dispersed it by the time it reached the air above.

Five large beda'gwigans ringed a large bonfire area, with several smaller wi'gwom around the periphery. The square beda'gwigans looked large enough to sleep an entire extended family, built like a log cabin with a birch bark roof. The wi'gwoms looked more familiar as Native dwellings to any child, built with tall poles gathered at the top.

A knot of women gathered to one side of the bonfire, working with several cones made of birch bark. Only a few young men mingled about young. The oldest male around seemed to be the one with the hunting party.

I squinted, trying to determine what the women worked on, and the details of their clothing. Then I sniffed the air and glanced to the trees surrounding the camp. Sure enough, taps hung from the surrounding maple and birch trees, small birch boxes slung around the trunks to catch the syrup slowly dripping from them. This must be a sugar camp, set up to collect maple and birch syrup and boil it all into sugar for easy transport.

Everyone stopped to watch as we arrived. The younger women whispered and giggled while the older women stared at us with blank expressions. Several young men sat up as Mattea walked by, and I restrained the urge to glare at them with menace. My protective instinct had already been primed by the hunt leader and now every interested glance made my skin crawl. I'm certain Mattea could handle herself. She's single and thirty, living in a major metropolitan area. She'll have learned how to fend off wolves most of her adult life. However, she had a history of poor relationship decisions. Also, being a stranger in a new culture always removed a veneer of confidence and the ability to read the danger signs.

The hunt leader took us to the back of the camp, where a larger beda'gwigan stood apart from the others. This one had spring flowers decorating the edge of the roof. We ducked into the doorway and as my eyes adjusted to the relative gloom, I discerned a figure sitting on a bench, stitching dyed porcupine quills into a piece of leather. I marvelled she could see such delicate work in this low light. She had white flowing hair and lined, mahogany skin. When she glanced up at our entrance, I saw the old woman's eyes, a startlingly young ice blue. The same blue eyes I'd just seen in Mali.

I shivered as my skin pebbled with a sudden chill.

We approached behind the hunt leader. He spoke to the grandmother, bowing low in respect. "Nokemes Di'dias, we have brought you visitors. They come seeking word of their relative. Will you see them?"

Nokemes Di'dias, which my translator told me meant Grandmother Blue Jay, peered at each of us, taking in details of our clothing, our stance, and our manner. As she studied us, I studied her. She wore several layers of fur around her shoulders, While I could discern beaver and bear, others remained less identifiable. The intricate beadwork necklace and quill embroidery on her leather tunic looked astonishing and beautiful, in deep shades of blue and purple. She gave the hunter a sharp nod. "Tema'kwe, I see them. Leave us now."

Tema'kwe's eyes widened. He hadn't expected her to agree so easily, nor to dismiss him. Her eyes glittered as he withdrew and then she turned her attention to us. She pointed at me with a gnarled finger. "You. Come forward."

138

With a glance at Mattea, who shrugged, I stepped toward the grandmother. I bowed as Tema'kwe had, clasped my hands in front of me, and waited for her to ask questions. As a guest, we must wait upon the host to speak first.

She let me stand there for at least five minutes under her intense regard. I recognised the technique, designed to make the subordinate nervous and likely to make a mistake. I refused to falter. While I didn't have the level of power she obviously enjoyed, I'd taken part in more than my share of power plays.

Finally, she nodded. "You are not easily intimidated. This is good. Long may you live. What shall I call you, strong woman?"

"I am called Wôbigo. My companion is Mekwi."

"I have not asked your companion's name."

"With or without your query, her name remains Mekwi."

After a tense moment, Nokemes Di'dias burst out laughing. The loud bray echoed through the large beda'gwigan to the point I wanted to wince from the onslaught. A few chuckles from outside proved others had heard her.

"Yes, I think I will like you. Come and sit next to me. If your knees are anything like mine, standing for a long time will be painful. I have room on my bench for both of you."

With great relief, I sat next to Nokemes Di'dias, but maintained my respectful posture. Mattea sat next to me with her back straight. We hadn't escaped the woods yet, but at least the path had inched open.

"Tema'kwe doesn't pass judgements to me unless something confuses him. He works out problems on his own and then asks forgiveness when he has broken something. Instead, he brings you rather than risk an error. What have you done to confuse him so?"

Her disconcerting blue eyes bore into me as I considered my answer.

"I must be a puzzle, Nokemes Di'dias. While I spoke your language, the decorations on my clothing appeared more Wolastoqiyik. I am neither. I came here from my home far to the west, in Ojibwe lands. However, I took time to learn your language and your ways as best I could before I visited. It seems some of my knowledge had been inaccurate. I apologise if my mismatched clothing has offended your warrior."

I'd expected Nokemes Di'dias to examine my clothing after I spoke, but she maintained eye contact. This told me she'd already taken in the details Tema-kwe had remarked upon.

"I can see how this might confuse him. However, your explanation needs some details. Why have you made such an effort to find us?"

I swallowed, realising I may have inflated my mission's importance too much. "I had planned on travelling to this area for many years. However, the need for travel became more urgent when a relative disappeared. Because I had already learned about your people, my people sent me to find word of him." While a painted miniature of the sort I showed people in Mali would not be an acceptable tool in this time and place, I could describe the traveller we sought. The man from Lima had been a Peruvian native, so his skin would be of similar color and facial feature to these northern cousins. However, he'd had short hair and the tattoo of a Chakana Cross on his arm.

"What is your relative called?"

I shook my head. "I am not certain what name he has taken on his travels. We called him Mario del Soccoro. However, he has his hair cut short and a distinctive marking on his arm, like so." Using a stick in the dirt, I drew the equal-armed stepped cross of the native Peruvian culture.

I held my breath while I waited for her answer. I didn't have long to wait. "I have not heard of such a man."

While it had been a long shot that I'd come across the tribe del Socorro had visited right away, my hopes sunk at her words. "Then I must seek another People to find word of him."

She shook her head. "Such a journey is unnecessary. You will not travel fast nor find where the People stay in this season. We move from winter to summer camps during the moon of smelts. Instead, I will send a runner out to our main tribe to discover if they know of him."

Working hard to let out my breath easily rather than in a rush, my head grew dizzy. I smiled and nodded to Nokemes Di'dias. "You are most generous. I thank you."

She stood more quickly than I could have after sitting so long. "Now, we shall eat together!"

Once outside the beda'gwigan, she spoke to Tema'kwe, and he sent for the kʷsiwa'mbe, or "pure man," an official runner. Such men must vow to touch no woman and live an ascetic life until such a time as another runner proved faster. They received much honour, even after their turn as kʷsiwa'mbe.

Nokemes Di'dias turned back after giving the young man the details I'd related. "He will be perhaps eight nights finding the main tribe, getting his answer, and returning. If he does not find an answer, he will inquire the surrounding tribes, but that will make his return longer. Perhaps twenty nights. Is that an acceptable time for your quest?"

Despite my itch to finish our mission quickly, I nodded, and she turned to him. "Go, now. Be swift."

The young man, perhaps aged fourteen at the most, clothed in an unadorned pale yellow leather tunic, dashed away into the afternoon sun. Tall trees quickly swallowed his slight form.

The two other hunters came forward, and Tema'kwe introduced them. The older man, he called Chansomps, which meant Locust. "Because he eats everything in sight."

Mattea covered her mouth to prevent her giggle from escaping, which elicited a cheerful grin from Chansomps.

"We call this hunter Wula'mbes." The word translated into Pretty Face, and the tall youth qualified. Tema'kwe didn't call Wula'mbes a boy. Nothing on their face or body indicated their gender. The shy smile and blush they gave Mattea might be an indication, but then again…

Mattea's smile grew deeper than normal, and I narrowed my eyes at her. However, she remained oblivious to my warning. I'd have to caution her later. The temporal maxims now forbade getting involved with a local.

While she'd been given this information, much of her training might have glossed past her, due to the condensed time. A judicious reminder wouldn't go amiss.

We sat down around the enormous bonfire, where other women had finished cooking a meal while I conversed with Nokemes Di'dias. First, the women passed bowls filled from a huge birch bark pot of three sister's soup, with beans, corn, and squash, flavoured with raccoon fat to the men. Next came corn meal mixed with maple sugar fried in raccoon fat, called pesida'men, followed. Last came muskrat tails fried between layers of fat.

Once they served the few men, the women received their portions. I noticed how Wula'mbes had sat amongst the men while they got food, but then took their food to sit with the women while they ate. This person became more intriguing by the moment. They sat between Mattea and an older woman who showed a missing front tooth when she grinned. After Mattea sat, the older woman showed her how to suck the muskrat tail by drawing it between her teeth and sucking the bones dry.

I enjoyed the soup the best, though the muskrat tasted sweet and juicy. Mattea licked the vestiges of grease from her fingers so, evidently, she concurred. No matter how primitive the culture, travellers usually ate as good as, if not better than, their modern counterparts. Perhaps they didn't eat as often, and lean times became disastrous, but when they had food, it tasted fantastic. Lack of preservatives made food either fresh and delicious or spoiled and disgusting, with few gradients in between. Perhaps I might bring some ancient food combinations and techniques to modern boutique restaurants. I'd never try cooking them. My own culinary skills, despite years of missions and living alone, remained pathetic. I might still suggest things to those who enjoyed such pursuits.

I doubted Devin or Reuben would want to include raccoon fat or muskrat tail on his Poké Bowl menu, no matter how delicious. Nami, however, might include them just to delight in the horror on the hipster's faces.

Once the last person finished their meal, stewed berries, like a compote, came around on another piece of the maple sugar corn bread. This melted in my mouth, and I wanted more.

After the women cleared the meal, everyone remained around the bonfire as Tema'kwe told a story.

Before he began, he passed around a drinking cup made of horn. Someone had carved the cup with a representation of a bear and a man sitting in a canoe. "This represents my mother. She was a Bear. This is the story of the origins of the Bear Family."

He related the tale of a family, a man, his wife, and a little boy, who left his village to go north for a great council. They walked up the river where they had to ford a half days' journey to the next river.

"The man carried the canoe first, leaving his wife and son to pack the rest of the supplies. While she packed, however, the boy ran away, to catch up with his father. However, the father had walked too far for the boy to find him, and he got lost. When the wife arrived with the supplies, they realised the boy had never arrived and they searched for him. They couldn't find him, so they returned to their village. The village searched for him for many moons, but none could find him.

"During the next spring, they found sharpened sticks near the river, and concluded the boy survived, and hunted for fish. They only found bear tracks, though, so they decided the boy lived with the bears.

"One man in the village had been well known, for his laziness. He didn't search for the boy before, and everyone yelled at him for this. They kicked and abused him until he agreed to look for the boy with the bears. He arrives at the bear's den, knocks his arrow against the rock outside, and calls within for the boy.

"Then the father bear comes out, holding a birch-bark vessel. The lazy man shoots him with an arrow and kills him.

"Next, the mother bear comes out, holding another birch-bark vessel. The lazy man shoots her with an arrow and kills her.

"Third, the cub does the same, and when all the bears are dead, the lazy man enters the cave to find the little boy, huddled and crying in the corner. He takes the child back to his parents, where the villagers showered him with gifts for his bravery.

"The boy grows bristles and acts like a bear, but the village turns him back into a boy before he becomes a full bear. We call all his descendants bears, and they draw pictures of bears on birch bark whenever they camp. My mother was of the Bear family. I am of the Bear family."

Tema'kwe sat down, and for a confusing moment, his hulking shoulders took a bruin cast. However, he may have sat that way on purpose, for just such an effect. I glanced at some of the audience to gauge their reaction to the tale, but they chatted amongst themselves with little concern. This tale must be well known and he'd likely told it many times. No one remarked upon it as unusual.

Mattea spoke with Wula'mbes, but I couldn't hear her soft words. I hoped they only chatted about the tale. I still needed to speak with her, but not among so many. As guests, we must act like such.

Another storyteller stood, relating a tale of a moose hunt almost gone wrong. This storyteller used body language and humour to flavour his tale. Soon, the entire campsite roared with laughter, some falling to the ground and holding against a stitch in their side.

I only paid half-attention to the tale as I remained preoccupied with Mattea's obvious flirting. Still, his antics elicited several smiles and chuckles from me.

As his tale wound down, a woman stood to relate a story. Her quiet words spoke of the origin of fish, frogs, and turtles. She told of a monster frog, Aglebe'mu, and how he forbade the People access to life-giving water.

Mattea's giggle distracted me from this new tale, and I glanced back toward her. She sat even closer to Wula'mbes and they held hands. I gritted my teeth to keep myself from jumping up and slapping their hands apart. Such a breach of etiquette would insult our hosts, if not create a criminal incident for striking one of their own. Still, Mattea ought to know better, damnit!

The meal sat in a heavy lump in my stomach as I tried to churn through thoughts. What if Mattea fell in love here? At over thirty years old, she'd be mature enough to understand her own heart. Temporal Agents had *defected* in the past, applying for permanent "emigration" to the past to be with their loves. While even the older maxims actively discouraged such practise, they allowed it more leniency than a casual dalliance. If someone emigrated, they became part of the past and integrated into the time stream. Such an action caused fewer problems than a life changed from a temporary visit or a child resulting from such a visit. The newer maxims weren't as forgiving.

I shook my head. I might have jumped the gun on this. She just flirted with a local. I'd remind her of her duties tonight and that would be the end of it. Mattea had always been a trustworthy, and mature, conscientious employee and a trusted friend. I had no reason to suspect a change in that attitude now. Just because a "pretty face" turned her head, she remained a modern woman with an addiction to modern conveniences.

The woman's tale ended, and several people drifted off to find their beds. Before our meal, Tema'kwe had shown Mattea and me to a guest wi'gwom, near the edge of the encampment. No one else stood to tell another tale, so it should be polite to withdraw now.

I stood and turned to Mattea. At first, I only saw the back of her head as she kissed her companion.

I stepped in front of them and cleared my throat. They did not stop kissing. I cleared it again and tapped Mattea on the shoulder. She looked up, her face flushed in the firelight. Her hair looked mussed, and her expression looked guilty.

"I'm sorry to interrupt, but I have an urgent matter to discuss with you, Mekwi. Wula'mbes, will you excuse us both, please?"

Without waiting for either to answer, I took Mattea's free hand and pulled her to her feet. I may not have been too gentle. Mattea stumbled as I led her to our wi'gwom. Once inside, I spoke in quiet but firm tones. "What are you bloody well thinking, Mattea?"

"What? What do you mean? It's harmless fun. They're sweet."

I gripped both her shoulders. "Did you doze off during that part of Agent training? I realise it was a lot to absorb, but you must remember we aren't to fraternise with the locals?"

Mattea set her jaw, and I saw the stubbornness shine through her eyes. "I thought they only forbid dalliances during more recent time periods? This is a thousand years past. What I do now can't mess up the time stream so horribly."

I let go of her shoulders and paced as well as I could in the tiny structure. "Everything we do now affects time. Every. Single. Thing. Most will weave back into the stream, but some few won't. We can't tell which those are, so our goal, our mission, our 'prime directive,' is to avoid serious complications at all costs. At all costs. Do you understand, Mattea? What if your relationship with this person keeps them from mating with someone else, someone destined to be the ancestor of a pivotal historical person? We can't know."

She crossed her arms, glaring at me. "Just being here changes time. That's the whole premise. We can't know what we'll change, so we have to trust time to correct itself."

I stopped pacing and glared right back at her. The dim light didn't allow much effect for the glare, but I used it anyhow. She knew me well enough to anticipate my expression. "There's informed trust, reasonable trust, and then there's blind trust. Blind trust is doing whatever you want and hoping it all comes out right. That's not how Temporal Agents work, Mattea. Frankly, I'm surprised and disappointed at this attitude. I thought you'd be more mature, more conscientious, than that."

She stared at her feet, chagrined. "I usually am. But, Wilda," she looked up, entreaty in her eyes, "Wula'mbes and I just connect. We understand each other. They said our souls were two parts, a whole separated until now. How can I fight against such a thing? Do you even know how long it's been?"

"Been since what?" As soon as the words were out of my mouth, I understood what she meant. Still, being on mission meant keeping control of one's libido. I hadn't given in to temptation since Paolo died. I clamped down hard on that memory and a rising sense of panic and glared again at Mattea.

"Don't play coy. You understand exactly what I mean. It's been years, and hard years at that. Who trusts modern lovers? No one. There's no truth in modern people, male or female or whatever. It's all games and contests. I don't want that. I want honest affection. What's so wrong with that? How can that be so evil?"

I sighed and sat on the log surrounding the tiny hearth. "It's not evil. Not in the slightest. That's a natural human need, and I'm not arguing against the need. But you must, must, *must* be circumspect when you're on a mission. It's paramount that we cause as few waves as humanly possible. If this wasn't such an essential mission, I'd pull us both out and return. However, that isn't an option. We have to stay to find out where del Socorro went, what he ate, who he met…whatever information we can glean."

She sat down next to me, and we stared at the low fire in sullen silence for several minutes, each lost in our own thoughts. Finally, she sighed and stood. "Fine. I'll maintain a friendly distance with Wula'mbes. May I still be friends with them? May we talk and work together while we wait for the runner to return with news? If not, this will be a long, difficult week. And snubbing them may cause more issues."

Time to relent. "I can trust you to be aware of which lines not to cross. Can't I?" I raised both eyebrows, needing her to verify my assumption.

She nodded. "I understand the lines."

"Good. Thank you. I'd already been tired before our talk. Now, I'm utterly exhausted. Do you want the spot on that side of the fire, or this one?"

"I'll take that one, so all you have to do is roll into your spot." She gave me a mischievous grin.

I poked her in the shoulder. "Yeah, I wish. I still need to relieve myself. All that fruit juice. What I wouldn't do for some coffee or better yet, a tot of whiskey. Now why did I remind myself of those two unattainable elixirs? I swear, sometimes I'm just masochistic."

"You're telling me."

Chapter Nineteen

If I expected the next week to be a chance to catch up on my rest, I was mistaken. Between helping the women gather and boil the maple syrup into sugar, taking my turn at coming up with stories to entertain in the evening, and crafting details about my home amongst the Ojibwe to satisfy Nokemes Di'dias' curiosity, my mind and body never powered down except for a few fitful hours each night. While the locals understood how to keep their beds warm with multiple layers between the sleeper and the ground, the cold still seeped through the furs and blankets into my bones.

The cold ground didn't help in the slightest, nor the still present blanket of snow around us.

While we hadn't made progress in finding word of del Socorro, I made new notes of the garb, customs, and social norms of our hosts. Each night, I wrote a diary page of the things I observed. This time and place had much less documentation than the more popular destinations in history. The Agency would add my notes to the Temporal Agent archive. Mattea wrote out notes as well, but since her Agent training had been cursory, her notes wouldn't be as refined.

Slush turned to mud which turned to ice. My muscles ached with careful walking all day around such treacherous places, made worse by sleeping on a hard pallet. Sure, I piled pine needles in a sack on top of the pallet, and the palette raised my bed a couple inches from the frozen ground, but none of this came close to the modern pillow-top mattress and warm comforters I had grown used to.

Mattea fared better. She made friends amongst the young women. She kept a cautious distance from both young hunters. I kept my eye on the latter as well, as I'd caught him casting leers toward Mattea. I would not permit such attentions forced upon her. Nokemes Di'dias also watched him when Mattea walked by, so the matriarch kept her eye on the situation. This reassured me. Nokemes Di'dias didn't strike me as a woman anyone crossed with impunity. I found a kindred spirit in the older hunter, the one named Chansomps, as we shared a wealth of experience and years.

The group spent the morning collecting full buckets from the maple trees and affixing empty ones in their place. Women canvassed the trees methodically, and while I worked slower than the slowest of them, I at least helped. Mattea learned quickly and soon became as deft as them.

Afterwards, I tended the fires to boil the sugar while Mattea learned some of the basket-making techniques. Birch bark baskets were the most common, though some had been made with the inner bark from different trees. Most of the birch bark baskets had been made by folding the bark into a square shape and then fixing the top with a strip of inner bark. They sealed the edges and corners with tree sap. A larger version, folded into the middle to form a stout handle, became my favourite. This basket had enough room for me to gather herbs, mushrooms, and other samples to add to my collection bag and bring back forage. These offerings became a welcome addition to each evening meal.

Nokemes Di'dias and the other women admired my embroidery skills. Once I got the porcupine quills in hand, I showed off my talent. This art form had always been a favourite of mine, and I'd made many pieces of garb and accessories with the dyed quills in my years.

I finished one piece, a medicine bag made with otter skin and a flap decorated in a decorative flower pattern. The dyed quills of blue and red showed stark against the dark brown otter skin, and I admired the effect. I handed it to Nokemes Di'dias for her assessment.

The elder examined both the internal stitching and the external quilling before nodding and smiling. She handed the bag around for the other women to study as the glow of approval suffused me.

Mattea also shared her basket, a solid square-bottomed affair. She'd found two different shades of inner bark to make a nice contrast pattern. While hers wouldn't be as waterproof as the birch bark baskets, it would work fine for holding solid items.

I made repairs to our gear, especially our footwear. The moccasins had been inadequate for the weather, and I ached for real boots. Well, my feet ached for them. Still, with enough rabbit fur, even my feet stayed warm while I re-stitched the soles and mended the hole where a stick had poked through. After a thorough washing and working the leather while it dried, the mud had disappeared.

Most of the women seemed frightened to talk with me. They might be wary of two women who travelled alone, without a male hunter to guard us, though Mattea made friends. Maybe they thought me a powerful protector instead of an older woman. While I would love to demonstrate that yes, it was possible to live and survive in the world without a man, thank you very much, that would run counter to the local culture and mores. At the least, it would stand out as an unusual attitude. If only a male travelling companion had been available, I would have been much safer. The Agency cautioned us to stay under the radar if they can. Unfortunately, being a proponent of women's liberation wouldn't qualify for subterfuge.

The older man, Chansomps, and I became friends after a fashion. Other than Nokemes Di'dias, he remained the only person close to my age in the camp. Our white hair gave us a shared heritage, a commonality of experience I pretended to and he shared.

Chansomps sat with me most evenings and discussed our lives, our pasts, and our philosophies in life. I modified most of my stories from my actual life experiences, but I might paint them in a patina of pre-Columbian life with only a few changes.

I had forgotten how pleasant it was to discuss such things with someone of my age and with a similar wealth of experience. Mattea was a great friend, and I loved Tarren's sense of humour, but they were both young women, and I had a full generation on them both. I came to treasure our talks and looked forward to each one.

On the evening of the fourth day, someone arrived at the camp. However, he didn't look like the young Pure Man runner we had sent out. In fact, his clothing and demeanour differed from ours. He turned out to be a messenger from the Pestomuhkati People, a related tribe to the east.

After a long session of speaking in low voices between the messenger, Nokemes Di'dias, and Tema'kwe, the two men left the camp. The bleak expression in Nokemes Di'dias' eyes forbade questions. The tension in her shoulders spoke volumes. I considered offering to help, but I reminded myself about interfering when I didn't need to. Instead, I sighed with relief that Tema'kwe, at least, had left the camp for a while. One less thing for me to worry about.

Mattea had kept her promise and maintained her distance from Wula'mbes, as far as I noticed. They still exchanged longing glances when they thought I wouldn't notice. I saw them speaking alone now and then, but always in full sight of the camp and with no public displays of affection.

Two more days passed amongst the women and the two remaining hunters. Chansomps and I discussed past loves and lives. He spoke of his first wife with such undying reverence and affection, I almost missed her myself. We sat on the bench next to the fire, waiting for water to boil for tea.

His eyes grew dreamy as he recalled her. "My Alsoomse had been a rare person. Someone who carved the spirit of an animal from the wood or bone. She coaxed out their true form using just a small knife. Her work brought great honour to us both."

"You must have loved her deeply."

"I mourn her every day these thirty seasons gone. She'd been a spring flower in my life."

I swallowed back the tears of memory from my own Paolo. "I've mourned my own husband as long. He and I walked the earth together and shared in our joy of the world."

Chansomps poured two cups of tea and passed one over. He lifted a chunk of maple sugar in question, and I shook my head. While it didn't compare with coffee, tea with sweet seemed a betrayal of a sort.

He shrugged and dropped two chunks into his own steaming cup, stirring with a stick until they dissolved. "Where did you explore?"

I chuckled with a rueful grin. "Anywhere and everywhere. We met amazing people and saw landscapes that took our breath away."

"Would you do it again?"

I caught my breath before I answered. Would I do it again? Even knowing I'd lose Paolo, would I take that last trip, the trip that stole him and my child away?

"How can I know? The Great Spirit saw fit to take him from me. I cannot argue against that decision, no matter how much my heart might wish to."

He placed a hand on my shoulder. I resisted the urge to flinch away. He merely offered sympathy, nothing sinister or salacious. I must school my reactions better. I gave him a half-smile and sipped my tea, staring at the fire.

We sat in silence, watching the flames shed sparks into the breeze. The sun had long since set, and the stars twinkled above us in chilly silence. Knots of women sat around the fire, chatting or laughing. I glanced around to find Mattea sitting between Wula'mbes and two young women. I frowned, but she did nothing wrong. Still, I had best keep an eye on her. I still couldn't believe her earlier intransigence. The maxims were so ingrained within my training, I forgot how quick her own training had been.

The sentry's voice echoed across the quiet night, a challenge in the darkness. A voice answered the challenge, strident and triumphant. We all stood to discover who approached. I glanced at Nokemes Di'dias, but her eyes remained shadowed in the dim firelight.

Three people approached Nokemes Di'dias in the glowing red of the bonfire. Tema'kwe and the Pure Man, I recognised. The third person seemed to be a stranger. Her dark clothing had beaded decorations of swirling floral designs, more like the designs on our own clothing. She must be from the Wolastoqiyik, the neighbouring tribe.

When she spoke Pa'nawampske'wiak, her speech carried a heavy accent which made her words difficult to understand. "I come summoned as I met a man who visited us several moons ago. I am told one of your people seek information from him."

Both Mattea and I sat straight. Nokemes Di'dias sought my gaze, and I nodded.

Nokemes Di'dias opened her arms wide in welcome. "It is true. We seek word of a visitor to your lands. Do rest this evening, and tomorrow we shall speak. Eat of our food."

The woman nodded and sat on a bench. Tema'kwe, full of solicitude, served her a bowl of stew from the fire. He brought her tea and sat beside her as she ate her fill.

She had flawless skin and refined features. I could see why Tema'kwe seemed entranced by her. If he escorted her back from the other tribe, they likely already struck up a friendship. This rival to his affections would relieve Mattea. I sighed as my shoulders relaxed.

With that relaxation, all energy drained from my body, and I let out a huge yawn. Chansomps laughed at me. "You must go to your rest. Let me walk you to your bed."

As I barely had the energy to stand, I let him. In fact, I even let him help me from the bench. My knees creaked and groaned as I stood, eliciting another sympathetic smile from the man. "Your knees sing as mine do. Sometimes I tire of the music."

"As do I, my friend. As do I."

Despite my exhaustion, I sleep evaded me. I stared at the sloped roof of the wi'gwom and waited for Mattea to join me. Sounds of laughter drifted in from the bonfire, and I tried to discern her voice. I recognised the new woman's voice and Tema'kwe's laughter. They'd sat closer to our wi'gwom than Mattea and her friends had, so that didn't surprise me. Still, I strained my hearing for a clue while I waited for sleep to overcome me. I waited in vain.

Did hours pass, or only minutes, before I heard the rustling of the tent flap? Mattea tried to be stealthy, but as she slid into her side of the wi'gwom, I finally relaxed and let sleep take me over.

*****

As the sun rose, the rain fell.

In the icy sleet that greeted me, Chansomps visited as we huddled inside the wi'gwom. "I remembered you had no large fire, and it would take time to stoke it to usefulness. Here, I brought tea for both of you. No, do not thank me. I'm off to bring hot drinks to our other guest."

When he left, I sipped the tea, grimacing at the sweetness. He must have forgotten I preferred no sugar. I glanced at Mattea through the steam and noticed the bags under her eyes. "Did you not sleep well?"

She shook her head but didn't elaborate. She closed her eyes as she sipped her tea. Then she put the cup down and ran her fingers through her hair, trying to tame the tangles. I rifled through my pack and pulled out my bone comb. She had her own, but she didn't look to be in any shape to find it.

I narrowed my eyes as she brushed out her hair. "Mattea, how late did you get in last night?"

She stopped brushing and glared at me. Half her tangles had been tamed and the other half still stood up like a demented Medusa. "Are you serious? You look nothing like my mother."

The chill made my skin pebble and itch. "Damnit, Mattea, we talked about this."

"You are correct. We talked about it extensively."

Gripping my knees, I glared at her. "You agreed to abide by the maxims."

She blinked and glanced at the roof while she attacked the other side of her hair. After wincing a couple times for knotty tangles, she gave me an innocent smile. "Did I? I don't recall that bit."

"Fuck. You did it, didn't you?"

She smoothed all her tangles but continued to brush her hair. The waves curled around her hand as she made each stroke. "'Did it?' Really? Are we children? Yes, I slept with Wula'mbes. But you can relax about any progeny. While they are called "Two Spirit," having both male and female essences, anatomically, they are female. I'd never get pregnant. So, withdraw your claws, if you please."

Her prim tone enraged me. "The possibility of issue is only part of the point, as you'll be well aware. What if they would have been with a male? Someone they might mate with and have progeny?"

"They don't identify as female. Wula'mbes would never go with a male. They assured me of that. And before you say they'd be forced to, Nokemes Di'dias assured me "Two Spirits" are honored amongst their people. They are considered sacred and lucky, being able to see life from two perspectives. She will not force Wula'mbes into any relationship they don't wish. We spoke of the possibilities at length before anything happened."

I had to admit, I could think of no counterargument to her action. Mattea had acted with some sense and foresight. I clenched my jaw, unable to argue but unwilling to give up the fight. I took a sip of my tea to collect my thoughts.

Mattea handed the comb back and took a sip of her own drink. "As a matter of pure curiosity, has anyone brought someone from the past as a permanent immigrant?"

Her question made me splutter my tea, almost coating her in a shower of hot liquid. "What? You can't be serious."

Her coy grin made me suspect she'd been angling for this question through the entire conversation. "I am quite serious."

An intense chill spiked through my spine. "Have you revealed your true nature to a local, Mattea?"

She shook her head. "No, no, of course not. I only asked if they'd ever considered moving to a different land. Wula'mbes expressed a deep desire to see new places and meet new people. I told them where I came from, people such as them had become accepted within society at a greater level than this one. They didn't believe me, but I wanted to explore if I might show them some day."

After placing my cup on the ground, I folded my hands. "Your training has been remiss. It seems I must recount to you the myriad of problems associated with taking a person from their native time. First, their panoculations will be wholly inadequate, even if we bolster them at the Agency. Second, the culture shock from a pre-historic, low-technology society, might be enough to damage their psyche, if not drive them to suicide. Integration into modern society would be a slow, almost impossible task."

"*Almost* impossible."

I held up my hand. "In addition to that, there is the matter of support. They'll have no way of making a living in the modern world, so you'd have to support them for the rest of their lives. That includes if you fight with them, get sick, or wish to move elsewhere. If you left them or died, they'd be alone in an alien culture and time."

"They might work at one of the living history museums! Those things are everywhere nowadays. They'd know better than the people running them how their culture had been. Wula'mbes would be giving tours in no time."

While I didn't know how such museums worked, I mustn't let her realise she had a point. "Also, it's so against the temporal maxims, they'd fine you heavily, fire you, and never allow you to travel again in your life." I let my voice drop to a gentler tone. "I know you always wanted to travel, Mattea. Would you give up your dream for the affection of someone you just met?"

This made her droop. "I don't think I'm eager for another trip once we're done with this mission. I mean, I've been attacked by brigands, sneezed on by a camel, and almost frozen to death. Hell, I can't even imagine what wonders await me in Scotland, but I think I'll have had my fill by then."

I put a finger under her chin, making her glance up. "It cannot happen. No matter how many arguments you make with me, it would never pass muster with PENDULUM. In order for Wula'mbes to travel to the future, they'd have to provide an implant for them, and we'd have to surgically insert it here. They will never agree to such a thing. In all my years as an Agent and since, I've heard of two other Agents asking similar boons. The Agency categorically denied both, even after many years of dedicated service. I'm sorry, Mattea. The answer will always be no."

She stared into her cup. I sipped my own, though the liquid had turned ice cold.

Chapter Twenty

Despite a full day of work with the tribe, I slept little that night. Between Mattea's betrayal and my imagination, I tossed and turned as the wind blew outside the wi'gwom. As the sun rose, I scrambled out and washed myself by the river. The icy water chased the fatigue from my body for the moment, but I knew it would return. I had little time for such bodily limitations. We would need to return with the woman of the Wolastoqiyik to her own tribe today.

As I returned to the camp, the visitor sat next to the large bonfire, coaxing a section to life. I hadn't yet spoken to her, so I took this opportunity to chat. Besides, I wanted to get a closer look at the features of her garb and memorise the curling flower designs. I brought water to boil for tea and we sat in silence. Once the flames grew strong enough, she placed the container in the embers to heat.

She poked the fire with a stick, causing a shower of sparks and smoke. "I am called Lintu. Are you the one who wants word of your cousin?"

I nodded with a smile. "I am called Wôbigo. My companion is Mekwi."

"And your cousin?"

I looked back to the fire. I didn't know what he called himself at each of his destinations. The Agency assigned most travellers their personas. However, since he used a rogue portal, we had no information on his identities. "I knew him as Mario del Socorro, but he may have used another."

"Can you describe him?"

"He's tall and thin with very short hair. He has a permanent drawing on one arm, a stepped cross with swirling designs inside."

At first, her expression only showed mild interest, but when I described del Socorro's tattoo, she perked up as she poured water into my mug. "I know this man! Yes, he came to us moons ago, a trader with reindeer skins from the north. He spoke of many years of walking amongst various tribes, and his exotic appearance gave truth to his stories. He gave his name as Gizos Igasho. This is your cousin?"

Gizos Igasho meant Sun Wanderer. What a perfect name. I nodded, eager for more details. "How long ago did he arrive? How long did he stay? Where did he stay?"

She shook her head. "He's no longer with our tribe. He stayed for a while with one of my sisters. She had a babe, but she was not the babe's mother. His mother had died of a fever last moon. The child interested Gizos, and he offered help in caring for him, but she would not allow it."

I cocked my head. "Not allow it? Why not? Wouldn't she appreciate the help?"

"She had a husband and would not undermine his status by taking help from another man, even for another's child. When Gizos learned this, he gave the child a gift of many furs and disappeared. He left maybe seven moons ago, after living with us for three. He stayed with our winter camp along the shore. I can show you where, but no one lives there now. We have gone up into the highlands to work our summer hunts."

Mattea groaned and emerged from her tent, her tangled hair mussed. She scratched at her side and stumbled down to the stream with a desultory wave. I hid a smile from the visitor, but she spoke. "Is she your daughter? Her skin is so light. I've never seen one so pale. Is she sick?"

I shook my head as my tea steeped. "That is her natural colour. Not my daughter, but I have responsibility for her. Her people come from the far north and east. Years ago, paler people came from across the sea to settle there." I didn't say Mattea had been part of the Norse settlers, but I left it as an implication.

"I've heard tales of such people but thought them mere rumours or fabrications. She looks so strange and ugly!"

This time, I let my smile widen, and I took a sip of tea. To the People, Mattea's pale Caucasian skin looked strange. While variations existed amongst the First Nations, most ranged from creamy coffee to mahogany. My skin could have been a latte. I regretted the use of this metaphor in my mind as I now craved a huge mug of black, bitter coffee. I sighed with long-suffering loss for the absent drink.

Mattea returned, her hair brushed and washed, dripping down her back. Her eyes flicked to our visitor, waiting for an introduction.

"Mekwi, this is Lintu. She will take us to where our cousin, Gizos, stayed over the winter. Can you pack our things? I'll want to leave as soon as we can."

A moment of panic and rebellion flashed within her eyes, which flicked toward Wula'mbes' tent. However, she nodded and moved to our own wi'gwom. I clenched my jaw and hoped removal from temptation would solve this issue. While it remained a faint hope, it's all I had.

My tea had steeped too long. The dregs grew too bitter for even my coffee-trained palate. I poured in more hot water to dilute them and drank the rest. I sought Chansomps out and made my farewell to him. He clasped my arms and made me promise to care for myself.

"You have a rare light, Wôbigo, a strength I have seldom seen in another, since my wife left. I would see your light shine for many years."

Unaccountably, I blushed at the earnest compliment. It had been so long since someone had given me one, I'd forgotten how to take them with grace.

Once we got our packs ready, we took our leave from Nokemes Di'dias. However, she had one more surprise for me, and not a pleasant one.

"Tema'kwe will serve as your escort. Wula'mbes has also requested to accompany you, as they have relatives amongst the Wolastoqiyik to visit. This will provide you with two skilled hunters for the journey."

I wanted to argue, but her eyes held no promise of yielding. I couldn't tell if she meant to keep Mattea and Wula'mbes in proximity or had another motive. As a fellow older woman, the decision seemed a betrayal, but it didn't matter. I'd just have to keep up my guard as the trip progressed. It shouldn't take longer than two or three days, and then I could bid farewell to the young hunter and the temptation they offered.

Mattea's joy at the decision couldn't be mistaken. She chattered like a schoolgirl on her first field trip. For their part, Wula'mbes seemed subdued, but smiled almost as much as Mattea did. Lintu and Tema'kwe walked together, which suited me. While I wanted to hear more about del Socorro's actions amongst the Wolastoqiyik, I also didn't want to deal with Tema'kwe more than I had to. I remained content to walk alone during the journey.

The weather gods smiled upon us, with bright sunshine and warmer temperatures. Since the snow from the week before had melted into copious amounts of mud, the journey became treacherous at points, but with five of us, we navigated all trouble spots with planning and assistance. It only became an issue when we came across a stream that had delusions of grandeur into a spring-melt river.

I eyed the raging water with dubious eyes. Lintu stared at it, a finger on her lip as she assessed the trees on either side. Tema'kwe, however, suggested we walk downstream. "If we find a ford, that will work. In the meantime, we can search for downed trees to work as a bridge. We're still headed in the right direction and will lose little time by following the banks."

I agreed with the wisdom of his idea. We headed downstream, but with more attention for material that we might use to pull us across. While I saw plenty of vines and felled trees, none looked stout enough to help us either make a raft or bridge for the crossing.

I'd just examined one ash tree and dismissed it as too short when I heard Mattea scream. I didn't see her with the others, so I scrambled up to the bank. Lintu, Tema'kwe and Wula'mbes peered down to the water where my best friend had slipped along the mud and fell into the river. She clung to a rowan bush but couldn't seem to get a strong grip as the rushing river tugged and pulled at her clothing. I wanted to run down to save Mattea, but I'd be a liability. I watched in nervous silence as Tema'kwe took charge of the situation.

Wula'mbes already picked their way down the bank, while Tema'kwe yelled orders to them both. "Careful! The rocks are slimy. No, you fool! To the right! There, you can reach her now. Mekwi, take hold of Wula'mbes leg. Form a chain. Not their hand, they need that to keep their own balance. Leg! Now, use both your arms and hold tight. Wula'mbes, climb slowly. It can take all day. We're not in a hurry. Slowly. Careful! There, take the root. You have it. Now, one more step."

He reached down to pull the younger hunter over the lip of the bank, where the river had washed away the dirt, exposing several roots. These roots became a ladder for both young people, and they climbed to safety. Mattea panted, covered in dirt and mud, while the young hunter lay beside her. I allowed myself to breathe again.

Travellers have died on mission. Many times, their luck ran out or the locals' prejudice became too strong. Agents sometimes can't return and correct things to keep it from happening, either out of caution for tangling the time stream or from lack of resources. Out of a hundred cases, about three are beyond saving. While this mission might be modified, at our current staffing, it would have been a while, and time, ironically enough, remained critical.

I held Mattea's hand as she brushed off the worst of the dirt and brush. She flashed me a weak smile. "I suppose you're about to tell me to watch my step?"

"Phrasing. And I don't need to, do I?"

She shook her head with a rueful smile. "Nope. Let's get going. I don't care for this place, for some strange reason."

We all laughed, with Lintu's high giggle cutting across Tema'kwe's low chuckle. For just that moment, I felt part of a well-oiled team, a group who worked together to do something wonderful. I'd missed that sentiment. Sure, I loved working with Tarren and Mattea, but the stakes remained low at the shop. At worst, dealt with officious idiots armed with rude words and imperious demands. No one's life stood in danger.

In this place and time, we'd formed a group and done something important. Not important in the grand scheme of the world, or within the timeline of history, but important to Mattea.

I missed that sensation. Paolo and I had worked together as a team. I swallowed the memories back into their little box, shut the lid, and turned the key. Such memories had no business intruding on my daily life, not while I worked on mission. They must remain hidden and locked until I could cherish them in privacy.

When I had the time.

*****

Evidence of a large group of people stood everywhere. Blackened pits for fires, cut trees, stripped bushes, detritus of an abandoned camp. A midden pile lay to one side, and the well-trodden path to the river lay muddy and trampled.

Obviously, no one lived here now. They must have moved on to their summer camp already. I missed the opportunity to detail their garb, but such research would be secondary to finding the traveller's path and contagion. "Where did Gizos sleep when he stayed here, Lintu?"

She pointed to the remains of a small wi'gwom, similar to the one Mattea and I slept in at the maple camp. "This is our visitor place. He stayed there with another visitor, a woman from the Mi'kmaw tribe. She came to visit her daughter, who married one of our hunters."

I nodded and ducked into the area. The structure remained for the tribe to repair next winter season, but for now the place stood as an empty hole, abandoned and lonely. As the darkness swallowed me, I closed my eyes and breathed in the place, searching for the essence of del Socorro, the trace of his presence. I found a tendril and smiled. I touched my pendant, the one to help me find other travellers. It didn't quite glow, but it did flicker.

I took samples of everything within the wi'gwom, including a slice of the wi'gwom itself, stuffing them into my collection bag. Mattea would be outside doing the same. I gathered bits of leather, a broken shell, several bits of food, flowers, and even crumbling ash from his hearth fire. The inside of his tent stank from disuse and rotted meat. A few flies buzzed into my face, but I waved them away.

When I emerged, I asked Lintu, "What did Gizos want from your tribe? Why did he visit?"

She glanced at Mattea, collecting the leaves from a nearby bush, and furrowed her brow. "I don't know for certain. He said he looked for family, but we did not quite believe him. Still, he seemed unthreatening, so we hosted him. His ways seemed strange, and he committed many rude acts. After several moons, we asked him to leave."

I snorted. That seemed likely, at least. By choosing a rogue portal, any study on the time must have been on his own. Such research would be inadequate. The Agents had much more extensive resources than others, as they had literal first-hand experience in most of history.

Rather than try to excuse his actions, which would do little good, I maligned del Socorro's memory. "He'd always acted rude. He didn't ignore rules out of ignorance, only out of nature. Still, he isn't a violent man, just an annoying one."

Both Tema'kwe and Lintu laughed and went down to the river to wash. Mattea and I continued to take our samples until we'd touched every branch, bush, and mould in the area. Wula'mbes, while they didn't understand why, helped Mattea with her collections. We took scrapings of wood ash, dirt, even the moose dung.

Wula'mbes called me over to ask about including a bright orange lichen. The shade looked so vivid, it might substitute for the blaze orange hunting paint in the modern world. It pulsed with sinister light. I nodded for them to include it in their sampling.

I wished the scientists at the Agency all the luck in the world in analysing all our samples. However, they asked for them, and we would provide them. We more than exceeded our projected number of collections, despite Pembley's admonition.

We had less luck discovering the reason for del Socorro's trip, not even a vague search for his ancestry. I wondered if the babe had been his ancestor, thus prompting his wish to care for the child. At least we brought back plenty of potential disease vectors.

After saying a silent wish that our panoculations would prevent said disease vectors from infecting us, I took solace in the fact del Socorro had made it this far without getting ill. At least with exhibiting no signs of illness.

I cradled that notion through the next several hours. When I determined we had enough bloody samples, I called down to Lintu and Tema'kwe. "We have found what we need. We must begin our journey back."

Mattea and Wula'mbes exchanged an intimate glance, and I glared at her. She cast her gaze to the ground and nodded. The young hunter must not come with us under any circumstances. I'm certain I made the situation crystal clear.

In the morning, we would make our way back to the portal to return to our own time, deliver our samples, and prepare for the next trip.

I only hoped our departure from this time would be kinder on Mattea's heart than it had been so far.

For once, I slept deep through the night, not even haunted by the past traces of del Socorro's presence in his abandoned wi'gwom. When I woke, bright sunlight greeted me as I emerged. I didn't see Mattea or any of the hunters, so perhaps they had gone down to the river already.

As I made my way to the water, I spied Lintu and Tema'kwe laughing on the rocks, but no sign of Mattea and Wula'mbes. Frowning, I splashed water on my face and returned to the camp. I searched our supplies and didn't find Mattea's pack.

With a scorching curse, I shoved my belongings into my pack. With a shouted farewell to Lintu, I marched toward the portal.

How dare she? How dare Mattea go against all the temporal maxims and try to return with a local? I know just how she'd try it, too. She'd likely try to wrap her arms around Wula'mbes and try to include her in the "clothing and supplies" bubble.

With each step, my anger waxed into outrage. Through muddy leaves, skeletal branches, and icy glades.

Mattea's plan wouldn't work. Did she not think people had tried this in the past? Temporal portal technology discerned between humans and inanimate objects. Her plan would only leave poor Wula'mbes alone, confused, even hurt and despondent. I marvelled at her selfishness and stomped forward, paying little attention to my surroundings as I rehearsed the blistering tirade I would give my assistant.

The incipient rage morphed into panic. What if I'd lost her? What if I never saw Mattea again, and she remained in the past forever? I'd lose my best friend and assistant. I'd have to leave here to die amongst the ancient trees.

My breath grew short and the grey closed in upon me, pressing me until I had to sit below a birch tree. The solid base at my back allowed me to keep my soul from fleeing in fear from my turbulent thoughts and fears. I concentrated on the pattern of pine needles on the ground in front of me, interspersed with a few old leaves left over from autumn. They made the shape of a dragon. I followed the outlines with my eyes, using the shape to focus my mind away from panic.

When my breath slowed once again, I mopped the sweat from my brow and cursed again, this time at my own weakness. I pulled myself up and leaned against the birch for a few moments before marching off again.

After several more hours' travel and several glances at my pendant, the portal location came into view. I checked the sun, knowing the day to be much too early for the portal to appear. The default appearance time was dusk, a time of liminal light and easily anticipated in primitive times, even in inclement weather. I saw no trace of either Mattea or Wula'mbes.

After placing both hands on my hips, I surveyed the empty glade. "Bloody Hell. Did it work?"

With a more purposeful examination, I studied the ground where the portal should appear. I saw no footprints in the snow. I cursed again, now certain something had happened to them on the journey here. If I didn't find Mattea soon, I might run out of creative curses.

Maybe I'd misinterpreted their absence? Or Mattea decided to run away and never return to the present day, living her life in the past with Wula'mbes. Her tracking device would fix that soon enough. She was fortune's fool.

I cast around the portal, searching for more signs. While I'd never be an expert in tracking, the muddy, slushy ground offered excellent evidence of human activity. Perhaps they'd come and left again,, and I could follow the tracks?

A deep, muddy depression of a footprint showed deep brown against the melting slush. "Aha! Gotcha."

I discovered two separate tracks leading away from the portal site to the west. I followed, careful not to tread on the tracks themselves. They led me out of the glade and down to the river.

There, as cozy as you please, stood a small lean-to. Two pairs of feet stuck out of one side in an unmistakable rhythm. Mattea's and Wula'mbes moaning voices filtered through the tent cover.

Embarrassed, I stomped back to the portal. They should finish soon and then both would get a piece of my mind. However, the rehearsed speech seemed so angry and petty. I only wanted to extract my friend and get her back to safety.

The voices faded but I gave them some pillow time before interrupting their interlude. I owed Mattea that much, at least. She still couldn't bring Wula'mbes back with her, but at least they got to enjoy a little time together before the break.

After a sufficient waiting time, I made my way back down the riverbank. Mattea had already emerged, adjusting her clothing and pack. When she saw me, her face flashed with resignation, hope, and anticipation.

I gritted my teeth, waiting for her to finish packing. Wula'mbes also emerged, glancing between us with confusion and rising distress. Mattea placed a hand on their shoulder and nodded. "I must go, Wula'mbes. My elders will not permit you to travel with me."

Chapter Twenty-One

Mattea crossed her arms with obstinate finality. "I won't go on the third trip. Find another partner. Take Tarren. Take Nami, for all I care."

We'd just dropped off our collection bags after much-treasured hot showers and headed to our debriefing with Pembley. While I didn't look forward to this session, I wouldn't accept Mattea's intransigence. We had a duty.

"Tarren has three young children. You can't ask her to go on such a risky mission."

She gaped at me. "But it's fine for me? Well, now I know how much you value my life."

I rolled my eyes. "You know I value you! You're the closest thing I've had to a best friend in…in decades. I trust you with my life. And that's precisely why I need you with me. I trust you to have my back, no matter what happens."

Mattea shot me a glare. "Even if I fall in love? You didn't even want to Agent again, and now you're forcing me to. You're a hypocrite."

She was spoiling for a fight, so I tried to disarm her with a different notion. "I'm getting to like it again. I might even go full-time again after this. You might join me, you know."

She didn't answer by the time we reached Pembley's office. We entered in sullen silence, knowing full well we hadn't finished this argument.

Pembley read over our preliminary reports and some paperwork from the science department before looking up. "You need to be more discerning in your collections, Wilda. The lab told me you brought back over two hundred samples from Mali and almost three hundred from Maine. They still haven't finished analyzing all from the first set."

With a shrug, I suppressed an amused glance at Mattea. "I'm no scientist. I gathered everything del Socorro might have come into contact with, per my mission instructions. Every bit of food, leaf, pinch of dirt, even hairs from our hosts. If you want someone more analytic in their collections, send a scientist instead of me."

He frowned at me, giving what passed for a "glare of patriarchal condemnation." I countered with "innocent Agent who knew damn well she'd made a point" look. He relented with a long-suffering sigh.

"Just keep them down to things more likely to be a vector for the third trip, eh?"

"Sure, I'll get right on that. When do I start my medical training?"

His growl made me smile more deeply.

"You also included in your report an incident with a local hunter. Do you care to elaborate on the matter?"

I glanced at Mattea, who only shrugged and crossed her arms, gazing at the ceiling. I took a deep breath. "We stayed with a local tribe as they collected maple sugar while we waited for word about the traveller's visit. While we stayed with them, my assistant developed a strong friendship with a local. The matter is concluded, and no further actions are necessary."

He raised his eyebrows as an indication for more details. I blinked back, refusing to comply.

Pembley shifted his gaze toward Mattea, but she still gazed at the ceiling. "Do you recommend your assistant for re-education?"

I sat up abruptly. "What? No, of course not. Don't be ridiculous. A minor violation, especially in view of her untrained status. She needs no correction."

He drummed his fingers on the report, glaring at me again. His suggestion rocked me. I'd forgotten about the severe solutions PENDULUM imposed for repeat offenders of the temporal maxims. The thought of re-education applied to Mattea horrified me. She no longer gazed at the ceiling but looked at me with entreaty and no small amount of fear.

"My assistant understands her error."

"And is she prepared to go on the third mission with you?"

I held Mattea's gaze. "May I have a word with Mattea for a moment, Pembley? In private?"

He glanced between us, narrowing his eyes, before standing. "Do either of you want more coffee?"

I stared into my almost empty cup. "Do you need to ask?"

"I asked more for her benefit than yours. Mattea?"

She gulped and handed her paper cup to him. "Please. One and one?"

He gave us both a curt nod and exited.

As soon as the door latched, I turned my chair to face Mattea. "Okay. Here's my proposition. Come with me on this last mission. When we return, I'll sponsor your application for permanent emigration to Wula'mbes' time, if you still want it."

Her eyes grew wide. "Permanent emigration? Is that even allowed?"

I frowned. "Allowed is a strong term. Not specifically forbidden is closer. Possible with a great deal of begging, copious amounts of paperwork, and a good dose of political clout is closer. Still, it's a possible path. Not likely, but possible."

Her eyes shifted several times as she considered the offer and the implications.

"I realise this is a huge decision and you don't have to decide right away. You can change your mind about applying when we return, if you decide it's not worth the risk."

"Risk. There's a lot of risk living in the past. I could never come back?"

I shook my head. "No. It's a one-way trip. I might visit you, but you will not have a way to return nor an easy way to signal me for my return. If you emigrated to a later century, or to a society more technologically advanced, you might store a letter in a lockbox with a stable law firm, but not pre-Columbian Maine."

She took a deep breath and clasped her hands. "Right. Well, let me give you a tentative yes. I will go on your mission. Will I have time to research when I return?"

I laughed, though my mirth contained a large dose of bitterness. "You have all the time you want, Mattea, on this side of history, at least within your lifetime. Besides, it'll take several months, at the least, to push such a request through the proper bureaucratic channels."

Mattea played with the sleeve of her shirt, rolling it into a curl and then straightening it out again. "Right. That's fine, then. I'll have…things to arrange. If I go. Those will take time to manage."

Pembley returned with their coffee. He raised his eyebrows at me, and I nodded. "Mattea will join us on the third mission."

He held Mattea's gaze until she nodded.

"Fine. The education for twelfth century Orkney is ready for you tomorrow. I wish you a good rest tonight."

That night, the final mission loomed large in my imagination. I'd never visited Scotland in either modern times or in history. I understood the horrible stereotypes. I'd seen Braveheart and attended the obligatory Highland Games. I even enjoyed bagpipe music, as long as they remained outside and not in a deafening enclosed space.

Though Pictish in earlier centuries, by the twelfth century, the Norse had lived on Orkney for several hundred years. Vikings had an even more stereotypical image in our modern world. Inaccurate horned helmets and elaborately carved longships aside, this would be a difficult trip.

As I lay in bed, begging my body to find the sweet bliss of slumber, I went over the many things I'd have to learn for this last mission. More customs, ceremonies, famous people, religion. At least they built with stone walls and iron this time. Cooking would be easier than during pre-Columbian Maine.

Dinah jumped on my lap and kneaded my stomach. I nudged her to my legs, to spare the soft tissues, but she ignored my relocation and moved back up again. With a sigh, I petted her, wishing we had the option to slough off this last mission.

Back before the first mission, I'd asked Pembley why he didn't go, or one of his Temporal Officers. He chuckled and pulled up his pant leg, revealing an obvious prosthetic. "Lost it in Afghanistan in the last war. Most of my force would be Agents if they possessed the physically capability to travel and blend in. While we can do anything physically, just having such a high-tech prosthetic is instant witchcraft fodder in most times."

"What about training someone else while we're on mission?"

"Remember, you're only gone from the present for one day each trip."

My body now wanted to find other arguments but my mind failed to construct them. At least we'd now completed two missions. What would happen if we didn't find the vector in this third trip? Would the lab be able to synthesise a cure from what we collected? Or would every traveller die?

Pembley gave us an update on the medical situation. Every prior traveller who came into contact with the disease fell ill, save three. Those three were me, an invalid who happened to be at the hospital when the traveller in Edinburgh, McKenzie, arrived, and a young man who left the Agency to become a nurse. The nurse couldn't travel any longer due to a heart condition. Of those who became ill, most remained in care within the hospital and related facilities. Ten others died after Josephus, though his cousin, Aminata, still survived. She hadn't yet recovered, but she continued to work on a cure despite her illness, along with a full staff of non-travelling scientists and doctors. Both del Socorro and McKenzie remained in their comas and were failing fast.

They'd not yet been able to locate the Toronto rogue portal, either, though Pembley assured me they came close a few times. The criminals either removed it or destroyed it when the Agents came close. They only found a warehouse full of empty promises and infrastructure so far. He hoped the assembly remained intact, so they might dissect it for clues when they caught the perpetrators. I shared his hope but doubted it would be so easy. The portals in Lima and Edinburgh had been found, but so utterly destroyed they defied all forensics. Anyone capable of sending unsuspecting travellers so ill-prepared cared little for the human condition or the effect of such wanton use would have on all of history.

Who created the portals? Someone with a great deal of financial resources, scientific knowledge, and no sense of morality.

Everything relied upon Mattea and me finding the proper disease vector. The weight of this responsibility made my shoulders ache. I'd never wanted such responsibility. If I'd craved power, I would have remained in the active Agent force, or worked my way through PENDULUM like Fionnuala. I only wanted to create garb for other travellers. Learning entire new cultures at the drop of the hat should remain an exercise for younger minds. To quote a cliché, *I was too old for this shit.*

Despite all my protests and ideas, only Mattea and I qualified for this mission. This didn't make me happy nor joyful. It would involve yet more danger, physical deprivations, and investigation.

For a moment, I wished she really were my daughter, rather than simply my assistant and my best friend.

An idea occurred to me, and I threw off the covers, to Dinah's extreme displeasure. I yelled, "sorry!" over my shoulder as I powered up my laptop. Within an hour, I'd discovered Josephus Konaté's family tree and pored through the branches. Would I find what I suspected?

There, amongst the African slaves shipped to Georgia to work on the rice plantations, I found the Malinké slaves within his tree. They dated from just the eighteenth century, but the tree went back four hundred more years in Africa. I found Baheera's name and Mansa Musa's. I took a deep breath as my theory coalesced. That's one connection.

With eager anticipation, I pulled up Mario del Socorro's records and found a family tree. After delving down two dead ends, my eyes alit upon the last name of Mitchell, a modern Penobscot name. I delved down further and found Nicholas, Francis, Slagger, and several others I recognised as Wolastoqiyik. These families I traced back to the seventeenth century when Jesuit priests gave them Christian Saint surnames, but couldn't get further back. The lack of a writing system before that time stymied my investigation, but the fact the branches showed that far back gave me hope.

Years before travelling, such genealogies relied upon guesswork and luck, owing more to decent records for those of status than the poor. However, with Agents and recreational travellers came those interested in personal genealogies. Several Mormons, for instance, commissioned extensive travels to find the truth behind their published genealogies. Travel filled in many gaps in with hard data as opposed to supposition.

Now I searched Emory McKenzie's tree for connection to Orkney. I found a McKay but it disappeared. Other northern relatives married English spouses and moved south. Maybe his Orkney ancestors were Norse instead of Scottish? If they dated from the twelfth century, the chances seemed about even. The islands had been Norse-owned until the fifteenth century, despite the Picts having lived there before the Vikings. What about this Sigurd Thorsson? Damn all patronymic naming conventions, anyway. They changed every generation, making genealogy much more difficulty. Each son took on a new last name reflecting his father's first name. So, Olaf Thorsson would be the son of Thor Magnusson, the son of Magnus Haraldsson, and so on.

Well, I'd found a link, anyhow. Sigurd Thorsson had been born in Norway but died in Orkney in the twelfth century. He might have been part of Earl Rögnvaldr's raiding party to take Orkney from his usurping cousin, just about the time McKenzie left.

With a mighty yawn, I closed my laptop. At least I'd found a starting point this time. I knew who to search for and might find a reason for each traveller's trip. Had this rogue portal cooperative, or whatever it was, set up the promise of genealogical trips in exchange for some smuggling repayment? There must have been something else to it, but at least that might be a start.

I trundled off to my cold bed and curled up around Dinah.

*****

When we entered the classroom, a large map on the SmartScreen showed the Orkneys, complete with their major settlements and extensive Neolithic monuments, in relation to the larger mainland of Scotland to the south.

Visions of earls danced through my head. Well, visions of earls, bishops and other Norse power players. What a convoluted, Byzantine thing Nordic and Scottish politics had been.

At least the living conditions felt more normal than the last two missions. Stone castles and thatched cottages felt homey after adobe palaces and wi'gwoms. And glory be! We get to visit during summer on this mission. Our destination would be the town of Birsay, known then as Birgisheraŏ, in the Orkney isles north of Scotland, in June 1136. Earl Paul Haakonsson ruled the area, but our studies warned a change of regime would be imminent. I meant to use that chaos to our advantage.

From what I could tell, Emory McKenzie's ancestor, Sigurn Thorsson, arrived with the invading force under Rögnvald Kali Kolsson. Perhaps invading force was too strong a term. The king had granted Rögnvaldr the co-earldom, but Paul took it for himself. Rögnvald became more of a liberator, an arbiter of justice. So the history books say, but the victor writes the history.

Men wrote the history. While we'd lucked out with meeting Baheera in Mali and Nokemes Di'dias in Maine, I found few records of strong females within Orkney hierarchy at that time. That didn't mean none existed, but I wouldn't hold my breath. Earl Paul's sister, Frakkok, might be a useful source, but she might not even be in residence. She'd tried to kill her brother once already.

The time we arrived should be just before a major power coup. Keeping clear of that shift in control would be difficult. Still, McKenzie's itinerary set our arrival time, not our own preferences.

While the politics remained important in a mission, so did the details of daily life. Mattea and I studied the roundhouses, brochs, and the Birsay settlement. A small kirk or church stood to one side of the settlement, with a new square tower, the single tall building in a sea of thatched huts and stone cottages. The broch on the cliff wall remained the seat of power until it shifted later that century to Kirkwall.

I took a sip from my fourth cup of coffee, savouring the bitter, black taste. I wished I had another chunk of the dark chocolate Mattea had brought. When I glanced over at her terminal, I noticed she'd finished her portion. We should be able to break soon, at any rate.

This culture of the Orkney Islands of Scotland around the twelfth century would be new to both of us. I'd travelled to the lowlands during the Jacobite revolution, but this group would be different in terms of genetic history, culture, and customs.

Mattea wrapped her arms around her shoulders and shivered. "It'll be freezing cold up there, isn't it?"

"Pretty much. While the Gulfstream hits Scotland and keeps the west coast mild, it's cooled considerably by the time it reaches Orkney. I visited once in the current time, during summer solstice, and it rarely got above ten degrees Celsius. Add the wind, rain, and lack of trees to block any of it, and you understand why the ancients built their housing complexes underground."

She shivered again, eyeing the map. "And what time of the year do we need to travel there?"

I checked my notes, flipping to the third dossier. "We're in luck. We go in mid-summer."

"Whew."

"You'll get used to it. We'll also have plenty of wool and fur in our garb. It shouldn't be much worse than a Toronto winter, and we'll never have to drive on the ice."

Mattea grimaced at me with a sidelong glance laden with mock derision. I grinned back at her with cheerful glee until we burst out laughing.

Peat bogs and not much else dotted the landscape both then and now. Any trees that scrabbled their roots into that windswept archipelago grew stunted and twisted. Rolling hills and rocky outcroppings dominated the landscape. I envisioned us tramping through hours of boggy land, looking for thistles, mushrooms, and marsh flowers. What I wouldn't give to bring a decent pair of waders or wellington boots.

Venison and heather ale would at least be palatable. A lack of spices would pale after a few days, but I could handle that. We travelled in June, but that didn't guarantee warm weather. I studied the average temperatures and shivered. Six degrees Celsius? In June? Bloody Hell. I'd better make certain we both added sufficient insulation in our garb.

The bell for a break rang, and we both stood from our monitors, taking a collective stretch. I turned to my assistant. "Fancy lunch?"

"You mean, you didn't hear my stomach grumbling over the video feed? I thought for certain it would drown out the posh Historic Scotland presenters."

"My own grumbled in counterpoint. Let's go check out the cafeteria. What intriguing wonders might they have for us today?"

They offered the usual boring options of hockey puck well-done burgers, greasy pizza slices, and a cup of wilted iceberg lettuce they were pleased to label as *salad.* The special today was soup, which possessed the added benefit of being brown so we couldn't tell exactly what the *cooks* added to it. Most likely, leftover pizza and burgers from yesterday.

Mattea pursed her lips, the disapproval clear on her face. "You would think, with the amount of money the Agency charges for a trip, they'd be able to afford better food for their staff."

"You would think so, wouldn't you? But then again, we keep coming back, expecting to find edible food. Who's more of a fool?"

"Fair. Still, we only have the half-hour break. Not enough time to find something on the streets and eat it. We have little choice. I suppose I should have brought a sandwich."

"That would involve effort and forethought. After this trip, I have the energy for neither."

We chose the pathetic lettuce cups and while I pushed mine around in the thin dressing, Mattea closed her eyes. "I'm only eating this in dread of worse food on our next mission. That venison jerky filled my stomach but I'm still pulling bits from my teeth."

"We should eat much better this time. Plenty of fish and tubers. They took pride in their feast-craft and there will be mead. The Norse even honoured a bathing tradition."

Mattea's eyes grew wide. "They did? Thank all the Gods I can name!"

"They took good care of brushing their hair, braiding their beards, even putting beads in the braids. Combs were some of the most common burial items for any of the Norse, whether in Norway, Sweden, Iceland, wherever they roamed. There's even a snippet of a complaint from an Anglo-Saxon around the year 1000 that the Norse must be killed because they were stealing women by being meticulous in their grooming. They were 'accused' of combing their hair daily, taking a bath every week, and even changing their clothes frequently. So scandalous."

She threw her hands up in the air, but then halted. "Fantastic. Wait...*hot* baths?"

I smirked, enjoying the news of our impending discomfort. "Ha! Dream on, buttercup. Only in Iceland. Hot springs dot the land there. Orkney offers more freezing streams than hot springs."

Her arms dropped and she hugged herself to shiver. "Dammit. Brr!"

"Brr, indeed. We'll be warm enough in our garb."

She gulped down the last of her pop. "I suppose we need to head back to the classroom now."

I refilled my coffee cup and took a second one. "Now that I'm re-supplied, yes. I think this afternoon's lessons is on hunting and wildlife, and local plants."

She grinned. "Well, at least I'll learn what I'll be stuffing into my collection bag."

I returned her grin. "Since we were so chastised for bringing too many samples back the first two trips, what do you say to beating our previous record this time?"

With a laugh, she grabbed a banana from the sideboard. "I'm game. We have to beat what, three hundred from Maine?"

"Three hundred and twenty-two."

"Right. I almost feel sorry for the scientists."

Suddenly sober, I frowned. "Don't. Feel sorry for all of us if we miss the important element because we were being 'cautious' with our sampling."

She nodded, her own expression serious. "Fair enough."

As I tried to sleep last night, Dinah kneading at my armpit, I tried to imagine what we'd find in Orkney. In contrast to our prior trips, I would stick out as unusual for my darker skin, instead of Mattea for her fair complexion. So far, we'd been lucky both for prejudices and for violence. Bandits and camels aside, we hadn't needed to fend off any attacks by amorous toxic males. I'd worried about Tema'kwe during the last trip, but his preoccupation with Lintu saved Mattea from unwanted attentions.

Our quarry this trip, Emory McKenzie, was a short, squat man with bright red hair and beard. My mind's eye made him a dwarf from Tolkien's Middle Earth, complete with braided beard and axe, though the Agency reports said he was an electrical engineer. I wished he had a defining characteristic like del Socorro's tattoo, but his stature and abundance of freckles would have to do.

While I'd not had a great deal of trouble with unwanted male advances throughout my missions, either now or in the past, some of that would have been due to Paolo's intimidating presence and my short, round stature. Few men, even during lean times in history, preferred a hobbit over a princess. Mattea stood tall and willowy; elegant by anyone's standards.

I hope our luck held true on our final trip.

Part IV
Chapter Twenty-Two

I pulled the fur-lined cloak around my shoulder as the wind whipped past us. We had barely gone through the portal before the weather almost knocked us over.

Mattea had to shout over the gale. "This is June? Are you sure?"

"Damn sure. Otherwise, there'd be snow on the ground. Be thankful it's only wind and icy rain."

She shielded her face with the edge of her own cloak. "Sure. Thankful. That's *precisely* the word I meant."

"C'mon. I see the village next to that rocky outcropping. Is that a church tower to the left? I can't tell in the rain. We can start there."

We chose to walk inland, which meant we walked into the wind. As we progressed with slow, cold, and painful steps to cross a treacherous tidal flat to gain access to the island. The tide remained low, but mud still slid under our feet.

By the time we reached the village of seven thatched cottages, my leg muscles ached as if I'd run a marathon. I'd finally thawed out in the three days back home, with the liberal application of hour-long hot showers and electric blankets, but my bones reminded me I'd grown old and shouldn't abuse my body with this crap anymore.

The tall broch stood out against the sea, a round stone tower with a snapping banner dancing in the wind. The banner had a black raven in the middle of a white field.

I shouted into Mattea's ear. "Let's try the large hall in the middle. The chances are good the most powerful man in the village has the largest home, and the Norse loved gathering in their mead halls on wicked days like this."

She nodded and gestured for me to lead. I ploughed through the still-strong wind until we reached the door. I knocked, hoping someone would hear it above the storm. My thighs already ached from the short hike through the gale.

Perhaps *storm* was an exaggeration. I suspected this wind and rain to be a usual occurrence this far north. Just a normal summer solstice day on the freezing edge of the known world. I shivered again as a tendril of chilly breeze wormed its way under my mantle and knocked again. I didn't even know if knocking had come into common practise. The Agency could only squeeze so much education into three days, and often minor niceties were abandoned in favour of major customs. Still, it would be hard to ignore someone banging on your front door as anything but a request to enter.

Only after a third barrage of knocks did the stone door inch open. The hairy visage peering at us through the crack examined us from head to toe. "I don't know you. Are you lost?"

I nodded, rubbing my arms in obvious distress. "We are. May we beg the hospitality of your hall? We can trade stories for warmth."

The door opened wide, revealing an older man with a long scar over his left cheek and eye. His salted beard and weathered face spoke of many battles. While his yellow tunic looked food-stained, it didn't appear ragged. His grin as he brought us inside deepened as we took off our outer garments. "You are welcome to my son's hall. I am Brusi Paulsson. What shall we call you?" Voices filtered in through from the main hall, but we couldn't see it from the entrance vestibule. Shreds of laughter and someone giving a toast punctuated the sound of the door slamming shut.

I dusted the last of the raindrops from my hat and hung it on one of many hooks near the door. As I turned, I noticed Mattea had done the same, and now stood pinned by Brusi's frank admiration for her. She crossed her arms under his regard and pursed her lips. As much as I understood her defensiveness, I hoped she didn't insult him so bad they sent us out into the weather.

"I am Valka, and my companion is Mattildr. We lost our way in the rain. Whose hall is this?"

He tore his gaze from Mattea and considered me. To my surprise, I received more of a leer than she had. In response, I straightened my shoulders and glared back, hoping my strength would keep him from pillaging before his son honoured us with guest-rights.

"My son is Gæðingar Jón Brusisson. He runs this hall for Earl Paul Haakonsson. Do you seek the earl?"

I shook my head. "At the moment, all we seek is a fire and some food."

His booming laughed quieted the muted murmurs. With a hefty clap on each of our shoulders, he steered us into the main hall. "We have plenty of both! Come, take of our bread and salt. You shall be our guests this evening. Let none say Brusi is a churlish host."

As the warmth of the hall thawed my face, I had to smile. Twelve adults and six children sat around an enormous wooden table. Bowls, platters, and several pitchers littered the surface of said table. I hoped at least one of them contained mead. After two trips without coffee or whiskey, I needed lots of mead to warm my blood.

After our introduction and a general toast of *Skaal!* to our good health, we sat between Brusi and an older woman. Thralls piled our plates high with roast fish, turnips, and most importantly, our mugs with mead.

I took a long, deep draught of the chilled, sweet honey wine before turning to Mattea. "So? Better than a cup of wilted lettuce and watered-down Italian dressing, yes?"

"Absolutely. *Skaal!*" We clicked our mugs and drank deep again. Brusi refilled our mugs to the rim and waggled his eyebrows in comic invitation. Mattea giggled and asked, "What's a Gæðingar? I remember the word, but not what it meant."

"He's an official in charge of the beacons, ships, and maybe even the sea wall, if there is one."

The older woman next to me, her long grey braids and apron dress decorated with bright milliflori beads, waited for me to take my first bite of fish before she asked, "Your name is Valka? That's a strong name. I'm called Káta. The brute who brought you in is my brother. Pay him little mind. He has a willing eye but a tired heart. He won't bother you much. If he does, he knows I'll skewer him for disrespecting our guests. Don't you, Brusi?"

The older man mumbled something and ducked, brushing his hair with his hand.

Káta cocked her head, making her beads click. I ached to examine them. "What's that, Brusi? I can't hear you."

"I vow not to bother our guests, Káta."

"So much better that way. Now, Valka, who is it you seek?"

I almost choked on my fish. Pushing back through the pleasant buzz already swimming in my mind, I tried to recall when I'd mentioned my quest to anyone on this end of history. With a glance to Mattea, who shrugged, I looked back to Brusi's sister. Despite the low light, I made out the details of her garb, including the bright tablet-woven trim of red and white on her cream apron dress. The glitter of silver turtle brooches flashed as she shifted.

"Oh, don't worry. I don't look deep. Only into your surface thoughts. He is a short, red-haired man, yes? Red like the setting son? We get some of those here in the wild north. I knew one well when I lived on the mainland. I almost lost my heart to one. Ah, those were days of daring adventure and quick blood!"

As the woman rambled, I studied her more closely. She must be a Seer of some sort. This wouldn't be the first time I'd come across such mystical powers in my missions, but true powers remained rarer than most historical romance novels would lead us to believe.

188

As the firelight glinted in Káta's eyes, I examined them, but couldn't tell if she had Bryonie's blue eyes. The recurring coincidence of the woman's prior incarnations almost became a given. I wouldn't look a gift horse in the mouth, not with so much at stake. Hadn't the woman mentioned Scotland when she first prattled on about my aura? I couldn't recall.

A flurry of activity behind me made me twist to see what occurred. New arrivals poured in through the vestibule and the main hall. These visitors appeared heavily armed and wore grim expressions.

The leader, a man almost covered with leather jerkin and fur mantle, held his spear in a stiff salute. "Jón Brusisson. You and your household are to come to the Broch at once, by order of Earl Paul Haakonsson."

The man at the head of the table, whom I had only briefly met, stood. His wife, a bulky blond woman twenty years his junior, also stood, shaking. "I will come, but my wife is heavy with child. The walk in the cold might be dangerous for her. Tomorrow, when the skies are clearer—"

The guard rapped his spear twice to forestall the offer. "You are all summoned now."

His quiet voice brooked no argument and increased the tension more than a shout would have done.

With quick, unobtrusive movement, thralls clad their masters in leather and furs while the dishes of the half-eaten meal disappeared. A young girl brought cloaks for Mattea and me, though I was far from being a member of the Gæðingar's household. I didn't think the guard would listen to any argument just now.

The guards herded all the free adults to the main broch en masse. The thralls would care for the young, and a few of the younger children cried out for their parents and siblings. The Gæðingar's young wife kissed a blonde boy on the forehead and urged him to take care of the other children, as he must act as man of the house until his father returned. She put on a brave face as she held her pregnant stomach, but the fear hid behind her eyes.

My stomach clenched. I knew we travelled in an unsettled time but having a crisis less than an hour after our arrival seemed patently unfair. As we marched through the stinging sleet toward the broch, I considered the wisdom of peeling off into the dusk. However, the three guards bringing up the rear carried long spears and didn't look afraid to use them.

As the wicked wind whipped into my face, I clenched my jaw and gave Mattea a grim smile. She returned the expression and plodded with me into the frigid night.

Chapter Twenty-Three

The journey up the steep slope to reach the broch almost sapped the last of my limited strength. I slipped twice in the mud, though Mattea's strong support kept me from falling onto my knees. The stone tower loomed in the deepening dusk and rain. The mist hid its true height, but it seemed at least three stories.

As soon as we walked inside the outer wall, the howling wind ceased and my muscles unclenched a little. Not completely, as we had been marched here under duress, but at least I no longer had to strain against the weather.

I longed for the gentle snow of Maine. From Mattea's chattering teeth, I gathered she shared the sentiment.

The guards took us up to the feast hall, on the second story and in the circular broch's centre. Except for us, the earl and a few of his courtiers, no one else occupied the hall. We stood in the centre as he regarded us.

Mattea and I inched to one side, distancing ourselves as much as allowed by the guards. I didn't want to get caught up in the local political squabbles, despite the bad luck of our timing and location. I hoped the earl would consider this as reasonable.

Because Vikings had such a strong reputation for being reasonable throughout history. Right.

As the captives milled into a knot, I noted the garb of the noble and thrall alike. Most conformed with my memories of Norse clothing and jewellery, though a few had elements more unusual, with perhaps a Pictish flair, or even Gaelic. These islands had become a melting pot at this point in history, with several warring cultures mixing into a creole of styles and languages.

The earl stood, sweeping his gaze across those assembled. He pointed at me and Mattea. "Those two. Who are they? I don't recognise them. Have you taken more wives?"

I snorted at the notion of anyone choosing me for a wife at my age, but stepped forward. "We arrived to the Gæðingar's hall a mere hour before your summons, Earl Haakonsson. Our presence was purely coincidental. We are on our own quest and had gotten lost in the storm."

"Storm? Storm! This is no storm. Where are you from that you believe this to be a storm? This is but a summer rain."

Biting back my sarcastic response, I gave him a small bow. "We come from the south, from the Scoti lands. We come in search of our cousin, gone these many months."

"Hmm. So you say. Sigurd, take them a guest antechamber. I'll question the women after I deal with Paul."

I glanced at the ginger guard who escorted us, wondering if he was the Sigurd I needed to speak to, McKenzie's ancestor. Eight centuries wouldn't have given me any clues on physical resemblance, but perhaps the rogue traveller had spoken to him. As he led us into a small room with naught but a bench and a waste basin, I placed a hand on his arm. "Are you Sigurd Thorsson?"

He shook his head. "No, my father's name is Dagr. Is Sigurd Thorsson the relative you seek?"

"No, but our quarry may have sought him out. We believe my cousin travelled under a different name, but he had bright red hair. He stood as short as I do."

A flicker of recognition flashed across Sigurd's eyes before he clamped down on his expression. "I'll send ale." He slammed the door before I had the chance to question him further.

Mattea sat on the bench and pulled her knees up to her chin. "Well, this is lovely. Truly. I'll be sure to recommend it as a five-star resort."

"I admit, this isn't precisely the reception I'd hoped for."

She glared at me. "You think?"

I closed my eyes and sighed. "Being as bitchy as I normally am won't help matters, Mattea."

She let out a short, sharp laugh. "At least you recognise the hypocrisy."

"I should have called ahead, you know. Advance reservations result in better accommodations."

Her bitter frown gave way to a reluctant smile. The smile turned into a chuckle, and we both shared a laugh. Neither of us had much strength behind our mirth, but the situation didn't allow for much.

The door swung open, revealing our erstwhile host, the Earl. The last vestiges of our mirth faded away.

He stood taller than I'd imagined, topping at least six and a half feet. His broad shoulders filled the doorway as he ducked in. He wore a long shirt of red linen and blue leggings, puffy at the top but tied close to his calves with long strips of cloth. A rabbit fur mantle covered his shoulders, clasped with a large silver brooch with intricate detail worked into the design. Two of his guards followed, though I didn't understand why he'd need backup when interrogating two females.

He watched us for a few moments, but I recognised the same tactic from in the main hall. His intention to intimidate me seemed clear. I glared back, refusing to back down or exhibit nerves. "What are your names?"

"Valka and Mattildr."

"From where do you come?"

"Most recently, from Caithness on the mainland."

He crossed his arms. "And before that?"

"We came from Galloway."

He narrowed his eyes, well aware I hadn't given Galloway as our homeland. I returned his gaze with all the strength I could muster in years staring down recalcitrant customers. This man had a great deal of personal power and it took all I had to push back against it.

He spun to confront Mattea, who still sat on the bench with her knees pulled up. "Why are you here?"

She stammered at being put on the spot. "We…we're looking for a cousin. A short, red-haired man. We know him as McKenzie, but we think he took another name on his journey."

He raised his left eyebrow. "Red-haired?"

She nodded, a little less nervous. "Red as glowing iron and covered in freckles. He would have come up from the mainland."

This statement gave him more information about us and our movements. However, it might even be to our advantage. He glanced at me, and I returned his gaze, again throwing up my wall of immutable strength. I didn't know how long I needed to maintain the barrier, but for now, I matched him.

He glanced between Mattea and me several times before he conferred with one of his guards, a man whose black hair had one white streak at the temple. I didn't hear the words, but the guard grew agitated at one point.

The earl hushed him with one hand and turned back to us. "Tell me why you search for this man."

"He is a relative of mine, my sister's husband. I have news for him about his son's health, urgent news I must deliver. We've been searching for him for some time and have traced his path to this area."

"And you came here from where?"

"Caithness, as I said earlier. From the town on the cliff, Thjorsá."

He frowned, crossing his arms again. "You came from Thjorsá."

I nodded and tried to take control of the conversation. "The other guard mentioned you might bring us something to drink? My throat is rough from the weather."

He ignored my request. "How long ago did you arrive on the island?"

"Even some water would help. I wouldn't want you to violate your host duties. Such a loss of reputation might have unforeseen consequences. It might be dire to begrudge a visitor their guest-right."

His jaw clenched several times before he flicked his hand at the second guard. I waited until he returned with a waterskin and two mugs. While they waited, I made a production of pouring for both Mattea and myself, relishing a long draught of the cool mead, and then smacking my lips.

"Now, what was your last question, my gracious host?"

The earl growled out the question. "How long ago did you arrive on the island?"

The mead helped me get a better grip on my glibness. "As I recall, we walked from the port at Hamnavoe, what about four hours ago, Mattildr? Perhaps five. The weather hasn't been helpful. I realise it may not seem fierce to you, but I assure you, we're soft southerners, used to more mild weather in mid-summer."

His pursed lips told me he didn't like my manner. I didn't care much for his at the moment, either.

"No ships came into harbour at Hamnavoe this week. The dock has been under repair for a moon, ever since a windstorm smashed the pier."

My stomach dropped at this intelligence. Damn me for making up too many details. Still, how would I have known?

"I will tell you what I think. I received intelligence that my previously loyal Gæðingar Jón would betray me. You two show up at his hall on the night of his betrayal. This cannot be coincidence. I believe you two to be spies."

Suddenly, his hand whipped to my chest and yanked at my necklace, pulling out the dull stone. No blue glow betrayed its circuitry, thankfully. Startled, I pulled back, but the chain wouldn't break. He shifted to grab my collection bag, and I panicked. He couldn't, under any circumstances, get that bag. I tried to pull away with no result when Mattea cried out. He turned to her, and I managed to get the bag back into the folds of my apron dress, between my legs. Let him rummage in there for it, if he dared. Mattea fluttered her eyes and fanned her face, the very picture of Scarlett O'Hara. When she'd had a drink to restore her color, he turned back to me and scowled.

"Now, who sent you?"

Despite the panic which gripped me, I wracked my brain for information on the political situation. The name Rögnvaldr bubbled up, and I grasped it, praying the bubble wouldn't burst. I played with the name in my mind, digging for details. He would take Orkney, and soon. Perhaps within a few nights, perhaps within a month. He would do so through treachery, betraying his cousin, my interrogator.

Digging deeper, I pulled out one more fact. The betrayal would have something to do with signal towers. Try as I might, further scraping revealed nothing. Mattea might remember further details, but my well ran dry.

I took a deep breath, trying to form a plan. Earl Paul Haakonsson glared at me as I took another. While the Agency cautioned us against interacting with major historical people as much as possible, I needed to save my hide and that of my friend.

I had one path remaining to me; to grasp power back from our captor. As a woman, only three paths of power lay open for me. That of an older relative, such as a mother or aunt, that of a visiting noble, or that of a *vǫlva,* a prophetess. Since I claimed no relation to the Earl, and the second required more knowledge of current political genealogy than I had, the latter remained my only option.

I rolled my eyes back into my skull and intoned in a sepulchre voice, "I see three things, three things I see."

By the gasps, either Earl Paul or his guard bought my vǫlva act. If I convinced him of my status as a prophetess, I might secure our safety. I wouldn't give him information that would change historical fact, but I might give him the illusion such information would help. Most prophecies remained so hopelessly clouded in ambiguity and allusion, people interpreted them a dozen ways. I only needed to hint at something he already knew to give verisimilitude to my powers.

"The first thing I see is a light on the ocean, a flame that licks high into the rainy night. Such a flame is the light of a disloyal friend."

"The second thing I see is a keel on the sand, a keel that digs into the native soil. Such a keel is the strength of your enemy."

"The third thing I see is the gleam of a blade, a blade that cuts into your heart. Such a blade will slice your veins and open rivers of blood."

With some unearthly moaning and swaying, I sold my prophecy until I collapsed in true exhaustion. I peeked through lowered lashes and bowed head to witness the effect of my words.

The earl whispered furiously with his guard, sending him out with panicked quickness. After a few moments, the guard brought back five more men. He gave these men instructions, only one returning. This guard came laden with trays of bread, milk, mead, and cheese.

In a much-changed attitude, the earl put a careful hand on my shoulder. "Please accept my abject apologies, sacred vǫlva. My hospitality is at fault, and I would beg your forgiveness. You appear much drained, and I would take you to a place to rest."

Chapter Twenty-Four

The storm intensified as I looked out of the tower.

Mattea just returned from her latest sojourn into the village, her hair still wet from the rain. "Does this infernal rain ever stop? Christ on a piece of toast, I wish I was back in Maine. We may have been there in April, but it still beats this so-called June."

I stared at the coastline, trying to make out any activity. "Now you see why trees don't like growing here."

"I can't see why anything would grow here. Rain, wind, cold, nothing but dour Norsemen running around. At least at Jón's hall, we enjoyed merriment and company."

I sighed. "Did you find anything out about McKenzie?"

She shook her head. "I tried, but I'm not as good at extracting confidences as you are. The men are more interested in bedding me. I've needed to fight off three more proposals just today. You'd think they hadn't brought their own wives for their needs! The women see me as competition and clam up whenever I get near. Are you sure you can't get out of here?"

Shaking my head, I peered at a boat on the sand, but it was just a fishing vessel. "You remember the last time I tried. The earl almost threw a conniption fit. If I'd known how valued I would be as a vǫlva, I would have pretended to something else. Suddenly I'm too valuable to let go. I suppose it's better than too dangerous to let live, but only marginally."

"Are you adding samples to your collection bag?"

"Of course. Anything I can get my hands on without attracting notice. I've also made notes about garb and stuffed them in the bag. There was this gorgeous brooch on one of the older women. She let me examine it. It reminded me of the Tara Brooch in Ireland, all filigree gold and silver."

"I wish I could have seen it. It sounds fantastic." After letting out a deep sigh, I gazed out the window again. I detested being this helpless. I wanted to smash something just to get a reaction from the Earl.

She flopped down on my mattress, brushing her hair until the damp curls untangled. "I think I've canvassed most of the surrounding farms, but there's another village on the mainland and down the coast. You'd think a red-headed dwarf would at least kick up gossip. Could we have gotten his placement or timing wrong?"

Another fishing vessel pulled up next to the first. The fishermen argued, one throwing a fish at the other, making me smile. "No, the Agency is excellent at tracing travellers. It's one of the few things they do extremely well. You keep investigating, while I work on a way to deliver me from the earl's clutches."

She fell back on the mattress, her hair making a damp spot on the canvas. "I only want to be warm and dry, for more than a few hours. Can you make that happen, O Prophetess of Orkney?"

With a roll of my eyes, I glanced at her. "Don't even joke about that. Remember what happened to Cassandra."

My stomach roiled at another memory, one long since buried within my psyche. Paolo's face flashed, as did Alessandro's, my son. The pain gripped my heart as I shoved the image away, but not before the awful spots on my son's skin burned into my mental image. The spots that took him from me. In a twisted way, seeing the future caused those spots. Despite my insight and my attempts to save them, it hadn't been enough.

Mattea rose and put a hand on my shoulder. "Wilda? Wilda, what's wrong? You look all pasty and you're swaying."

I pushed her away. "Nothing, nothing. Just an old pain come back to haunt me. You said there's another village? How far away?"

She narrowed her eyes. "About a half-day's journey along the coast to the south. I can ask the earl for an escort, as the tension has increased each day since we got here. It's like something'll burst if someone sneezes."

The fishermen increased their hostilities below, until a wave swamped them. The water made them both scramble inland, dragging their skiffs behind them. I gave a low chuckle and turned back to Mattea. "I wish we had the date the coup took place so we could ensure our departure before such event. The records aren't clear on the date, just listing it as *close to mid-summer*. Still, if I can't remove myself from here, you need to follow whatever clues you find. Understand?"

Footsteps outside saved Mattea from agreement, but I glared at her to pound home my determination. She answered with a tentative nod before the knock on the door drew our attention.

A guard opened the door, the same one who fetched me each evening for the last four days. "If it please you, honoured vǫlva, the earl requires your presence for the evening hall. Follow me."

With a parting glare at Mattea, I pulled my fur stole around my shoulders and followed the guard.

By the time I descended into the central hall of the broch, the earl already sat at the head of the table with his family. Perhaps thirty warriors and landsmen sat along the tables, in various levels of armour. Some only wore indoor clothing, while others looked ready for battle. The latter seemed more vigilant, their eyes shifting amongst each diner, searching for the slightest sign of treachery.

I'd been to Norse evening meals before, though in Iceland and in Sweden. The standard fare was meat, root vegetables, mead, and song. Bragging and poetry took up much of the conversation, with a staggeringly high level of male swagger.

Most attendants suffered from severe testosterone poisoning before the evening finished.

Earl Paul's table, however, held much more restraint. A few men at the lower tables laughed in drunken joviality now and then, but most of the guards with higher status, judging from their armour and arm-rings, kept their mead consumption to a minimum and their vigilance at a maximum.

Even the small amount of conversation silenced as I walked in and took my place. My chair sat in a place of honour, next to the earl himself. As a guest and a vǫlva, I enjoyed a special status, even higher than his sister, Frakkok. I nodded to the elegant woman in green with solemn grace and she returned the gesture. The other evening, I'd asked her about McKenzie, but she steered the conversation to weaving or food preparation, refusing to even acknowledge the subject.

I glanced to the earl's daughter, sitting next to her aunt. The young lady's flaxen hair framed bright blue eyes, but they held little spark of intelligence. I'd tried to corner her the night before, hoping her lower level of cunning would allow easy manipulation, but she proved too stupid to question. Either she knew nothing of a red-headed visitor, or she'd been too frightened to reveal her knowledge.

The guard who collected me each night likewise remained too conscious of his duty to reveal any details, if he knew any. My frustration grew at each blocked attempt to the point I felt ready to scream in exasperation.

"Don't you think so, honoured guest?"

I turned to the earl who had obviously just asked me a question. With a cough, I swallowed my bite of turnip. "I'm so sorry, can you repeat that? I couldn't hear over the noise."

The earl glanced over the quiet hall and raised an eyebrow. "I said, the nights have stopped getting shorter. We should approach mid-summer. Don't you think so?"

With a quick mental calculation, I smiled. "Yes, the solstice should have been two nights ago. It's difficult to see the sun setting with the constant cloud cover of the last few days, but the nights will be longer now. Not by much, but they will increase."

He narrowed his eyes and nodded. He leaned forward, addressing his sister. "Have you heard from our mother yet, Frakkok? The messenger yesterday had been most insistent upon delivering his words to you personally. Most urgent."

If I imagined the hall to be quiet before, I'd been mistaken.

No one breathed while Frakkok sipped from her mug before answering. "I'm afraid not, brother dear. Simply another request for my presence in Norway. Not even from Mother; this request came from King Harold."

Earl Paul's scowl deepened, but Frakkok concentrated on her meal, choosing a morsel of fish from her plate, carefully chewing it, and washing it down with a drink of mead before choosing another. She continued in this way for at least a minute before she glanced to the Earl. "Did you have another question, dear brother?"

He stabbed his knife into a slab of lamb and tore off a chunk with his teeth as an answer. The rest of the hall returned to their meals, though with even less conversation than before. Several guards standing behind the earl placed hands closer to their weapons. When nothing further occurred, they relaxed marginally.

I'd extracted more historical details about our earl from Mattea's recollection, including details about Frakkok and her mother trying to murder Earl Paul earlier, using a poisoned shirt, much like Medea had in Ancient Greece. Instead of her intended target, however, their brother had fallen dead.

I forced myself to swallow the last bite of fish. I needed to escape this hall, before the next betrayal occurred. From the exchange with Frakkok and Earl Paul, I didn't have a lot of time. I felt like a mouse at a cat show, and I didn't much care for the sensation.

Chapter Twenty-Five

Once the rain eased, I watched the sunset from my tower window. In fact, it was about my only entertainment. This time of the year, the sun didn't set until around midnight, and the light, when not dimmed by storm clouds, remained twilight until it rose again in a few hours. I should sleep but my brain wouldn't stop whirring with political intrigue and a desperate need to figure a way out of my mess.

I'd tried everything. Frequent guard patrols foiled the trope of using bed cloths to tie a rope. These patrols increased, ironically, from my own predictions. Talk about being hoist by one's own petard. Bribery with gold had resulted in horrified denial and a hasty exit by the young guard in question. While I would never ask Mattea to give herself in seduction of a guard toward a similar end, she'd suggested the plan herself.

Not even such an extreme measure had worked.

However, Mattea had discovered rumours of McKenzie in one of the coastal villages. Even now, she'd journeyed to the mainland to follow up on this rumour. As the third night of her mission dragged on, I scanned the area for her return, anxious for her safety.

If only the earl had been literate, I might have asked for some reading material. I didn't read Old Norse, but I might have done my best to puzzle it out. Despite the advances in technology that made the translator implant possible, no one had figured out a similar technology for reading languages.

The work would have kept my brain occupied and away from the constant disastrous imaginings I assigned to Mattea and her mission. Alas, neither the earl nor his priest kept any written documents. I suspected the priest of illiteracy as well, though the ancient man wouldn't admit to such a thing.

I'd tried enlisting that official's help, but since I'd set myself up as a pagan prophetess, he wouldn't speak to me, much less heed my imprecations.

A scratch at the door heralded my one friend in the broch other than Mattea. I creaked to my feet and opened the door a sliver to let in Asta, a white cat who had adopted me as her own.

With a plaintive meow, she jumped into my lap as I sat next to the window. She purred and curled into a ball as I stroked her soft fur. I sighed and smiled at her. "I wish the rest of this place would be as accepting as you, sweet thing. If only the earl would be as trusting."

To be fair, I'd given him little reason to trust anyone with my hasty and ill-conceived prophecy. While it would prove true, which would cement my status and honour, in the meantime it only threw every single person into suspicion, including me.

The betrayal might occur tomorrow, or it might be next year. I didn't want to remain imprisoned for a year, damnit! I needed to be out there, helping Mattea find McKenzie's tracks. My mind needed to do something, anything other than pining away at a stone window, watching the twilight creep over the countryside.

No fishermen stood on the beach at this time of the night. The only movement I saw was the constant rhythm of the waves and an occasional animal skittering across the shadowed grass. I took in a deep breath, the ever-present brine scent of the ocean overlaying the woodsmoke and less pleasant scents of a medieval human village. The wind died for once, leaving the land below still and silent.

The plaintive cry of a sheep broke the quiet. A lamb answered her mother's call.

Asta leapt from my lap, raking her back claws across my legs. I yelped and stood, scanning the room for what made her run under my bed. Finding nothing suspicious in the room, I glanced out the window.

The scene below remained as still and dim as it had before the cat freaked out. With confusion, I cracked open my door, to see who was down the hall.

A torch guttered in its sconce, its flame flickering as it burned. Other than that, I spied nothing that might have spooked the animal. After shutting the door firmly, I glared at the bed. "Bloody stupid feline. You'll have me jumping at ghosts next."

The cat disdained to answer me, or to come out from her hiding place. I blew her a raspberry and resumed my seat next to the window. The calm night worked as an anodyne to my nerves, despite jumpy cats and their sharp claws. I counted each wave licking the sandy shore below as I rubbed the place where she'd clawed my thigh.

Folklore said each seventh wave reached higher than the others. I tested this theory but gave up when the premise became destroyed in just three cycles. Still, counting the waves soothed me, more than counting sheep ever had. My eyelids drooped, and I pulled the tapestry off its hook and crawled into bed, pulling the scratchy wool blanket up to my chin. The tapestry did a creditable job of keeping the chill out when the wind didn't blow it aside, but the cold still seeped through the stones of the broch.

Once I had shifted into the depression in the straw mattress, tucked the wool blanket under my chin, and stared at the ceiling, my brain refused to sleep. I strained my ears for the sound of the surf, to count the waves from bed, but I couldn't distinguish each one enough to relax. Bloody damn insomnia to all levels of Hell.

I rarely suffered from insomnia, but periods of great stress made it more likely. Worrying about Mattea and her mission made for sleepless nights and drooping days. At least I'd been able to walk the grounds of the broch and add samples to my collection bag. The earl had even permitted me, with a proper escort, to walk along the beach. I picked up seaweed, shells, rocks, whatever I found amongst the flotsam and sand. However, I'd been stymied in every line of inquiry on our quarry. I hoped Mattea had encountered more luck in finding information on McKenzie.

Today at the evening meal, I'd gotten a glimpse of a new kitchen maid. Her skin was dusky, similar to my shade. I recalled the Vikings had been to Sicily, Constantinople, and even north Africa. If she came from another land, perhaps she'd heard of the traveller we sought, another stranger. When the guard brought my morning meal, I'd argue with him and insist to be escorted to the kitchens. I might see her there, if my luck held.

Luck. Such a fickle mistress luck was. I'd been lucky in my youth, until our trip to China. Then, I'd been lucky in my later life, until Josephus arrived on my doorstep. I'd been lucky on these missions, and now that luck had fled like a raven in the night.

The caw made my eyes fly open. The tapestry had somehow flipped up over its hook, revealing my metaphor come to life, an enormous black corvid perched on my windowsill.

Shoving down the irrational panic, I sat up and glared at the bird. "What the Hell do you want? If you're looking for Edgar Allen Poe, he hasn't been born yet."

The bird's gimlet eyes glittered in the dim twilight, and he cocked his head, considering me.

"Well? If you've some inscrutable message from Odin, speak your piece. Otherwise, bugger off. I'm exhausted."

He cawed again and ruffled his wings, but he didn't leave. I had no wish to emerge from my now-warm wool cocoon to shoo the pest away and unhook the tapestry. With a growl, I turned my back to the bird and pulled the blanket around my shoulder. The blasted thing would do as he wished. Maybe Asta would murder it.

This cheerful thought put me to sleep.

Chapter Twenty-Six

That night had been the last sleep I got for the next three days. As each night fell, my worry for Mattea grew. The kitchen maid turned out to be yet another dead end, as she professed no knowledge or rumour of a short, red-haired stranger in the villages.

Earl Paul's subtle feud with his sister eased for a few nights, at least. She travelled to a neighbouring town, to visit a cousin. This decreased the tension in the hall, but the earl still searched for the vehicle of betrayal in every glance and sigh around his table.

I'm amazed my stomach didn't rebel with all the unrest. At least the Norse knew how to cook. Their bread and fish stew tasted savoury and delicious. Most of their other cooking tasted wonderful except for pickled herring. Pickled herring could go take a deep dive in a shallow pool, for all I cared.

A scuffle at the door made me glance up. I'd done the same at every change in routine, hoping it signalled Mattea's return, but the door revealed a male messenger, still clad in the oilskins of a sea voyage. He ran breathlessly to the earl's side, pulling him aside for a secret conference. After a few words, the earl took him out of the hall for a full consultation.

Glances across the table became legion and the muttering began, speculating on the messenger's information. Before the conjecture could gain too much steam, though, the earl returned and silenced the budding rumours with a stern glance. The messenger hadn't returned with him.

He stared at me and narrowed his eyes. I pretended nonchalance and took a bite of my fish. "The salmon is excellent tonight, Earl Paul. I commend your headwoman. What sort of seaweed is it flavoured with?"

He didn't answer but continued to watch me. The weight of his stare followed me as I broke off a piece of rye bread and dipped it onto my plate. I mopped up the juices and closed my eyes in appreciation. I hadn't lied; the fish had been delicious. I wanted to secrete the seaweed into my collection bag, but with the earl watching me, I daren't do such a thing.

I almost missed the next disturbance, concentrating so hard on appearing innocent and unconcerned. When Mattea's face came through the door, I almost shouted with relief. However, I contented myself with a deep sigh and a smile. I stood, my bench scraping loud in the silent hall. "Earl Paul, Mattildr appears exhausted. She needs rest and sustenance. Do I have your permission to take her and with some food up to my room?"

The look of relief on Mattea's face fueled my entreaty, but the earl didn't look pleased. He frowned and glanced at his head guard. The man didn't hint at an opinion. The earl shifted his gaze to where his sister normally sat, but she hadn't returned from her visit. Lacking any reason to keep us, he gave me a curt nod.

I grabbed Mattea's unresisting arm and pulled her from the hall. My stomach rumbled with the tension and worry, but I waited until we arrived safely in my room. Asta darted in just as I shut the wooden door.

"Where have you been all this time! It's been a week. I've been sick with worry. Are you well? Hurt? Injured?" I examined her up and down, searching for bandages or wounds.

She shoved me away. "Stop that! I'm fine, thank you very much. I didn't find the village right away, nor the source of the rumour. I didn't realise you wanted me to trudge back each day for a status report, or I would have wasted my time with that!"

Her rebuke stopped me short. I relented and dropped my gaze. "Of course, you're right. I'm just being a paranoid old bat." I took a deep sigh and gestured to a stool. "Now, sit. Eat. Tell me what you found."

Mattea took one stool and tore off a chunk of rye bread. She slathered butter on it and took a bite, closing her eyes to savour the food. "I've had little but dried meat the last few days. I daren't eat anything in the village I found."

While she ate, I waited impatiently for her to continue. She chewed the bread forever before doing so.

"About three days' walk down the west coast, I found a small village. Twenty small cottages, no church. One of the young girls there remembered the short red-haired man. He'd come through two moons before, a pack full of trade goods. He used his real name, Emory, and he'd walked many leagues, searching for his family."

I smiled in self-satisfied glee. I wondered if he'd found the same relative I'd found in my research, Sigurd Thorsson. But why had he searched out such distant ancestors? This detail I still didn't know.

"The girl hadn't wanted to tell me where he lived at first. She'd looked frightened and run away into the barn. I coaxed her out, but she still didn't want to talk. I convinced her I needed to find McKenzie.

"Inland about twenty miles, I found his village." She swallowed and looked out the window. The sun still sat high in the sky, despite the late hour. "The place," she took a deep breath, "looked deserted at first."

"At first?"

Mattea closed her eyes and swallowed again. "At first. I saw no one about, no livestock, no children running around, and no men in the fields. When I approached the first cottage and knocked on the door…"

Her skin turned ashen and the freckles stood out strong on her cheeks. I poured mead for her and made her drink it.

After she swallowed the drink, a small measure of flush came to her cheeks. "The wife sat at the table with her head down over her arms. At first, I thought she slept, so I knocked on the doorframe, loud enough to wake her. She didn't move, so I shook her shoulder, which felt freezing cold.

"When I lifted her head, the skin rotted from her face and bits… fell off. That's when I noticed the red slash of gore on her stomach and her intestines spilled out. I backed out of the cottage as quickly as I could, almost tripping on the threshold.

"After that, I didn't want to enter any other cottage, but I made myself. Each one showed the same. Everyone had died. Some showed horrific expressions of pain or terror on their faces, while others looked as if they slept peacefully. All had been killed with sword or knife, some slash or gash upon their bodies. Most rotted. The cold kept the odour from hitting me at first, but soon it was all I smelled."

She shivered and downed another cup of mead. I refilled it, putting a hand on her shoulder as she shivered.

Mattea shrugged off the comforting hand, continuing her story. "I decided I needed to find out what happened. I took samples, catalogued clues, and did my best to trace the progress of violence. It looked like the first casualties happened at the north edge of the village. I found the highest incidence of peaceful deaths there, people who must have been asleep. The cries of the first victims must have alerted the rest of the village."

I nodded in approval. She'd done well, despite the obvious horror of the incident. "What happened next?"

"I walked out of the village from that first spot, searching for where the killer may have come from. It took me a full day, but I remember the tracking lessons from Maine. I discovered a cave where someone had sheltered for a while. In the back, I found the remains of a fire, skins, fish bones, and something else that made me certain of what I'd found."

I raised my eyebrows, inviting her to continue.

"I found a piece of paper."

"What?"

"Paper. Not parchment, but real, wood-pulp, modern paper. It had been folded and scuffed, but real paper, with ruler lines and everything.

The edge had been torn from a spiral notebook. The writing had been made with ball-point pen."

I sat straight on my stool. "Did you take it? Can I see it?"

She smiled with grim satisfaction. "You can hardly think I would have left it, can you?"

Mattea reached into her bag and brandished a much-folded piece of ruler-lined paper. She unfolded it, revealing a scrawl of messy handwriting. Several names connected with lines covered the sheet, with McKenzie's name at the top.

I glanced at Mattea. "A family tree?"

"That's what it looks like, though there are places where he's skipped several generations. Still, this name looks like his latest quest." She pointed to a name in the lower left corner.

I expected to find Sigurd Thorsson's name. However, it read: "Ótama Sigurdsdottir." The birthdate read 1135 AD. Sigurd was listed as her father, and Sigga Bursisdottir as her mother.

I furrowed my brow as I stared at the chart. "She's barely a year old right now. What would he want with his ancestress as a baby? Was she a victim in the village?"

Mattea glared at me. "I didn't stop to check their IDs. Shall I go back and do so?"

"Stop trying to be as nasty as me, Mattea. I appreciate you suffered through a horrific experience, but—"

She stood, her stool clattering behind her on the flagstones. "But what? Do you want to hear the rest, or would you rather berate me some more for having a human reaction?"

I slouched onto my stool. "You're right, you're right. I'll shut up. Sorry."

She glared at me for a moment more before continuing. "I found someone else alive in the cave."

Chapter Twenty-Seven

"Someone else?" The words sounded stupid even to my ears.

She nodded and stood, pulling the tapestry aside to peer outside. She hooked it and gazed out at the beach. "He stood in the cave entrance when I turned to leave. I just about jumped out of my skin, but you'd be proud of me." Mattea turned to give me a feral grin. "I whipped out my knife, and crouched in a menacing pose. He took a step back and the expression of surprise on his face gave me immense satisfaction. His words, however, made me break my stance."

"What words?"

"It wasn't his words, 'who are you,' but how he said them."

I raised my eyebrows in invitation for her to continue.

"He said it in English."

Recognisable English didn't exist in the twelfth century. In this time, the Old English of Beowulf reigned, barely beginning the journey to Middle English, the English of Chaucer. The languages spoken on the British Isles today would be scarcely recognisable to modern English speakers, and even then, only with copious footnotes and glosses.

"Modern English?"

She sighed and nodded. "Near as I can tell. Complete with British accent, highborn, and posh. In fact—and you'll never believe this—I recognized him."

"You *what?*"

"I recognized him. Remember that posh idiot from the London police?"

"Sir Algernon the Pompous? Are you fucking serious? He's here? Bloody Hell and an order of Timbits." The memory of his curly brown hair and his haughty expression assaulted my mind's eye.

"There's something else. My pendant didn't glow for him."

I stared out of the window. "So, he's here through a rogue portal. Bloody Brits. Do they think the rules don't apply to them? Did he come through in Toronto, like Josephus, or do we have yet another rogue portal to worry about now?"

She shook her head. "I couldn't extract his entrance portal from him. In fact, he stayed canny with his information other than his name, once he recognized me. I believe he's here on a similar investigative mission, though."

"What did you tell him about yourself?"

She shrugged and sat on the stool. Asta sharpened her claws on Mattea's leg. "Ow! Stop that, infernal feline. Not much other than my name and that we worked for the Agency. I could do little else, since he recognized me from the shop. I didn't want to give away too much."

"Well done. What else?"

"That we stayed in the broch. He may come searching for me here. I asked about the items in the cave, but he shrugged and said he'd just gotten there himself. Still, I'm not sure I believe him."

I picked up the cat, despite her protests, and plonked her on my lap. I petted her until she curled up, saving Mattea's leg from needing a transfusion. "What makes you say that?"

"His eyes kept shifting around the cave, as if waiting for someone to emerge. I'd already had the chance to do my collecting, including the piece of paper and many other things. Foodstuffs, water, skins, and such. However, he seemed familiar with the cave and how low the ceiling sloped, for instance. He'd been there before."

My smile grew wide. "Very well done, indeed. So, what do you recommend as our next move?"

"First, we've got to get you out of here. Then I suggest we go back to the cave. You're sure to see something I've missed. Then we canvas the area farther inland, to see if McKenzie came from that direction, and if anyone remembers him."

The cat fell asleep on my lap, her purrs rumbling against my stomach, which growled in response. I realised how little I'd eaten at supper. "That's a sound plan, but the first part is the most difficult."

"Sir Algernon St. Clair the Pompous may come in handy for that part. If he shows up, I'll urge him to ask you for a prophecy. In response, you'd insist on being on location at that village. It would at least get you out of the broch."

My stomach growled again. "Earl Paul would send several guards as escort, if he even agreed to such a thing."

"Guest-right should require it, and St. Clair struck me as the sort to have brought plenty of tradable silver to do what he needed to do."

"What makes you think he'd expend such a resource to help us?"

She grinned. "A British gentleman give up the chance to save two damsels in distress? His sense of chivalry would explode in frustration if he denied us so heartily."

"Hmm. Maybe. I won't hold my breath. You'd be amazed at how few men actually act chivalrous when his peers aren't watching."

With a glance out the window again, she stood. "Then again, we may get our answer to that soon. Look."

Two figures walked along the shore from the south, a man and a woman, from their gaits. "Is that him?"

"It walks like him."

"Who's with him?"

She shrugged. "I have no idea. He didn't mention a companion."

"Then perhaps we'd best get back to the main hall. I'm hungry enough to eat a horse."

She chuckled. "They don't have many horses here on the islands. Better make it a whale."

The hall only held about half its normal complement this late in the evening, but both Mattea and I snagged fish and bread from a servant as we came in. I'd only managed a few bites before the visitors entered.

The man stood tall, over six feet, slim despite the bulky furs he wore. His brown, curly hair tumbled in curls as he took off his fur cap, framing a slightly hooked nose and green eyes. He must have a translation implant similar to ours, but he spoke Old Norse with a posh British accent despite this. I masked my grin by stuffing more fish into my mouth. To my surprise, I recognised the woman. Brusi's sister, Káta, walked next to St. Clair, her colourful wrap a riot of clashing colours. I hadn't seen her since our brief conversation the night we arrived. An enormous black bird stood on her shoulder. His eyes gleamed at me, and I felt sure it was the same blasted bird who had deviled me the other night. I glared back at the corvid.

Earl Paul stood as the visitors entered. "Who comes to my hall this night?"

Káta smiled, her grin wide. "My earl, I have brought you a visitor from across the sea, a man who comes on a quest. This is Algautr, in search of prophecy from your new vǫlva.

The earl swivelled around to glare at me, but I returned my most innocent gaze. With my eyes, I told him on no uncertain terms if he meant to keep me as a pet, he'd have to deal with others who sought my wisdom.

With a growl, the earl turned back to Káta. "I've only had this *vǫlva* for a few days. How did he hear of her?"

She blinked with a feigned innocence similar to my own. That's when I saw the blue eyes more clearly. Yes, Bryonie's eyes gazed back at me. For once, I welcomed the knowledge of this strange woman's past lives. So far, her previous incarnations had all been helpful to my quest. I only hoped that continued to be true. "Why, I told him, of course. It only increases your status to have such a renowned *vǫlva* at your court, my Earl. Why hide such a prized possession?"

Why, indeed. I renewed my look of bemused innocence as the earl shifted his gaze between me and Káta. Finally, he addressed the visitor. "What wisdom do you seek from my vǫlva?"

He bowed deep, full of propriety. "If it please my host, my quest is of a particularly personal and intimate nature. I must not divulge the details in such a public forum. I'd be pleased to expend an appropriate measure of silver for the privilege of speaking with your vǫlva in private, if such a thing might be possible."

His translator didn't work well. Old Norse had been a much more direct language than modern English, but he still spoke with the circumlocution of the upper class of British nobility into the coarser, simpler language. I didn't know how he managed it, but such skill earned a measure of my respect, despite his rogue status. I turned to Mattea, but she smiled as well with a nod. He exhibited a rare charm, despite his formality. His grin seemed engaging, even for Earl Paul. Either that, or the mention of an "appropriate measure of silver" piqued his interest.

The earl didn't even glance in my direction. Despite the fact that speaking with the visitor would be to my benefit, such disdain irked my sense of pride and independence. I stood and glared at him. "Pardon me, Earl Paul, but do I get a say in the use of my gift? Or am I mere chattel to be sold off at your pleasure?"

Several people swivelled to stare at me with surprise, including the Earl, Mattea, Káta and St. Clair. Realising my situation, I cleared my throat. "My visions must be inspired. They are not yours to conjure at the snap of your fingers."

The earl growled again.

"You should get that seen to, Earl Paul. You might be coming down with an ague. Do you have a healer?" I blinked several times as a titter swept through the hall.

Chapter Twenty-Eight

Once Mattea, St. Clair, Káta, and I arrived at the door of my room, I turned to Káta. "I thank you for bringing this man to Earl Paul's court."

She shook her head. "The least I would do for a fellow vǫlva. Wise women must stick together, particularly against the ignorant but powerful men who rule our lives. Is that not so from your own home?"

With a rueful chuckle, I nodded. "Very true, no matter from where one hails. We are the quiet strength behind the bravado."

Her head rocked back from her loud laughter, which echoed against the stone walls. "You put it precisely, Valka. And yet, without the men, we would be forced to deal with all the dreary political machinations of the world. I, for one, am happier without that burden."

"What can we do to repay you for your help, Káta?"

"I ask for nothing, nothing at all. You are someone I must help, you see. Your colours demand it."

I furrowed my brow, trying to make sense of her words. She laughed at my expression. "You must not see them, either. Most people have colours about them, colours I can see but others don't. Your own colours are that of a seeker, someone on a quest. Algautr wears similar colours. I had to get the two of you together, no matter the cost." Her expression grew pensive with the last comment.

"Cost? Káta, if your actions have gotten you in some peril, I must do what I can to ease that."

She shook her head. "My peril, indeed, that of all of us, is not of your making nor for you to correct. You are not to blame for anything that happens, and I shall be sound enough where I am. I needed to bring this man to you. You are kindred spirits. Just heed me in this: complete what you need to do this night. We have little time."

With that, she nodded and left, the raven cawing as she walked down the curved hallway. After she disappeared, I opened the door to my room. In English, I spoke to St. Clair. "If you will join us, fellow traveller?"

His eyes widened as he preceded us into the small room. I sat on the cot while Mattea and our visitor used the stools.

I crossed my arms and glared at our visitor. "Well, Sir Algernon St. Clair. Where shall we start?"

He raised his eyebrows and glanced between the two of us. "I had no idea I would encounter you once again, my dear woman. The young lady showed kindness in informing me of her own first name but forbade to supply a surname. In addition, she wouldn't inform me of yours, though I do remember you from Toronto."

His English sounded as complex as his Old Norse had. Overly verbose to the point of ridiculous. "I am Agent Wilda Firestone of the Temporal Agency of Toronto. This is my assistant, Agent Mattea Jardine. From where and whence did you travel?"

He cleared his throat and ran his right hand through his curls. I noticed edges of silver peppered through. "I came through in London, in the year 2037. I arrived in this time a month past."

2037. The same year we travelled. I glanced at Mattea, her mouth set in a grim line.

We didn't have an official portal in London. "London, you said. Not Paris."

His gaze dropped to his feet, which he shuffled. "That is, unfortunately, precisely correct, Agent Firestone. Despite all our efforts at the Met, I proved unable to get the appropriate permission to travel from the Parisian Agency in time, or indeed any of the registered portals. Their bureaucracy became much too onerous for the required speed of my mission. As did your own."

"And what mission might that be?"

He stood, walking to the window. Looking over the darkening sky, he stared at the scenery for several minutes before answering. When he turned back toward us, his eyes looked more tired than I'd yet seen them. "Surely you are not ignorant of the traveller plague which has beset us? I am searching for the source of such illness. An unregistered traveller came here, and I mean to find out why."

"What have you found?"

He flicked several imaginary bits of dust from his woollen cloak. "My dear lady, you are most direct, I must say. No guile in the slightest. I do believe I prefer this to the more common methods of interrogation."

I clenched my jaw. No sweet-talking Brit would charm me away from my mission. "Save your flattery for your constituents and answer my question. What did you find?"

He sighed and clasped his hands, still standing. His posture reminded me of a choir boy getting ready for his first solo performance. "First, I am no politician, my good lady. I am an Inspector of the Metropolitan Police. I am looking for one Emory McKenzie, who travelled to this time and place via a rogue portal in Edinburgh, without official sanction."

If he traced the same man, I might determine that from his itinerary. "Where and when?"

He cocked his head. "Will you allow me some reciprocity for these questions, my good lady? Might I similarly discover details about your own mission forthwith?"

"Did you just say *forthwith?*"

He puffed up as if I'd insulted his Labrador puppy.

I waved that away. "In time, in time. Where and when?"

He clasped his hands more tightly, glancing between me and Mattea. "I do believe time will be of the essence, no matter what our missions are, Agent Firestone. Do, please, answer a question for me, first?"

I sighed and rolled my eyes. "Considering you travelled through an unauthorised portal yourself and are on a rogue mission to begin with, no matter what your modern authority, you are in no position to demand a thing from us, as official Temporal Agents. You must be well aware of this. Are you even trained as an Agent, Sir Algernon?"

The wind picked up again, fluttering the tapestry aside with a sudden gust. Sir Algernon drew himself up in umbrage and opened his mouth to answer. However, something outside drew his attention back to the window. "I say, what the devil is all that?"

Chapter Twenty-Nine

Despite my burning need to hear more, I joined him. Mattea came to his other side.

In the distance, through the sudden rain and flashes of lightning, I saw the flickering of a signal flame burn bright, then go out. Men scrambled from several longboats on the beach, armed and running toward the keep. The rain may have masked their noise. Perhaps the earl watched them approach. Either way, I wanted nothing to do with a coup. Coups often turned violent, and invaders didn't stop to ask which side someone fought on, or if they only visited.

"Bloody Hell and an order of Timbits. It's happening. That's what Káta meant. Quick, pack everything. We're getting out of here, now."

To her credit, Mattea sprang into action. She'd hadn't unpacked from her quick trip down the coast, but she shoved some of my stuff into her bag while I grabbed the rest. St. Clair stood next to the door while we scrambled. We finished in short order.

A quick glance outside showed an empty beach. The shouts and clashes of steel sounded from the other side of the broch, the front entrance.

"Down to the kitchens. Mattea, you remember where? There's a small back entrance there. It's shielded and only opens from the inside. It leads to the stable yard, for easy access to the chickens and goats."

Both my companions nodded as we crept down the outside hallway of the broch, down the stairs, and into the kitchens. The place looked deserted, as it should be so late at night. The dim twilight helped us see as we ran through the stable yards and to the stone wall surrounding it.

I gave thanks for my foresight in finding a tall companion. St. Clair helped us up over the six-foot stone wall, and then pulled himself up when we stood safe. I scraped my hands and one cheek on the way down the other side.

The noises of battle came from the right, so we turned left. I considered appropriating horses, but the creatures had considerable valuable, and their absence would be noted. Besides, we had no way of getting them out of the yard undetected.

Under the dim twilight of the endless dusk, we escaped along the coast as the inevitable coup took the Earldom of Orkney from Earl Paul and into the hands of his successor and rightful heir to the islands, Rognavaldr Kali Kolsson, the event I had *prophesied* to escape interrogation. The result of which had been, rather than freedom due to a vǫlva, an enemy's imprisonment.

I wished no harm to befall Earl Paul, despite his role in this fiasco. I shouldn't have given in to the urge to impress him with my knowledge in the first place and found a wiser course. As far as anyone knew, he wouldn't lose his life this night. However, his future remained shrouded in mystery and no Agent had yet investigated his life after this event. Perhaps he'd suffer a mortal wound or be imprisoned for the rest of his life.

I didn't think I could muster much sympathy for him in the latter case.

I refused to dwell overlong on his fate. Instead, I concentrated on our route. We walked south, along the beach and rocky shore, through two villages before we allowed ourselves a rest.

We found a small, abandoned cottage and explored it with caution. Sir Algernon declared it safe, and we entered. "I dare say no one has occupied this dwelling for at least a year. No hearth ash remains, and the stable is almost scent-free, as much as any such structure can be after housing kine. No, I do believe we shall remain unmolested, at least for one night."

I surveyed the small space. "Well enough. The new Earl won't be searching for us in the chaos. He'll concentrate on securing his own space. I hope Káta found safety, regardless."

Mattea's wrinkled her nose as she glanced at the bare floors and uncovered windows. "Damn it. I hoped to spend at least one night in a warm, comfy bed after the last week. Can we at least have a fire?"

Looking down the beach, I couldn't see even a hint of the broch. "I think a small fire inside the house would be fine. In fact, I think we'll need it to keep warm through the night. Can you gather fuel?"

"Ugh. I suppose I asked for that, didn't I?"

"You absolutely did. Have fun."

She grumbled as she dropped her pack and stalked outside, searching for the animal dung the locals used for fuel on this tree-scarce island. If no one had lived here for a year, she might find some. Sheep on the hills would have left pellets, but those might be difficult to find in the midnight gloom. But, as she'd said, she asked for it. I left the disgusting task to her, despite lingering guilt.

I busied myself by making nests for the two of us, trusting Sir Algernon to make his own arrangements. Once we settled, I'd grill him further on his purpose. How much of my mission did I dare reveal to him? All of it? None of it? I wouldn't lie, but I might misdirect. Even if we were, ultimately, on the same mission, he was not of the Agency.

Unlike prisoners of war, Agents put in comprising situations wouldn't be bound by honour and duty. Their first duty must be to the time stream, then their own lives. If required, they might be expected to remain in the past rather than disrupt the time stream beyond repair. Rare as that would be so far in the past, it remained a possibility.

Once Mattea returned with her cape full of sheep scat and cow dung, she dumped them in the middle of the cottage, where I'd placed several rocks to contain the flame. She wrinkled her nose again and shook out the cloak, beating it a few times to get the bits off.

"Oh, look what lovely horse hockeys you've brought me! You spoil me, Mattea."

She growled and marched off again, grumbling about getting enough fuel to last the night.

I chuckled under my breath as I arranged the larger chunks in the middle and the smaller ones around the edge. Then I took out my fire-starting kit and clicked the iron pyrite a few times to the flint. Soon, a workable spark flew in the right direction, and I carefully fanned the tiny smoulder into a decent glow. The noxious odour of burning dung smacked me in the face and stole my breath. I coughed a few times before my brain functioned again, cataloguing the stench into a compartment of my sensory perception.

"So, Sir Algernon. Before we were so rudely interrupted, you'd been about to present your credentials as a trained Temporal Agent, had you not?"

When I looked up after my question, I arrested him in the act of shaking out a blanket over his own nest. He looked guilty and sheepish at the same time. I waited.

"Yes, well, not as such, no. I did receive some rudimentary instruction on the rules an Agent is expected to follow while on his or her erstwhile mission, of course, and some basics in the periods I would be visiting. However, since I had been denied official access to both the Toronto and Parisian portals, well, you understand, I'm certain. The practicality of the mission trumped the requirement, quite."

I stood to face him, my hands on my hips. Even though he towered over me by more than a foot, I instilled a great deal of authority in my stance and answer. "Quite nothing. There is an excellent reason to use the official portals, or did they not tell you that tidbit of information? Rogue portals can subject their travellers to irreversible cellular degeneration."

He swallowed and nodded. "Yes, well, quite true. The Yard did inform me of the possibility, nay the probability of this eventuality. Nonetheless, I maintained my willingness to volunteer, knowing full well it may be the only mission I would ever complete in my albeit staid and heretofore uninteresting lifetime."

This bald statement stopped my fury cold. He knew the risks and took the trip anyhow. I set my jaw and considered my next move. Instead of a foolish, reckless scion, similar to those who paid outrageous fees at my shop, Sir Algernon might be a soldier, someone who knew they might die, and sallied into the breach anyhow. A member of the Forlorn Hope of old. He deserved my help, at least, and perhaps even my humble respect. He might lie, but something in my gut screamed at me to believe his earnest expression.

With a nod, I dropped my hands from my hips. "Very well. I'm relieved they warned you of the dangers. If you would trust me at the conclusion of our trip, I can return through the official portal and come back with a proper mechanism to allow you to come back through the Toronto portal. This will help to minimise the damage and prevent a possible instant death through the rogue one."

He blinked several times, a wave of relief washing across his face. "That is a most genteel offer, my lady. You have my thanks. Indeed, you may even have my life, for such is forfeit."

"However, we currently each have a mission to complete."

Mattea returned with a second load of shit. She dumped it and, sensitive to the tension, looked between the two of us for an explanation.

"I was just explaining to our new companion about our mission. Sir Algernon, we received a strange visitor to my Outfitting shop one day. One Josephus Konaté collapsed in my shop, in obvious distress from illness. Despite our efforts to get him quickly to the traveller hospital, he died several days later. Two other rogue travellers were reported in other parts of the world, both now in comas from a similar malady. From the tests performed, they brought a plague with them, despite any panoculations.

This plague seems to infect any traveller who had used the portals in recent years."

He nodded as I spoke. "This sounds similar to our experience. Approximately a month before McKenzie arrived, a young woman, a native of this time, came to the Met, quite out of her mind with madness and excessive perspiration. She had the temerity to expire before we could extract good information from her, despite one man's familiarity with Icelandic. We'd originally decided her linguistic aberration must be a side effect of the rogue portal she'd utilized. We later determined she had been speaking Old Norse, a language too far removed from Icelandic for his ready comprehension."

He sat on his pack and placed his hands on his knees as he continued his account. "The first person to take ill, a recreational traveller, worked for the force. When they admitted him to hospital, since we don't have one dedicated to travellers, it took us a long time to isolate the vector, much less contain it. From what our scientists have been able to ascertain, it only affects those who have travelled, but it is highly contagious and can be carried by non-travellers."

I sat on my pack and Mattea took a seat. "Our scientists believe the vector could be a substance, some sort of fungus, plant, or animal item the travellers brought back."

He put a finger to his lips in thought. "We had a similar idea. The patient who came to us, Sigga, ranted about a violent madman who tried to steal her baby. We thought perhaps some sort of psychotropic drug might be to blame for the unfortunate incident, but the illness had no resemblance to such a thing, at least not in its first stages."

A cold ball formed in the pit of my stomach. "First stages?"

He nodded, his expression bleak. "One of the few people to survive the plague grew increasingly irrational and violent, until, by necessity, we had to isolate him in an armoured room. By the time the Yard sent me on my mission, he required extensive personal restraints to prevent him from harming himself or others."

We all sat in silence. Mattea's description of the carnage at the village flashed in memory and my imagination continued with what would have happened if McKenzie had reached this stage of the illness.

Mattea sat up. "Wait, what did you say the woman's name was?"

He blinked. "Sigga. Sigga Bursisdottir, I'm quite certain. Why, do you know of her?"

Chapter Thirty

When we reached the village, Mattea insisted on waiting for us at last camp. "I'm not afraid to admit I don't want to see all that again. My nightmares are vivid enough, thank you very much."

With reluctance, I agreed. "Keep vigilant, though. We'll be back before dusk falls."

She snorted at that. "That's a long day, by any measure. I'll keep the fire lit. Maybe I'll write an epic saga about the whole thing to keep my mind occupied."

With a half-smile, I nodded. "I'll look forward to your performance of it tonight."

In silence, both Sir Algernon and I trudged to the village in question. With extreme trepidation, I approached the first cottage, its door swinging open in the chilly breeze. A hint of misty rain caressed my face as I walked in. The smell didn't seem strong at first. I had hoped the rot had progressed enough to be less noxious, but as soon as Sir Algernon came in, the fumes assaulted me. I staggered from the impact and pushed the erstwhile traveller aside as I ran out.

With several gulps of fresh air, I calmed myself and my stomach. When I re-entered the cottage, Sir Algernon's face tinged green. That he wasn't unaffected helped salve my embarrassment for my reaction. Still, we had work to do.

I took samples of everything I could find, explaining to Sir Algernon why and what we looked for. He pointed out several things for me to add to my collection, including what looked like their last meal. I gingerly took bits of the meat, turnip, and mushroom from the plate before moving to the next house. As I sampled, I deliberately did not examine the woman whose head lay on her arms at the table, after Mattea's most graphic description of her. I didn't need to watch her rotting bits fall off into her intestinal soup. Mattea had already seared that image in my mind, along with other horrifying incidents.

I pulled up happy thoughts as I made my collections, veering my memory from the horrid parts. Laughing with Paolo on a beach in aboriginal Australia or climbing a mountain in the pre-Columbian Andean Range. The day I gave birth to our son as we vacationed in modern Iceland. I had to argue with the doctor to name our son Alessandro Firestone. He urged us to name him in the Icelandic tradition, Alessandro Paolosson. Paolo, just to be contrary, had championed this notion, until I reminded him I'd just given birth, and if he argued further with me, I'd tuck the little bugger back in and walk away.

This made me chuckle, even as I scraped blood from the doorway of a new cottage. Sir Algernon flashed me a quizzical glance, but I shook my head. My memories remained my own, and I refused to dilute them by sharing them with a stranger.

Little Alessandro's smiling baby face floated in my memory as I canvassed the next place. He'd grown to a sturdy toddler, and we took him on some of the safer missions.

Safer. What a laughable concept.

I walked outside of the latest cottage and gulped fresh air again. This time, it didn't work. I vomited beside the wall on the straggled remains of what had once been someone's garlic crop. The miasma which sprang from that novel mixture made my stomach rebel afresh and added even more to the malodorous mix.

Soon, I had nothing left to heave. With a swish of cool, fresh water from my waterskin, I rinsed my mouth, spit, drank more, and squared my shoulders for the final house.

This last house hit the worst. A child lay amongst the slain, a child about Alessandro's age when he…when he left us. I couldn't do it. I beat a hasty retreat, shoving the bag at Sir Algernon. "You take this one, be a dear? I must…"

I ran outside and knew it for a cowardly retreat. Some Agent I turned out to be, unable even to gather samples to save thousands of lives. I swallowed several times, trying without success to pull the happy memories back into my mind's eye. The laughing times, the romantic times, the adventurous times. Any of those will do. Anything but the bright red spots and the rasping, dry breath of my dying son. Anything, anything at all. Please, all that I ever held holy, let me banish this dreadful ghost from my mind, just for this day. I'll promise the world on a platter.

My attempts at staving off the panic attack failed miserably. The sweat dripped into my eyes, making them burn. I sat against a stump someone had used for chopping firewood. Splinters lie around, forming pale patterns against the green grass. They swirled in my vision as it grew foggy, making me dizzy and faint. Pick one and stare at the details. Pick a second one. Find a third. A fourth and a fifth, and my breathing came back under control. I mopped the sweat from my face. I pulled myself to my feet twice before I succeeded.

When Sir Algernon emerged, he handed me the bag in silence. I nodded thanks and secured it to my belt. "Shall we search the village for other items? After, we complete this task, we can check the cave."

Whatever gods might have listened, they granted me a reprieve for the rest of the day. Perhaps it helped that I didn't gaze upon any more stricken children. Regardless, we collected fungus, stones, food, dung, plants, and fabric from the village and the cave without further attack on my psyche.

When we returned to our campsite, however, Mattea had disappeared.

I'd had just about enough of this day. I crossed my arms and surveyed the site. "Bloody Hell. Why would she wander off?"

"Agent Firestone, I believe I have discovered signs of a struggle. Do examine this spot." Sir Algernon pointed to scuffmarks in the dirt to one side. "Unless she decided to entertain herself this afternoon by dancing an Irish jig, I do believe the lovely lass has been taken against her express wishes."

"Bloody, bloody, bloody Hell and an order of Timbits. Right. There's her pack. Gather what we can, and we'll track down her kidnappers. They'd better be ready for a fight. I've had enough of this crap. My patience had never been strong to begin with and this day sapped the rest of it away like mist in the sun."

Sir Algernon watched as I shoved several items into a bag before I swivelled and glared at him. "Well? Have you something to add? Or are you going to stare as if you've just been informed your prom date worked the royal court as a noted courtesan?"

He put his hands up to ward her away. "Oh, no, my dear woman. I wouldn't add a single thing. In truth, I'm quite in agreement of your assessment of the situation. I simply don't believe I'd wish your temper upon my worst adversary, not in a month of Sundays."

Despite myself, I chuckled. "Well, you can be taught, I'll give you that. And please call me Wilda. The Agent Firestone crap is much too formal at this point."

If I'd expected him to offer a nickname for himself, he left me disappointed. This made me smile even more. The Brits acted so hopelessly stodgy with formality. At least Sir Algernon's intransigence seemed to come from a kinder place than Lady Prissy-Pants insistence had.

Once we packed the camp, we followed the churned earth back along the beach. When I realised it would lead us right back to the broch, I found more creative ways to curse. From his blush, I'm certain I scandalised

Sir Algernon's tender ears. Excellent. I cursed more, just to see his colour shift through several shades of red. His ears darkened first, then his cheeks. The progression distracted me from worrying about Mattea.

Chapter Thirty-One

As we walked back to the cursed broch, I told Sir Algernon of the paper Mattea found. "Therefore, I theorise Josephus sought his ancestors in Mali, but I have no idea why. The other trips to here and to Maine seem to correspond with genealogical research for each traveller as well. But what would McKenzie do with a baby? We found no one of that age in the village. Did you see…a baby in that last cottage?"

He shook his head. "A toddler, yes, but not a baby as you described. It might be the child wandered off in the chaos and lay somewhere in the surrounding countryside, hidden from our sight. On the other hand, he may have taken the baby himself, secreting her someplace safe. He may have wished to bring the child forward in time for his own opaque purpose."

I snapped my fingers. "That's it! The genealogical record must stop here, and he sought to save the child by bringing her forward rather than dying! But no, that would mean she wouldn't bear descendants, leading to him. She must have lived regardless, in this time, long enough to have children of her own. Damn it all to Hell. This is getting too complex."

"As you say, my dear, as you say. Now, if he sought to save this child from the slaughter, the slaughter which wouldn't have occurred if he hadn't travelled in the first place, would that be a possibility?"

I grabbed the branch from a bush as we passed, breaking it off. After I pulled leaves from the branch one by one, venting my frustration,

I replied. "I hate the Grandfather Paradox. It's possible he learned of the slaughter and came back to prevent it somehow, not realising he'd be the perpetrator. But what would he hope to do? Time is time. The time stream must be kept complete, no matter the tragedy. The Agency pounds the Maxim into our heads."

"But he didn't train as an Agent, dear lady Wilda. He travelled rogue, as I did, and perhaps sent with a less noble purpose."

I stopped in my tracks. "Sent? You believe someone sent him?"

He nodded, waiting for me to continue walking. "I do. Do you not believe it odd each traveller had the monetary wherewithal for such expensive journeys? Did they strike you as a wealthy individuals? Three trips, particularly from a rogue portal, would require a great deal of money, would it not? If, however, some individual had sponsored their costs, or sent them on a mission…their own purpose would be secondary pursuits to the main mission."

I stepped forward, intrigued by the idea. "Hmm. It's a possibility worth considering. Let me ponder for a while."

The wind brought sea spray as it whistled across the beach to the seaside track we walked. Somewhere in the distance, a cow mooed. I hadn't considered the theory that each man had travelled on a larger task. Would the purpose be to find something for biological warfare against travellers? Or had that simply been an unfortunate side effect? Who would bankroll such a mission? Terrorists? New Americans? As far as I'd heard, no religion had set up a restriction or commandment against travelling, though who knew what the Bible-thumpers south of the border believed nowadays. The technology might be as yet too new to offend priests and prophets. However, perhaps I shouldn't underestimate the power of the easily offended, much less of religious zealots.

I massaged my temples. I needed Mattea's clear insight. She had a fantastic habit of cutting through the crap to find the kernel of the problem while my mind swirled around the fog of possibilities until it became lost in the chaos.

Worry for my friend plagued me again. I hoped her captors treated her well, for their sake. I harboured little doubt the new earl, one Rögnvaldr according to our briefing, hosted her now. It might be necessary to don the vǫlva persona once again to spring her. This time, however, I'd try to be more circumspect in my prophecy and not make myself a prisoner again.

With a glance at Sir Algernon, I considered sending him back with the information and samples we had gathered so far. However, that tiny seed of doubt still niggled at my conscience. He may still turn out to be a consummate player, someone in the employ of another interest. I couldn't demand his identification as an officer of the Metropolitan Police. He'd not be foolish enough to have brought such an anachronistic thing with him.

Still, if the new earl captured me, we'd need someone on the outside to spring us both. I turned to my companion, ready to ask him, when the sound of running feet made us both turn around.

A child, perhaps ten years old, ran toward us. Beneath the rags and the grime, they might be male or female. The tangle of hair streaming behind them held no clues and they seemed too young to show any defining characteristics. When they reached us, out of breath, they flung themselves at my feet, their arms entwining my legs.

They pleaded in a hoarse voice. "Please, please, take me with you! Please, there's a monster. I ran, but the monster took everyone."

I glanced at Sir Algernon but received only a confused shrug. With strong arms, he hefted the child into his arms. "Never fear, my dear child. We head to the broch, where the earl lives. He shall see you fed. And cleaned. Definitely cleaned." He wrinkled his nose at her strong odour. Yes, the delicate features must be female.

Monster. Did she mean McKenzie? Had she been living rough for so many days? On each of our trips, we tried to arrive shortly after each traveller left, but the Agency didn't have precise dates. This trip, it seemed, we'd gotten closer by a good measure. It might have been a week since McKenzie left this time.

For a resident of twelfth century Orkney, living rough wouldn't be as dreadful or unpleasant as someone from modern Toronto would find it. They already knew how to hunt, trap, and guard themselves from wild beasts and the weather. The biggest difference would be the lack of a family to comfort them, to protect them at night, and regular food.

She must have lived through an atrocious experience.

I hoped she remembered enough to give us some clues.

*****

As we searched for a place to camp that night, the child lost some of her wariness. Once we found a sheltered spot, ducked her in the stream to her vociferous protests, and gotten some dried fish and bread into her gullet, she choked out her tale. It took a great deal of cajoling, comforting, and some sweet songs, but she told us of the Night of Madness, as she'd dubbed it.

"My name is Tóka. My parents and I live…lived…in the village by the river. The red man came one night, looking for my cousin. I don't understand why he wanted her. She's just a baby! All she does is cry and poop." The girl stared into her cup for a moment before continuing.

"He took her away. I don't know where. But I hope she's safe wherever she is. Her mother left with her and never returned."

Sir Algernon interrupted her recount. "What did her mother look like? Do you remember her name?"

The girl glanced up. "I called her Auntie Sigga. She was tall and dark, very pretty."

I glanced at my companion, and he nodded. This must fit the description of the woman who he'd discovered in modern London. I gestured to Tóka to continue.

"Several weeks passed. We never saw Auntie Sigga or the baby again, but the strange man kept returning to our village. He wandered the bogs, poking around and looking for something."

I cocked my head. "Did he tell you what he searched for?"

She took a deep breath. "A mushroom. We're not supposed to touch it, but he wanted it. My brother said the mushroom would kill me. Witches use it for spells or curses. It's an evil fungus."

An evil fungus? May my ancestors help us from superstitious natives. I clenched my jaw. "Can you describe this fungus? Or show us where it grows? It's very important that we get some."

She glanced between us before giving a shy nod. "There's some in the bog still, near my…near where I lived."

Her eyes welled up with tears, and I gathered her in my arms. "Shh, child, the madman is long dead. He cannot hurt you now."

A suspicion grew in my mind, one which might make sense if I found this evil fungus. Still, to ask the child to return to the scene of such tragic violence would be cruel. I glanced at Sir Algernon, who seemed to have the same idea. "Perhaps you described where this particular specimen grows, my child. Can you draw a map? I might go fetch a bit and bring it back, to see if I chose the correct item."

She shook her head in confusion. "Sir…uh, Algautr, the child is likely not literate in the slightest. A map would be well beyond her knowledge. Be reasonable."

He huffed slightly. "I only wished to spare the child further trauma."

"I'm well aware. However, I need to decide which is more urgent. Saving Mattea or getting a piece of that specimen. In the grand scheme, I must choose the latter." I held Tóka out to look into her eyes. "Tóka, I understand you're scared to return to the bog, but can you do it, just this once, for me? It's important we find that mushroom. Someone's life depends on it. I promise, I'll be with you the entire time, and won't let anyone hurt you. Then we can leave straight away and head to the broch, where I'll make sure you have a bed, warm clothes, and a fire. Will you do that for me?"

Sir Algernon crossed his arms. "If I might, I would continue in an attempt to free your younger companion. Or do you prefer to have me along in case of marauding Norsemen?"

I narrowed my eyes at him, unable to determine if he spoke with flippancy, sarcasm, or just cluelessness. I decided the latter to be the most likely choice. "I prefer we both accompany our young charge. The more protection she has, the better, don't you think?"

He harrumphed a few times but didn't argue.

In the night, Tóka screamed in her nightmares. Her skin soaked in sweat, I held her close until she quieted into a troubled slumber. I tried hard to shove away the burning memory of Alessandro's dying screams. They wormed their way into my mind and soul, shattering the careful armour I'd constructed over the last thirty years. Screams tore away each layer, one by one, until my soul lay bare and quivering from terror.

Chapter Thirty-Two

When I woke the next morning, it took a while for me to recover my mental strength. I masked the time by groaning and complaining about my hip and sleeping on cold ground. After several missteps and attempts, I'd erected makeshift walls against my past.

We trekked back toward the village of carnage, my trepidation rising as we grew closer. Tóka, never talkative to begin with, grew more silent with each league. When it came into sight, she tugged my arm to the left, pointing to the land behind the village. I nodded to Sir Algernon, and we followed her lead into the boglands.

Scottish bogs could be treacherous. I suppose all bogs, by their very nature, would be treacherous, but the dim light of an overcast sky, and the false firmness of undulating landscape made this one seem more dangerous than most. Not that I made a habit of walking in bogs.

With each step, I tested the ground before putting weight on my foot. The child must know a safe path through, for she almost scampered between the sawgrass tussocks and dips. We almost lost sight of her on more than one occasion. We came to a low area filled with bracken, bushes, and a few spots of a dark blue, sinister-looking fungus.

Just as we reached this specimen, as I opened my bag to take back a sample, the sun cut through the clouds. As the sunbeam sought the fungus like an angelic clarion, it glowed bright blue, almost phosphorescent in the sunlight.

In an instant, the sunbeam disappeared, but the fungus still glowed. A raven crowed in the distance. The haunting sound made me shiver.

I stared at the fungus and took a piece of my cloak to grab it. If this fungus infected McKenzie, touching it might be dangerous, and I couldn't take that chance. Tasting it would be even worse, but it looked familiar. Where had I seen it before?

As I broke off one piece, the stench hit me in the face. The smell of rotten cheese or something. Maybe old laundry. I packed it into my collection bag, I scoured my memory. Where had I heard about mushrooms? I hated the things, so I wouldn't eat them. I pictured the menu at the Poké Bowl, the restaurant next to my shop. It seemed like forever since I'd enjoyed a meal with Nami, Reuben, and Devin. They'd had something new on their menu, something Bryonie had mentioned…

Tóka's cry brought me back to the present. I glanced around but didn't see her. When I stood, I spied both the child and the man, and the latter struggled with something.

As I picked my way toward them, Sir Algernon's voice took on a note of panic. Stupid man must have gotten himself stuck in the bog. He stood waist-deep in creeping muck, looking utterly disgusted. Tóka held tight to his arm, but the child lacked the leverage to pull him out. She only kept him from sinking farther into the muck.

I put my hands on my hips. "Well, here's another nice mess you've gotten yourself into, Ollie."

"Do hurry, my good lady, there's a dear. I don't relish such an ignominious termination."

I searched the surrounding ground for a solid foothold. Spying a flat rock, I perched on the edge and stretched out both hands. "Get a good grip. No, idiot, hold on to my wrists, and I'll grasp yours. There you go. Now, rock with me and lean into it on the count of three. One, two, *three*.

Again. One, two *three*. A third time. One, two, *three*. Can you get your foot free yet? One, two, *three*."

He pulled his foot out of the sucking mud and get it to the rock. I leaned back, putting my back into the struggle, and he dragged himself out of the bog. I staggered back, trying to regain my balance. It took longer than it should, but I found my equilibrium.

Sir Algernon studied his mud-covered leggings and leather shoes with disgusted disdain. "How perfectly revolting. I am eternally glad this is not my—"

"Algautr! Remember where you are."

"Oh…uh, glad this is not my home. Farther south, yes, indeed, I live in a much cleaner place far to the south of this island."

I rolled my eyes at his clumsy prevarication and stalked away. At least we had what we came for; the fungus specimen nestled in my collection bag along with all the others. Since we had reasonable intelligence that this might be the trigger, we might return to our present time.

Once we retrieved Mattea.

Once again, I considered sending Sir Algernon back with the samples, but I still didn't quite trust him enough. He still might be a mole of some sort. Too much relied upon the successful mission to entrust someone who had come here illegally and through a rogue portal, even if I believed him to be of the Metropolitan Police. Besides, he couldn't even keep from falling into a bog. I did, however, give him a small sample of the same evil blue fungus, so he had something to bring to his own scientists. Even if he hadn't told me the whole truth, the more scientists working on the problem, the better.

Would I hold the same level of distrust for someone professing to be of the Toronto police, or somewhere else in the United States of Canada? If he professed to be from New America, I wouldn't even trust him to watch over me as I slept. That part of the continent which remained after the secession had been left to the isolationist conservative religious zealots, from all the news reports. They'd built an enormous wall around their entire nation and rarely spoke to the rest of the world. I wondered what would happen when the Texas oil fields ran dry, as Alaska had seceded to Canada. However, that wasn't my problem.

At the moment, my first problem was Mattea.

After Sir Algernon did his best to scrape the worst of the muck from his clothing, and amidst his constant grumbles, we trekked back along the beach. We moved with alacrity, only stopping when we must for bodily necessities. Sir Algernon and Tóka ate as we walked, but I wasn't hungry. I had grown to know this stretch of track too well and would rather not walk it again.

Two days later, we reached the broch. We approached just as the sun hit its zenith, and for once, the wind had stilled, and the sun shone bright. I almost had a spring in my step as we approached. The temperature even approached a high enough level that I took off my fur-lined cloak. In a pinch, I'd even describe the day as summer. Sort of.

Before approaching the front gate, I turned to both my companions. "In this keep, I am known as a vǫlva, someone who can see the future."

Tóka's eyes grew wide. "You are a vǫlva? Truly? I am so sorry to have touched you, honoured one!" She threw herself at my feet in abject genuflection. Embarrassed, I crouched to pull her to her feet. "Child, none of that. Yes, I know things about the future, but you need not abase yourself to anyone. Do you understand me?"

She shook her head but remained standing. I glanced at Sir Algernon. He regarded me with calculated assessment. "Yes, I can see how you might intimidate with such a persona. You can rely upon my assistance in your clever ruse, my dear lady. For your young companion's sake, I do hope you are successful in your endeavour. How may I best ensure your victory?"

With a deep sigh for his annoying level of verbosity, I turned back to the broch. "I'm not certain yet. The old Earl was a right bastard, make no mistake. He imprisoned me for being a valuable asset as a vǫlva, and I only escaped when the coup occurred. I've not met the new earl."

"That would be Earl Rögnvaldr, from my studies, is that correct?"

"Earl Rögnvaldr Kali Kolsson, that's the lad. Half the earldom had been granted to him by rights through his mother for the last seven years, but the prior Earl, his cousin, had taken possession of all the islands anyhow. I seem to remember Paul survived the coup, but not what happened to him afterward."

Tóka looked between me and Sir Algernon, her voice a whisper. "How do you know all this? Do you also have a *vǫlva*?"

Sir Algernon smiled down at the child and patted her head in a horribly awkward avuncular manner. "I have my own vǫlva, child. I asked her before I travelled here."

True enough, as far as that goes. At least it offered a reasonable explanation. No need for the child to grow frightened of us at this point.

"Right. Shall we ask for entry?"

In a misplaced show of ridiculous chivalry, he offered his arm. "Let us do so, good lady!"

I rolled my eyes and did *not* take his arm. Instead, I took Tóka's hand and marched off, trusting him to follow. He harrumphed a few times, but his footsteps echoed on the flagstones.

Chapter Thirty-Three

The guard went inside to inquire about our entrance. While we waited for the verdict, I squeezed Tóka's hand to reassure her. She'd turned back into the terrified mouse as soon as we approached the well-armed guard. Sir Algernon stood behind her, or I was afraid she'd have bolted into the hills, and we'd never find her again. My stomach flipped several times, nervous about our reception.

The guard returned with a smile on his face and escorted us into the hall. I almost didn't recognise the place. Where the previous incarnation of this room had been bare and gloomy, now three times as many torches, even at the height of daylight, made the room bright and cheery. Vivid tapestries had been hung on the walls, with scenes of action and heroism. One in beautiful shades of blue and red caught my eye as I passed, and I resolved to examine it later, if I had the chance.

The new earl sat at the head of the hall behind his long table. He looked younger than Earl Paul had, with light chestnut hair and a medium build. He stood as we got close. "Welcome, welcome. Do come in. I understand you have visited this hall before, under Earl Paul, is that not correct?"

While I glanced around for Mattea, I found Káta, her grin fit to crack her face. I smiled back, but still searched for my friend. Absently, I remembered the earl waited on my answer. "Yes, Earl Rögnvaldr, though the previous earl did not consult me on his decision to keep me here."

He nodded, a look of embarrassed sympathy on his face. "I understand that. Káta gave me the details of the unfortunate incident. Will you accept my apologies on behalf of my cousin? I would not have an honoured vǫlva angry with me for any reason, especially one so talented."

So talented? Then someone must have informed him of my words to Paul. The coup had involved beacon fires. I'd recalled such detail and couched it in the language of my prophecy. The warning had been vague enough to keep Earl Paul from mounting an effective defence against the midnight attack, as evidenced by the new earl standing before me. I bowed my head once in vague acknowledgement. "I am here in search of my friend and companion. Her name is Mattildr. Have you perchance seen a young woman, about two handspans taller than me, and in the middle of her fourth decade?"

His eyes widened. "Oh! Oh, yes, of course. She is helping with some of our children now. Sigurd, go fetch the young lady, would you?" He gestured to one of the younger guards, who skittered away through one of the side doors.

The relief flooded my body, and I almost lost strength in my legs.

"Now, can I offer you food and drink, as your guest-right? And for your companions?" He raised his eyebrows in a strong hint for introductions.

I turned to Sir Algernon. "This is Algautr, a fellow traveller. He came from the mainland in search of a friend." I pulled Tóka in front of me, though she refused to release her vice grip on my legs. She peered up at the earl and then buried her face in my knees. We'd washed her, but her hair remained tangled, as she wouldn't still long enough to brush it.

"We found this child on the road. Her family's been killed. Would you, by chance, have a place for her to stay? She's a good child, from a farming village down the coast." I clenched my jaw. "There is evidence of violence there. You might send some guards to investigate. I don't believe the aggressor remains in the area, but the place needs some…attention. There may be another child, a baby, lost in the area." I could do little else for the child. If McKenzie's meddling had changed her timeline, then so be it. Somehow, the time stream would compensate. She'd have been found by another village nearby, or by the guards from the broch. Somehow, she'd survive and grow up to be McKenzie's ancestor, even without her mother. At least she wouldn't remember the carnage.

I swallowed back the memory of the smell of the village and commanded my stomach to behave before smiling up at the Earl. He'd already dispatched another guard to fetch a nurse when Mattea entered.

She clutched me in a fierce hug. Tóka moved aside at the last minute before she got crushed. The earl beamed at us as if he'd just witnessed a miracle.

My stomach continued to rebel, despite my happiness at seeing Mattea. I clenched my jaw again to staunch the nausea, but it still bubbled up. Trickles of sweat formed on my forehead, and I wiped it away with confusion.

Mattea's face swirled before me, as did Sir Algernon's concerned visage. When I fell to the ground, Tóka held my head so it didn't crack against the flagstones. I tried to speak, but my words only came out in a mumble. The swirling wouldn't settle and then the grey closed in.

My senses abandoned me. Flashes of Earl Rögnvaldr's worried face, Mattea, Sir Algernon, and even Tóka swam in and out of my view, interspersed with grey and swirling chaos. Cold compresses dripped down my face while heavy blankets made me swim in sweat. I know I spoke, but I couldn't tell you what I said. My body grew wracked with pain from constant dry heaves. I faded into a world of memory, a trip I'd avoided so many times in the past.

I turned to Paolo and surveyed the landscape from Zijin Mountain. The twinkling torches below sparkled in the morning dawn as the sun drowned them in brilliance. The Yangtze River shone in the glare, blinding them both until they shaded their eyes. Jiangning had always been a lovely city…from afar. Now that the First Opium War had ended, the Agency had deemed it safe for travelling, as long as we left by 1855, a good five years ahead. We had no wish to be subject to illness, nor become embroiled in the violent politics of the Taiping Heavenly Kingdom rebellion

This period represented a calm lull between the atrocities of one war, which led to the outrages of the next.

Ostensibly Protestant missionaries, both Paolo and I packed translations of the Bible in our bags. I'd argued against bringing our son, Alessandro, but Paolo had insisted. "How is he to learn to be an Agent, and follow in our footsteps, if you coddle him at every turn? The lad must learn to blend into new cultures. If he learns this young, he will have no problem when he gets older. Isn't that right, my clever lad?"

He'd addressed this last comment to the young lad in question, not yet aged three. He smiled at his father and laughed at his funny face. Paolo had waggled his eyebrows and wrinkled his nose as Wilda sighed in long-suffering impatience.

"He'll learn nothing if we don't get on with it, Paolo. Come, I want to settle into the Mission before darkness falls, and we still have a great deal of walking before we even get to that village. It looks close, but at least a couple hours' walk lies before us to get to the south gate. Unless you've learned to fly when I wasn't looking?"

"Your mother's being a silly hen, isn't she, Alessandro, my lad?"

I huffed and adjusted the straps to my pack "I'll thank you not to denigrate me to the child, Paolo, there's a good man."

With measured steps, I walked away from Paolo, carrying Alessandro in my arms. The child reached for his father in protest, throwing me off balance. I cursed under my breath and adjusted him. Ungrateful brat. When Paolo got into this mood, he became insufferable, and I had no desire to let him teach such habits to our son.

Within a few minutes, Paolo had collected himself and caught up with us. "Wilda, dear, I do apologise. I shan't do such again, I promise you."

He would, and we both knew it. I also knew I'd forgive him now and the next time. I turned with a half-smile on my lips. He kissed them as soon as I turned, startling Alessandro. He whined. "Mama, I want down. Can I walk? Please?"

I set him down reluctantly, holding fast to his tiny hand. While the path seemed well-maintained and wide, as many people walked these high tracks, I didn't want him running off into the trees and tumbling down a mountainside. I already regretted letting Paolo change my mind about bringing him.

The rest of the walk delighted all three of us. The day grew bright and warm. No clouds marred the sky as we descended into the valley below and approached the impressive city curtain walls, both outer and inner. Another two walls surrounded the city centre and the palace, but we didn't need to travel there.

Massive, blocky, stones surrounded the ancient city to over twelve metres. The eastern gate, one of thirteen around the outer wall, loomed as we came close. Alessandro stopped his fussing as we joined other people walking into the city as the press of people grew claustrophobic when we passed under the gate.

We weren't supposed to be here. Missionaries must work in five coastal cities until the Second Opium War in 1860. Nanjing stood a good three hundred klicks inland from Shanghai, and our supervisor wanted specific data from this area. However, we had deemed it a minor infraction compared to the alternative.

The Agency had begun a new program they called "panoculations" to guard us from the most virulent of local diseases. However, its purpose had been more to protect people in the past from our modern diseases. Any reciprocal protection still needed testing and refinement. Therefore, we'd rather take our chances on being politely deported than dead of the plague. There remained the chance the authorities would execute us for spreading Christianity, but since we didn't intend on spreading any Christianity, but merely pretending to the role, we should be safe enough. I detested the thought of converting people content with their own belief systems to a foreign one in the guise of *doing them good.*

What we hadn't counted on, what none of us could have counted on, was that the dates of the plague were incorrectly reported. At the very least, the plague hadn't been recognised when it first showed. It shouldn't have been active in Nanjing in 1850 when it originated in Yunnan, twenty-five hundred klicks away, forty-five years later.

But time research remained an ongoing process, and we were still in the early days of the craft. Agents had discovered many historical facts to be false, exaggerated, wholly mythological, or horribly underestimated.

I glanced at the harried woman next to me, dragging her five young children in a line behind her, like dark-haired ducks. They shuffled their feet, which is what had caught my attention. Their exhaustion was apparent in the lines on their drawn faces, even the children. Though I searched nearby faces, I saw no man nearby, no husband, but she shuffled off. I stared after her, my mind trying to catalogue the marks on her face and arms. My memory recognised those marks. We'd been schooled to look for those marks as part of our Agent training.

I held Alessandro closer. "Paolo, we need to leave. Now."

"What? Whatever are you on about, Wilda? We need to cross the city to get to the Mission. We're expected by sundown. Our papers were sent ahead—"

"No, Paolo, we must leave. Immediately."

I grabbed his sleeve, but he pulled away. "Wilda, what the blue devil has gotten into you? You know how important this mission is."

"Important enough to lose our lives?"

He retreated in confusion, looking around us. "I see no violence. No danger. Wilda, are you well? You've gone ashen. Here, let me take the child. I'll find a place where you can sit. There are steps there, near the gate."

I slapped at my arm in horror. It itched. I examined it for flea bites, but I saw nothing. At this point, I didn't trust my own sight. I couldn't have mistaken those buboes. Black, pus-filled circles of death. I shivered and felt my forehead, certain I'd already contracted the disease, silly as that sounded.

Had we come close to anyone on our journey from the portal? We'd journeyed two days and we'd walked along several groups over that time. Some had dogs. Dogs had fleas. Fleas bit people, transferring the bubonic plague. I could see the page of our medical textbook as if it were here, the graphic, colour pictures seared into my mind.

I felt up and down my arms, feeling for lumps. I probed my armpits, to find any hard masses, but found none. I dripped with sweat, but that might be the heat of the day and my sudden distress. Paolo had pulled out his canteen and tin cup, pouring a measure for me. "Take it, Wilda, do drink up. I'll pour you another. The canteen kept it rather cool, truly." He poured another splash on his handkerchief and placed it against my head.

"The woman, with the children. They walked next to us…"

He looked about as if he expected a family to jump upon his back. "Where?"

"No, they're long gone now. But I saw marks on her skin. Spots. Black spots."

"Like pox?"

"Like buboes."

My words finally penetrated his worry. He sat on the step next to me and took a drink for himself. "Bloody Hell and an order of Timbits. Now I see why you want to leave."

I turned to him, incredulous. "Why I *want* to leave? Don't you mean, you see why we must leave immediately?"

"Of course, of course, dear. Let's do this. I'll take you and Alessandro into the countryside, to a small village, safe from the pestilence of the city. Then I'll go fetch the scrolls Campbell needs and collect you on my way back from the portal. I should be able to complete the mission on my own. In fact, it might make things more efficient. I know you wanted a holiday in a new city, but—"

I stood, my eyes wide. "How can you even consider staying? Don't you remember the history? Bubonic plague, wiping out eighty thousand people in Yunnan alone!"

"Be reasonable, Wilda! And do moderate your tone, there's a lass. That's Yunnan, half a country away, and fifty years from now. This must be just an isolated case."

I moderated my voice, but only to make my point more urgent. "There's no such thing as an isolated case of bubonic plague, Paolo."

Alessandro burst out in tears, reacting to the tension and anger. I picked him up absently and rubbed his back. He whined and wiggled, making him difficult to hold. With apprehension, I checked under his shirt.

Tiny red dots showed on his arms.

Flea bites.

As fast as we rushed out of the city and marched back to the portal, I hadn't been fast enough. Despite my modern medical knowledge, I had no way of curing the plague. Not in nineteenth century China, in the wilds of Nanjing, trying to find the portal to limp home before my child died.

Neither Alessandro nor Paolo made it back through the portal alive. I could only fashion a travois and drag them back across rough country. Alessandro's final screams echoed in my ears, as they would for many years.

Part V
Chapter Thirty-Four

My brain hurt.

I clenched my jaw against the pain but that only hurt worse. Next, I tried to open my eyes, but either I'd gone blind, or something covered my eyes. I suspected the latter.

My arms wouldn't move, but I twitched my hands. That told me I wore restraints.

I cast my memory back. What had happened? A vague maelstrom of confused images swirled in my mind, unconnected, tragic, nonsensical, and troubling. Flames lit on hill beacons, glowing blue mushrooms, and a massive brick wall were the strongest flashes, but they didn't fit together. The jigsaw seemed broken.

Someone coughed. I tried to speak, but only moaned. However, this brought someone to my side. Mattea's voice sounded calm but worried. "Wilda? Have you woken?"

I meant to say, "Of course, I've woken. I'm not a zombie." It came out, "Ugh." This witty repartee gave no indication that I was not, in fact, a zombie.

Her cool skin touched my arm. I grasped her hand, eliciting a surprised gasp. "Doctor! Doctor, she's awake this time!"

A flurry of activity came to life, with people talking, machinery beeping, and the sound of many hurried footsteps.

"Will you get this stupid cover from my eyes?" sounded more like, "Et...stoop...ayes?"

A male voice responded, "She's trying to speak. Do go easy, my dear Wilda. You've been in a coma for a quite a while. In time, your vocal cords will remember how to form words."

I remembered the voice. I recognised it but couldn't place the reference. More flashes of memory came up, and I shuffled through them like a slideshow, trying to pull up the visual to match the audio. The manner of speaking sounded familiar...there! The pompous, verbose rogue traveller we met in Scotland. Sir Algernon St. Clair. *Bloody git.* Who was he to give me advice? He couldn't even get himself out of a bog.

A person who I presumed had medical authority shooed them out. "Go, at least out of the room. We'll fetch you when she's ready for visitors. Yes, both of you."

I sighed in relief. I didn't yet want to communicate with anyone, much less Sir Algernon, who required a great deal of mental effort just to understand. Still, I hoped he came back through an authorised portal. Since he hadn't died a horrible death, I presumed as much.

With the non-medical personnel cleared from the room, those remaining fell into a routine of tests, commands, and checks. They left the cloth over my eyes, but ran my body through a series of exercises, moving each arm and leg.

They poked me with sharp objects and asked if I felt them. "Of course, I bloody felt that! That hurt! When can I take this cloth from my eyes? I want to see."

"Soon, Agent Wilda. Your reintroduction must be circumspect."

For a moment, I imagined Sir Algernon had snuck back into the room, but I sensed a pompous doctor, rather than the pompous police officer. I growled at him.

The doctor spoke as he moved around the room, telling me to point to where I thought he stood. I wished my pointing conveyed sarcasm, but even my considerable creativity failed at such a task.

I grew tired despite having just woken. My skin itched and my full bladder needed emptying. "I need to pee. Help me up."

I struggled against the restraints. They'd re-attached them after checking each limb. "Stay prone, Agent Wilda. You're restrained for your safety for now, but we'll free you soon. We've hooked you to a catheter. You can just let go with your bladder."

Wrinkling my nose, I tried. I really did. I'd never been able to use a catheter, even when I'd been in mandated bedrest after Alessandro's birth.

The thought of Alessandro halted my impatience and took my breath away. China seemed so recent, so strong, I burst into tears. The doctors scrambled, unaware of the reason for my outburst. I couldn't wipe the tears or snot from my face, so I coughed, almost choking on my phlegm. Still, I couldn't stop. A dam had burst, the fragile shell which had shielded me from the brunt of my grief. The barrier shattered into a million sharp pieces, raking cuts into every part of my soul. The death of a thousand cuts, leaving my psyche bleeding to death.

Nami would have been proud. I wished she sat beside me.

A nurse used a syringe to clean my nose, but it filled right back up again. My throat grew hoarse from wailing. The doctor ordered a sedative, which inspired me to pull myself together. I would not submit to a forced unconsciousness, not with this fresh pain running rampant in my mind. I would lose all vestige of sanity if forced to sleep with Alessandro's death so raw.

"No, I refuse! You will not force me to sleep!"

The doctor must have paused, as all noise ceased. My breath shuddered as I continued sobbing, but in a much subdued tone. "Agent Wilda, you must remain calm, then. We can't have you so upset. This extreme emotion will harm and delay your healing."

"I'll be fine. Just leave me alone for a while. Or send in Mattea. She calms me."

A few of them held a whispered conference before the door shut. A minute later, someone took my hand. "Mattea?"

"Yes, you silly woman. I'm here. What the Hell did you say to the doctor? He looked ready to cry."

"Tell him to join the club."

"You look rather rough. Here, let me wipe your face. Do you need to blow?"

She held something to my nose, and I let loose a honking blast. I almost apologised for the snotball she received, but I figured after the camel, nothing else would compare.

"Eww. Thanks for that gift. I'll treasure this forever."

Grateful for the normality in her voice, I responded, "You're most welcome. Don't say I never gave you anything."

"Want to tell me what happened? I've never seen you cry."

I didn't mask the resignation and exhaustion in my voice as my breath caught in a final sob. "Nothing. I'm just tired and hurting."

She made a noncommittal sound of acknowledgement without agreement. However, she didn't press, for which I remained grateful. "So, I'm sure you want to hear what happened. What's the last thing you remember?"

I scoured my brain for an answer. "I remember a bog. A village. Horrid deaths. Oh, I remember coming back to the broch and seeing you. After that, my recollection's a blur. Memories. Things I'd rather not have relived."

"Hmm. That's about when you collapsed, so that makes sense. You burned with fever and sweats. Sir Algernon convinced Earl Rögnvaldr to supply us horses and we got you to the portal within the hour. Good thing, too. We got you straight to the traveller's hospital and into care."

I swallowed. I needed the answer, though I really didn't want to know. "How long?"

"About three weeks. We weren't certain you'd make it, but evidently, you lacked one of the essential ingredients for the full plague."

"So, the mushroom turned out to be the vector? The girl had been right?"

The smile came clear in her tone. "Partially. It took a partnership between both the British and Canadian scientists, but they distilled the unique set of circumstances to create the disease.

"The mushroom was the initial vector. Eating the mushroom might make any given person hallucinate or sick. Odds are about even between the two options. However, once the travellers brought the fungus through a rogue portal, the mechanism mutated the mushroom's molecular structure. The illness mutated the spores, turning airborne and deadly. Still, the disease only affected those who had gone through a portal, any portal, probably primed by the same mechanism that mutated the spore."

"But I'd travelled in the past. Why didn't it hit me before?"

"Either you didn't get a strong enough dose with that initial contact, or the earlier portals mechanism worked differently. Perhaps it primed you but didn't get you sick. At least, that's what the doctor here said. When you came near the fungus in Scotland, though, after travelling through a modern portal, all bets were off."

"And you? Sir Algernon?"

"I didn't get exposed in Scotland. You'd already stuffed it in the collection bag. Sir Algernon escaped exposure the first time, as he never met Sigga; his colleagues had. He still had a layer of protection, so to speak."

I considered the implications, the concatenation of events that had resulted in this disaster. "Wait. Why did the travellers bring the mushroom here in the first place? Why had they sought the infernal thing out?"

Mattea didn't answer at first. My skin itched, and I wanted to scratch my arm, but the restraints held me in place. "They haven't shared all the details with me about that, but the rumours in the Agency say there's a smuggling ring for gourmet foodstuffs."

I struggled in vain to sit up. "They're smuggling a deadly disease? Are they mad?"

She placed a hand on my chest. "Stop that! You'll hurt yourself. Just lay down, will you? Or they'll make me leave."

Fuming, I forced myself to relax. I clenched my fists, though. I had to satisfy myself with that.

Mattea patted my fist. "Crap, we need to clip your fingernails. You're cutting your palm. Stop that. There, much better. They smuggled the fungus, not realising it would turn deadly. Besides, non-travellers didn't fall ill. They marketed it to boutique restaurants as a delicacy."

"Seriously? 'Here, try this. This might kill you, but what a way to die?' What the actual fuck?"

Her laugh held and edge of irony. "It worked for fugu, didn't it?"

She had a point. Stupid foodies. How many must die in their pursuit of a titillating gourmet experience? I couldn't believe how banal and ridiculous this had turned out to be.

"Now," she continued, "once the doctors proclaim you ready to be questioned, the Agency will send someone to debrief you. They've done so for both me and Sir Algernon already. Let me tell you, I'm not anxious to repeat the experience. But I told no lies, so you don't have to remember anything to cover for me."

"Did you tell them everything?"

She hesitated. "Everything of relevance."

Which meant she hadn't mentioned her relationship with Wula'mbes. I nodded to convey my understanding. That incident remained none of their business, anyhow, and regulations be damned. You couldn't legislate the human heart.

"All right, I've got to get out of here. I still have paperwork to complete. Oh, and I put down the costume details I remembered, but you'll want to add to them, I'm sure."

"Wait! What about Sir Algernon? Are they prosecuting him for using the rogue portal?"

She let out a bark of laughter. "That one! No, I assured the Agency that neither you nor I would have returned alive without him. That went a long way in alleviating his crimes. He still may get docked a hefty fine, but from what I understand, he can stand the cost. He's thinking about quitting the Metropolitan Police to start Agency training, you know."

That made me chuckle, which turned into a half-hysterical laugh. Mattea laughed with me and when we both ran out of breath, she rose to leave.

"Wait, I have one favour to ask before you leave."

"Sure, Wilda. If it's within my power, I'll do it."

"Get me some coffee? Please?"

Chapter Thirty-Five

It took another week of angry arguments, legal threats, and abject pleading to get the doctor to release me. The Agency had indeed been by several times, with several interrogators, to debrief me and suck me dry of every memory I could relate of the things I found, the people I met, and the historical details they wanted for their database.

I'd almost forgotten that part of being an Agent. The debriefs were brutal. The ones after Mali and Maine had only been stop-gaps, a partial debrief until they had the time to drill deep into my experience. Costume details were the least of it. Food, customs, people, animal fur colour, smells, even the taste of water. How the Hell does one describe the taste of water from one river to the next?

The questioned drained every ounce of precious energy I'd stockpiled as I recovered. The doctors only allowed them in an hour at a time, three hours a day. For once, I felt grateful for their stricture. Still, it would be so wonderful to sleep in my own bed once again. I left Dinah at her boarding for one more night. Dusk already approached, and I didn't want to make another stop. I wanted to get home and collapse on my own bed, with my own comforter. Perhaps I'd throw on an episode of Cracker to get my mind into a sufficiently cynical mood for my re-entry into my old life.

I had to jiggle the key in my door a few times before the lock snapped open. Once I pushed into my flat, I stared at disbelief.

Gone was the neat, spare living room I had left behind, with everything in its place. Instead, a chaos of overturned furniture, ripped chesterfield cushions, and broken glass lie strewn across the room. With a curse, I backed out of the flat and yanked out my mobile. I jammed in 911 while trying to calm my racing heart. A young man in a black hoodie approached as I waited for the operator, but I glared at him until he stared at the sidewalk and hurried past.

The phone crackled and a male voice asked, "Toronto Police and Fire, this is Officer Morris, where is your emergency?"

"I came home, and someone's tossed my flat."

"What's your address?"

I gave him my address and flat number, still trying to get my heartbeat under control. I still hadn't regained all my strength from the coma and had no desire to confront a burglar even if I'd been in excellent condition.

"What's your phone number?"

My anxiety burst into temper. "What the Hell do you need my phone number for? Just send someone over, for my ancestor's sake!"

"I need your phone, ma'am, in case we get disconnected."

"Fine." I gave him the number.

The operator continued, his tone mechanical. "Is he still there?"

I sighed. "I don't know. I didn't go in."

"Are you safe?"

"I'm a middle-aged woman standing alone on a street at night, so you be the judge."

My response didn't rattle him. "How far away are you?"

"I told you, I'm standing just outside on the street."

"Did you see or hear anyone?"

"No." I glanced down the street, but other than a tram blocking traffic, no one walked nearby. In my current paranoid state, I wouldn't have hailed a stranger down for help anyhow.

"What distance are you from your flat?"

"Down the stairs and out the vestibule. Call it thirty metres."

"Remain on the line. We will send someone there. Is anyone injured?"

"No." Right now, I felt frightened, alone, and vulnerable. I hadn't much experience with any of these sensations, and I didn't like them one bit. Anger, my trusty standby, stepped in to take over. How dare someone violate my sanctum? Especially after I'd risked my life on this mission. To come home to this outrage made me want to punch someone.

Footsteps sounded behind me, and I spun, crouching into a martial arts stance despite my bare training in such things. The young lady walked by while texting, not even noticing me or my quasi-threatening pose. I forced myself to breathe slowly. My heart had just about calmed before this, but now returned to its former racing state.

I put the phone back up to my ear, but the operator said nothing. I scanned for an emergency vehicle, squinting at each light I saw. The streetlight above my building had burnt out, but the ones to either side glowed with sulphurous yellow light, illuminating cones in the evening mist. The fog rolled in. Why wouldn't it on this night, of all nights?

A siren wailed in the distance, but I couldn't see the lights. Ah, there they came. Two police cars had just turned the corner. Soon they'd pulled up to my street, and I hurried to meet them.

"Did you call emergency services, ma'am?"

"I did. Someone broke into my flat and trashed the place."

"What's your address? Can you show me some ID?"

I clenched my jaw against a smart answer and pulled out my wallet. I handed it to the officer, a young man with black hair and a chiselled jaw. He examined it and glanced up at the building. "Flat 21, is it? Second floor?"

I nodded, looking up the stairs, which had taken on a sinister veneer since I left my flat. "I don't know if anyone is still there. I left as soon as I saw the destruction."

"Wait here, ma'am, while we clear the flat. We'll tell you what we find."

An obviously junior officer stood with me while the other three walked upstairs, guns drawn, to clear the residence. I tried not to compare their actions to the hundreds of episodes of British detective shows I'd watched. The officer's radio crackled but I couldn't make out the dispatcher's words.

Another siren wailed in the night, but soon faded away.

My mobile buzzed, startling me out of an exhausted trance. I recognised Mattea's name and answered.

"Wilda? I'll be late tomorrow. It looks like someone had fun in my flat today. The place is a mess. And yes, I called the police. They're just arriving now."

My blood grew cold. "They turned my flat, too. Tell your cops about the connection. I'll call the Agency. There's no way this is a coincidence."

I turned to the junior officer, whose nametag read: Monroe. "Officer Monroe, I just spoke to my assistant, Mattea Jardine. She told me her flat had also been broken into. We are both Temporal Agents and we recently returned from a mission together. You'll want to inform your supervisor."

The poor young man looked flustered when I mentioned the Agency, but he flipped open his notepad and began writing. I dialled Agent Pembley's number. His sleepy voice answered but perked up as I explained the situation.

When I'd finished, he thought for a moment before responding. "Agent Firestone, you and Agent Jardine need to come into the Agency. We can put you up in the dorms."

"Are you serious? Those beds are like rocks. After all this, I want to sleep in my own bed."

"I realise it won't be as comfortable as your own place, but I would rather you and your assistant stayed safe tonight."

Granting the wisdom of his recommendation, I sighed. "Fine. I'll give Mattea a call. Expect me in about an hour?" I glanced at Officer Monroe for confirmation, and he nodded. "Do you have toiletries and a change of clothing for us?"

"We keep the necessities on hand for any Agents who need them, Agent Firestone."

"Didn't I tell you to drop the 'Agent Firestone' crap a long time ago?"

He gave a long-suffering sigh. "You did, Wilda. I apologise. Also, when you arrive, I have more information to share."

"Information about the case? Or about my flat?"

"Possibly both."

Chapter Thirty-Six

Clearing the scene with the police took longer than I expected, but after an hour, they let me leave. They'd allowed me inside my flat to check for anything missing, but I noticed nothing. I checked to ensure my ageing answer phone worked. They asked questions about when I left the house, if I knew who did it, or if anyone else had a key. I pointed out the security cameras for the building, but they'd stopped working aeons ago. The supervisor took my Agency credentials and promised a report in the morning. While they said I might stay in the flat that night, I surveyed the damage and decided the dorms would be more restful. Otherwise, I'd be up all night putting things away.

I took an Uber, picked up Mattea, and arrived at the Agency. The concrete block building loomed in the night, forbidding and bereft of elegance. All windows looked dark save one in the upper right corner.

We badged in and climbed to the dorms in the back of the buildings. Each Agent dorm comprised a single bed, a wafer-thin mattress, and a single thin blanket, with a small nightstand of dubious sturdiness, sporting a small lamp. We checked out clothing and toiletries from a basic commissary. The dorms had all the charm of a prison room with none of the fascinating roommates.

Mattea and I shuffled through the motions of getting toothpaste, deodorant, soap, shampoo, scrub-like pajamas, and extra blankets. I felt certain I'd be freezing in the night without an extra cover.

The yellow walls pulsed as I placed my horde on the bed and walked back down the hall toward Pembley's office. He'd told me he'd be there in an hour, which told me I'd woken him with my call. Good. Someone else should lose sleep over this, especially if he'd withheld vital data from us.

When Mattea and I entered his office, a wave of regret for my ill-wish washed over me at the sight of the bags under his eyes and his pale skin. I'd seen him once last week during my debriefing, but he didn't look like he'd slept since then.

After we sat, I folded my hands. "Sorry to have dragged you from bed, Pembley."

He nodded and closed his eyes briefly. "You aren't the first this week, and you won't be the last. This case has been running us ragged. We might be on the cusp of finding our quarry, but they keep slipping from our grasp."

"Your quarry? You mean, who's behind the rogue portals? Or the smuggling of this fungus?"

"Both, it seems. They're one and the same. The fungus isn't the only thing they're smuggling, just the most dangerous. We'd had feelers out on a couple of things, but this is the first time they've coalesced into a clear picture. However, we still haven't found the ringleader. All his minions clam up. I wish this worked more like the movies, where a small dose of coercion made them *sing like canaries*."

I gave a rueful laugh. "May the ancestors save us from trite cop clichés. You could always pull the 'good cop, bad cop' farce."

He grimaced. "That never works. You've been watching too much bad telly."

"I watch too much *great* telly, thank you very much. Just not accurate. Still, there must be something we can do. What do the break-ins tell you? There must be a connection, considering they targeted both Mattea and me."

He folded and unfolded his hands several times, cleared his throat, and stood to pace before he answered. We turned around to watch him. As he walked back and forth, he said, "There's a leak within the Agency, which is how they knew about your mission. I've already sent a detail to Sir Algernon's new place, but he missed being targeted. They wouldn't have known about him ahead of time."

Mattea piped up. "Sir Algernon is staying in Toronto?"

He nodded. "We've set him up in a temp flat downtown, but he's only just moved in yesterday. I've discovered this leak may be one of my own team, and I've had the devil of a time investigating it around that possibility."

"How big is your team?"

"I have twenty Agents within my current team, plus five on leave or holiday."

I shook my head. "Damn. That's a lot. And you can't investigate them all yourself. Can other teams help?"

He clenched his jaw and clasped his fingers together. "I called in a few trusted friends to help, but it's still a tricky business. We don't wish to telegraph this knowledge before we have proof, for fear the mole will go to ground. It infuriates me someone of my own would betray me."

"I don't doubt that in the slightest. What can we do to help?"

He grimaced and sighed. "I'm uncertain how you can help. What are your ideas on the matter?"

"Are you more interested in finding your mole or finding the smuggling ringleader?"

He shook his head, utterly defeated. "Anything at this point. I'm flummoxed."

I glanced at Mattea and we both shrugged. "Give us a copy of what you've got so far, and we'll comb through. It's been a long time since I worked as an active investigator, mind you, but fresh eyes may help."

He sank into his seat. "I have few other options at this point. At least no one else is dying. We've synthesised a palliative measure to keep patients alive until the worst of the disease has passed. Now we just have to find whose idiotic ambitions made this fiasco possible."

*****

The next morning, Mattea, Tarren, and I loaded Pembley's flash drive onto the workroom SmartScreen. We talked through each of the details, including the places the rogue travellers had visited, the samples we'd brought back, and the testimonies and backgrounds of the smuggling ring so far. We pored through for hours, trying to find connections, correspondences, coincidences, anything that might help us find the ringleader.

After lunch, we switched to the backgrounds of Pembley's team. We compared the personal details with each of the suspects from the smuggling ring to find any matching data or shared associates.

Tarren stared at me as we went through one of the sample lists. "Wilda, how well did you sleep last night?"

I shrugged. "Not well. The beds in the dorm are about as comfortable as a concrete driveway."

Mattea narrowed her eyes. "You only got out of the hospital yesterday. Didn't doctor tell you to ease back into work?"

Placing my hands on my hips, I glared at each of them. "And?"

Tarren frowned. "You're swaying, Wilda. If you don't go upstairs and grab some rest right now…"

"You'll what?"

"I'll…I'll sit on you."

My laugh possessed a hysterical tinge, but I turned it into a cough. When I got the cough under control, the wave of weakness which washed over me made me collapse into my chair.

Tarren crossed her arms and loomed over me. "Right. Do I need to argue further?"

"Fine, fine. I'll rest. Just don't let me sleep too long, eh?"

From the look my assistants shared, I knew they would, but I no longer cared. I needed their help getting up the stairs and admitted they must be right. I needed my rest and recovery remained elusive. That coma took more out of me than I'd realised. The break-in and conversation with Pembley hadn't helped.

Possibilities swirled in my mind as I tried to grasp the fleeting prize of sleep. Names flitted through my mind, mixing as I matched each one with little to no reason to be matched. I must have drifted away as my world grew black.

I jumped awake when I heard a shout. I bolted upright and searched the room, looking for the cause of alarm. Nothing but rows of slumbering garb surrounded me, but female voices drifted from the workroom below.

Hoping I'd gotten at least an hours' rest, I grumbled as I creaked to my feet and shuffled to the spiral staircase. I descended with care, listening for clues in tone. Had the shout been happy or angry? Alarmed or thrilled? Tarren laughed gleefully, so I guessed they must be happy.

When I opened the door of the workroom, both women leapt and rushed to me. Mattea grabbed my arms and shook me until my neck cracked. "We found her! We found her?"

"Ow! Her, who? Your true love? The Messiah? The lost Goddess of Atlantis?"

Tarren giggled, but modulated her excitement, perhaps out of respect for my ageing bones and coma-tired body. "The smuggler. It must be her! There's no way that could be a coincidence."

I rubbed my eyes and ran my fingers through my hair, making it stick up. "Talk sense. What did you find?"

Mattea glanced at Tarren, who nodded in return. "Tarren found it. Do you remember the woman who came in a few days before Josephus? That prime snob, Lady Xanthippe?"

"Lady Prissy-Pants? Of course, I remember her. Who could forget that stench?"

Tarren beamed. "Exactly! The stench. Now, do you remember the fungus you collected?"

As soon as she said it, I made the connection. Of course! How could I have missed that horrible stink? Rotten cheese, dirty socks, a tinge of gasoline…however you described it, the odour seared my memory.

Mattea and Tarren waited for me to figure it out, practically bouncing in anticipatory glee. "But she acted like such a patent idiot! How could she be the ringleader of such an outfit?"

Mattea clapped like a girl with her first tiara. "Once we requested a sample of the fungus to compare the odour, and agreed they matched, Tarren delved into her background once we figure out the match."

I held up my hands. "Hold on a minute, Speedy Gonzalez…*once we requested*…how long was I asleep?"

They exchanged a guilty glance. Tarren started, "Well, you slept so soundly…"

Mattea finished with, "We knew you needed your rest."

I crossed my arms. "How. Bloody. Long?"

Mattea took a deep breath. "Twelve hours."

"Twelve hours! Christ on a piece of toast!"

Tarren shrugged. "Do you feel better?"

I closed my eyes and prayed for patience. Since the ancestors didn't work that way, I knew prayers would do no good, but it helped me calm my irritation, regardless of other results. When I opened them again, they had both transformed back into gleeful children with tiaras.

Tarren clasped her hands and put them under her chin. "So, I discovered that Lady Prissy-Pants is the CEO of a gourmet food distribution company, The Posh Nosh Emporium, if you can credit that. This didn't jibe with her helplessness when she visited, so I dug deeper. This company, Posh Nosh, is the *only* source of this new gourmet mushroom that's become all the rage in foodie circles."

Mattea picked up the thread. "It's listed as dangerous if not prepared right, and will make someone ill, but not like the illness Josephus got unless they're a traveller. Of course, she doesn't share that tidbit."

I bit my lip in concentration. "But why would she come here, of all places?"

"Tarren surmised she wanted to scope our operations out, looking for ways to improve her own portal. That way she could send more unsuspecting would-be travellers to smuggle the foodstuffs. Dollars to doughnuts this fungus isn't the only proscribed food she's importing from the past, just the deadliest."

Tarren added, "She must pay them with a recreational trip before they can do the final, payoff mission, or else combine the two into one. That's why Josephus was sent to Mali, and McKenzie to Orkney, etc. She wouldn't be telling any of her smugglers about the cellular degeneration."

I nodded, comprehending the scope of her operation. "Which is why she needs more after a few trips. Right, a true heartless bitch. And all of this for a damned *mushroom*, no less. She's killed people. Killed them! Over a culinary delicacy." I paced as I got more and more agitated over the idea of this woman and her machinations. I halted mid-stride. "Have you told Pembley this yet?"

They shook their heads in unison. "We decided he'd listen more readily if you delivered the theory."

"Fair. I'll call him now. But you need to be right next to me. I mean to give you all the credit for this discovery."

Chapter Thirty-Seven

We fell back into our old routine with only a few hiccups and detours. Mattea took to more intensive research into the pre-Columbian period, while I started the paperwork to request permission for her permanent immigration. Tarren proclaimed an interest in learning Mattea's job, so she spent countless sessions with both of us, learning the garbing requirements for different times and locations. We hired on a new receptionist named Jerry. Despite his youth, he seemed qualified to deal with just about anything that came through the door.

He explained at his interview. "I grew up in a rough neighbourhood down in New York City, before the revolution, ma'am. I've learned when to be diplomatic and when to give no ground."

"These aren't meth heads or gang members we're dealing with. Many are members of the aristocracy and must be handled with precise, gentile manners." I didn't mention my own thin layer of sarcasm. He'd learn.

He frowned. "Canada doesn't have an aristocracy. Does it?"

I chuckled. "Not technically, no. However, the vestiges of rank have filtered over from Britain, and have never quite been wiped away. *They* still believe they're aristocracy and expect to be treated as if they retained such status. Do you think you can handle that?"

He nodded eagerly. "Yes, ma'am. My grandmother taught me how to treat all manner of folks properly. She would whip me if she thought I'd forgotten."

With Tarren training Jerry and Mattea training Tarren, several months went by in controlled chaos. Bryonie came by when she came to town, but I daren't discuss seeing her…what, her prior incarnations? Her soul? My mission details must remain confidential. Still, Mattea had formed a lovely friendship with her, and they met for tea whenever Bryonie came to town.

Pembley sent me occasional reports of their investigation, but they remained skimpy, as he only divulged a few facts. Until the trial opened, the case details remained confidential. I hope they nabbed Lady Prissy-Pants in an embarrassing situation. Perhaps while she hosted a posh dinner party, or during a concert. Mortification before their peers would be a worse punishment by far than any fine or penalty.

Even better would be an extended prison sentence. I had to admit, I had no clue what the penalty for smuggling might be. It was on the list of forbidden acts for an Agent, at the risk of severe penalties. Out of curiosity, I looked it up the penalty section of the temporal maxims. $950,000 in fines and up to seven years in prison. A woman of Lady Prissy-Pants' wealth would laugh at the fine, but the prison time might be problematic. I grinned in delighted anticipation.

We'd all be required to testify at the trial. Pembley had already handed us the subpoena with abject apologies, but I told him we'd be thrilled to do what we needed to. Mattea and Tarren had been most eager at the thought of adding their testimony. Even Sir Algernon wanted to assist, though I doubted they'd served him a subpoena. He'd begun his official Agent training and therefore had little time or energy for socialisation. That downtown flat had lasted all of two days. He found a permanent flat in short order and confided in me he felt as if he mooched to stay in such a place.

I smiled at the memory of our last conversation. He'd dropped most of his officious manner, though his word choice remained ponderous. Still, it had been rather charming when he declared his infatuation with Toronto and his intention to stay and join the Agency. The Met in London had been rather miffed at his sudden resignation. They had even sent an officer to retrieve their errant man, but he fended off the retrieval.

When had I last spoken to him? It must have been a month ago. Time moved strangely for me since the mission. Days sometimes slipped together or disappeared. My panic attacks came more frequently. My doctor assured me such things could be common side effects of being comatose for so long, and they may clear up. It may also continue to happen. I had always been meticulous in keeping a calendar for future appointments, but now I added notes of what happened each day, so I might refer to them later, almost a bullet point diary.

I sipped my sixth coffee as I added my notes for today. It had been slow, but we had one Agent come in around noon for an eleventh century Kiev outfitting, as well as the final fitting for a tourist heading to eighteenth century South Africa. As I'd already lectured him when he came in the first time about the volatile situation, I forbade to warn him again. He looked determined and eager for his holiday. I finished our alterations and wished him well. I hoped I'd see him again, as he'd been polite.

The door opened just as I finished his entry. I glanced through the door to see Jerry questioning someone, but I had the wrong angle. Then he stepped to one side to pull out his identification, and I recognised Pembley.

He never came to the shop, but always summoned us to his office. I hastened out with a glance to Mattea and Tarren at their workbench. They put down the pre-Renaissance ruffles and stood to stand in the doorway.

"Pembley? What's wrong?"

He turned, his eyes widening. "Oh, good. You're here. Thank you, young man." He nodded at Jerry. "Is there a place we might speak in private?"

"With me, or with us?" I nodded back toward Tarren and Mattea.

"Us is preferable, as horrible as that grammar sounds."

I chuckled and led us to the workroom, closing the door behind me. "Jerry, if we're still closeted by five, lock up and head home."

"Yes, ma'am."

Rolling my eyes at him, I said, "Please, stop calling me ma'am."

He gave me a wicked grin. "Of course, ma'am."

I shut the door with a little more force than necessary. "What's wrong, Pembley? You never come here."

"I felt the need to be urgent and didn't trust a subordinate or the phone. They've moved the trial date to tomorrow morning."

Mattea gasped. "Tomorrow? The trial wasn't set for another three weeks, is it?"

"True. But we've received intelligence that an attempt might be made to suborn the guards at the prison where Lady Xanthippe has recently been…convinced to enjoy our hospitality."

I narrowed my eyes. "Have you been speaking with Sir Algernon? You used to be more straightforward in your speech."

He dropped his gaze to the floor. "I admit I've conversed with him rather often. He has some interesting stories from London."

"Great. That's just what we need. Two Agents with more words than sense."

He shook his head. "Don't distract me. Will the three of you be ready to testify? They may not call you tomorrow, but the trial will start. It should be sometime this week, at least."

I glanced at both the other women, and they nodded in unison.

"We are. But I still don't understand why you didn't just call with this."

"There's another part. I need you all in the dorms tonight."

I groaned. "My back doesn't like that suggestion."

"It's not a suggestion. The same parties who seek to engineer the accused's escape may try to break into your flats again."

I crossed my arms. "Not good enough. They've not bothered us all these months."

He glanced up at the ceiling. "I may not have told you the extent of the security we've placed on all three of your flats. However, I've stretched my squad too thin tonight. Remember that mole? We need to ensure your safety."

"You *what?*"

He refused to meet my eyes. "The added security was necessary."

"How *dare* you not tell me about such measures!"

His jaw clenched several times before he answered. "I didn't dare risk the mole discovering the other guards, Wilda! The few I trusted utterly watched your place and Mattea's. Necessary precautions."

Mattea cut in. "Isn't this all like 'guarding the barn after the horse escaped?'"

Exhaustion rushed over me, and my resistance faded. I waved Mattea's question aside. "Fine. Let me get Dinah back to the vet for boarding. She's barely forgiven me for the last time."

Tarren pulled out her mobile. "I'll let Ray know."

When I glanced at Mattea, she pursed her lips. "I have no one to tell. Can I at least pack a bag?"

Pembley nodded. "I'll have officers escort each of you to your homes for an overnight bag and to make whatever arrangements you need. Also, bring anything you'll need for court tomorrow."

Chapter Thirty-Eight

"All rise"

The shuffle of feet and bodies to stand drowned out the tension in the courtroom. Lady Prissy-Pants still hadn't arrived, but all four of her counsel had. The team had designer suits and chiselled features. Had she chosen them from a modelling agency? Bloody Hell and an order of Timbits. This would be a bloody circus, wouldn't it?

I glanced at the royal seal and a painting of Queen Elizabeth II behind the bench as the judge, an elderly woman with iron-grey hair in a black robe, white collar and red sash, walked in and sat behind the bench. Her podium nameplate read Ruth M. Wells.

"This Ontario Superior Court of Justice is now in session. You may be seated."

A full jury sat to the right, which rather surprised me. Not only because of the changed trial date, but because a jury usually only sat on the most critical of criminal cases, and then only by request of the accused. Lady Prissy-Pants would in no way consider normal, everyday people from a jury to be amongst her *peers*.

The doors opened behind us. Despite the trial being considered *in camera* and thus, not open to the public, the courtroom looked packed with people associated with the case. I wondered how many of the attendees bore relation to travellers killed from the disease.

Lady Xanthippe Thundergrast-Hickenbotham strode into the room as if she hosted a Parisian soirée. She surveyed those assembled with pompous disdain before giving a bare incline of her head to the bench, rather than the required bow. Instead of her prior pink and purple ensemble, today she wore white and silver. Seriously, silver. Lace frothed from every hem, like an enormous virginal sacrifice. I'm certain her allusion fooled no one.

Perhaps she fooled herself. It might well be, in her addled world of narcissistic superiority, she considered herself a true royal in medieval times, subject to no one for her actions. I hoped this trial would horribly disabuse her of this notion. In fact, such a comeuppance would be delicious. I looked forward to the reckoning.

She sat next to her counsel team, refusing to acknowledge any of them. Instead, she watched the judge. The judge looked as if she smelled something nasty.

As the notion struck me, so did the stink. Lady Prissy-Pants still stunk of that damned fungus. She must eat the stuff every day from her odour. It oozed through her pores like garlic on a hot day. The people assembled began polite coughs and several produced handkerchiefs and serviettes from purses and pockets. A brief conference between the judge and her clerk resulted in several windows being opened. I breathed in the fresh air with relief, a relief echoed by the rest of the attendees.

I laughed to myself. She must not notice her own body odour, and none of her associates either cared enough or were too frightened to tell her. The odour itself gave evidence of her complicity in the proscribed substance. This should work in the crown's favour. This also meant we must endure the funk for hours, if not days.

I hoped they called my witness statement early in the proceedings. When I glanced at Mattea and Tarren, their expressions showed own thoughts must have marched with mine.

The clerk stood. "The first matter to present is The crown against Lady Xanthippe Thundergrast-Hickenbotham. Will the accused please stand?"

With a great deal of fluttering and shuffling of her lace petticoats, she complied. The haughty expression on her face suggested she stood in front of her own court as queen. Her team stood beside her as the clerk of the court rose, shuffling his papers. The accused didn't even blink as he read off her charges. She might have been waiting for her servant to finish pouring the wine, for all the mind she paid. Six counts of accessory to smuggling illegal substances, one count of operation of a rogue portal, and seventy-two counts of involuntary manslaughter as a result of a crime.

"Defence, are you ready to proceed? How do you plea?"

She stood, not even glancing at the judge. She held her nose so high, I worried for the dust on the ceiling. "Not guilty, Your Honour."

I tuned out as the Crown presented their evidence and studied Lady Prissy-Pants. She held herself straight, refusing to meet anyone's eye. I wondered what went on within her mind at this moment. Did she consider herself innocent? Surely not. She must be cognizant of the counts against her. In fact, the Crown had listed them, one by one.

They called the first witness to the stand. I didn't recognise the man, but he wore an Ontario Provisional Police uniform. He attested to the discovery and confiscation of the rogue portal, which police had discovered a few doors down from my shop on King Street. They'd found it above a self- serve laundry. I couldn't even imagine Lady Prissy-Pants entering a laundry for any reason, even to enter her own illegal time travel portal.

Next came two Temporal Agents who had attempted to interview Josephus when I'd brought him to the hospital. He'd gained consciousness for just a few moments before dying. He'd been able to describe the portal's location.

"I call the next witness, Temporal Agent Wilda Firestone. Please take the stand."

My knees wobbled as I stood and walked to the wooden dock. The clerk offered the Bible, but I asked for eagle feathers instead. I scowled as he gauged my skin tone and nodded. I fumed that he believed I must be a certain darkness to be granted such a request. However, I put my hands on the feathers and swore my oath anyhow. Now wasn't the time to make a stand.

"Agent Firestone, can you please recount your recollection of the day the accused came to your shop?"

Doing my best to stick to the facts and not my judgement, opinion, or feelings upon any of those facts, I spoke in short, precise sentences. "The defendant came in. She requested a fitting. She stank to high heaven."

"I beg your pardon, Agent Firestone. Would you repeat that final point?"

"Her odour was intense and most unpleasant, much the same as it is today, sir."

The jury gave a muted laugh and Lady Prissy-Pants pursed her lips. She shifted, and for a moment, she looked as if she might stand to defend her aroma, but I remained disappointed. So far.

"And had you ever encountered such a singular odour before?"

"Not before. Afterward."

Court counsel raised his eyebrows. "Can you describe where you encountered this odour later?"

Defence counsel stood. "Objection. Assumes facts not found in evidence."

Judge Wells said, "Overruled. Jury, please keep in mind this is the witness' opinion on the similarity of odours. If the witness would continue?"

"When I travelled to twelfth century Orkney on a Temporal mission, I obtained samples of a fungus. It had the same horrible odour."

Crown counsel addressed the judge. "If it please the court, the Crown presents exhibit C, a sample of said fungus from Agent Firestone's mission."

The judge asked to examine exhibit C. She urged the jury to do the same. The bailiff helped me step down, while Mattea and Tarren took the stand, corroborating my recounting of that day.

State counsel brought other evidence to bear, including financial records from local restaurants. I glanced around and noticed more people had entered during the proceedings. I caught Nami's eye, and we shared a smile. Of course! She'd had the noxious stuff on her menu.

The Crown didn't conclude their case that day. When we recessed until tomorrow and we exited the courthouse, I took a deep, sweet breath of clean air. Mattea, Tarren, and Nami did the same. We all exchanged glances and burst out laughing.

To this day, I'm not certain what we'd found so hilarious. Perhaps the shared experience of watching Lady Prissy-Pants' noose grow tighter and tighter, all the while knowing not one person in that courtroom could stand to be in the same room as her stench.

Tarren shook her head. "You would think someone, anyone, would have told her how much she stank. Does she have no friends at all?"

I chuckled. "I tried to, the day we visited, don't you remember? And no, I'm sure she has no friends. She'd probably walk into public with a chunk of toilet paper on her shoe and no one would say a thing, I'm certain. She doesn't precisely endear herself to anyone. I'm certain she frightens her staff."

Chapter Thirty-Nine

The court gave us all the option of returning the next day for trial but didn't require us to stay in the courtroom. However, we needed to be nearby in case they called us back for follow-up questions. We spent a cozy night at our flats and returned the next day.

To save our olfactory sensibilities, Mattea, Tarren, and I settled into the Timmie's across the street for the day, while I had my mobile in case counsel called.

I didn't frequent Jarvis Street, but the people-watching proved to be entertaining. When several characters went by with clothing which we could only charitably term "colourful," I turned to Mattea. "Have you heard from the Agency yet?"

She shook her head. "I sent in my second appeal last week. The first application and then the first appeal took a month each time, so I won't hear until at least then."

Tarren raised her coffee. "Third time's the charm? If they grant your immigration request, when would you go?"

Nami piped up. "Fun fact. Immigration to from Old America to Canada increased twenty times the normal rate as the Second Civil War ramped up. By the time the states had seceded from the United States, the population of Canada had almost doubled."

I raised my coffee cup to her in a toast for the trivia and returned my attention to my assistant.

Mattea didn't answer at first. Instead, she stared at her maple doughnut and picked a few crumbs from her plate. She ate those in silence before looking up. "As soon as I can get out of my lease, I think. I don't own much stuff. I'd always lived pretty sparsely. Dad was in the military, so I didn't keep stuff. We didn't always have enough room in our new digs when we moved."

I pressed my lips together. "That habit might help a great deal for adapting to the past. Conversely, you also have to save everything you come across in case it's useful. No corner shops, and all that."

"I'm aware."

Her pensive mood brought the conversation to a halt. I regretted bringing up the subject but couldn't think of how to shift things to a more pleasant subject. The mobile saved me with a buzz.

"Hello? Yes, definitely. We'll come now."

As I hung up, Mattea asked, "Do they need us for more questions?"

I shook my head. "They are ready to announce a verdict. He asked if we wanted to be present.

With a wrinkled nose, Tarren said, "I don't want to enter that room again."

I patted her arm as I tossed my empty cup. "It'll be worth it."

Mattea popped the last bite of doughnut in her mouth. Around the pastry, she muttered, "You hope. And I hope I keep that maple doughnut down when I walk in that room."

The building front looked like a cheese grater, with lots of little, long rectangular windows. When I entered, the faint whiff of Lady Prissy-Pants' odour lingered. I'm sorry to say I could follow my nose to the proper courtroom, even if I hadn't remembered its location from the day before.

When we entered, the malaise smacked me in the face afresh. A look at the accused showed she still believed in her complete vindication. A glance at the jury told me she should shake in her boots. Their expressions appeared either grim or angry.

We took our seats as three more people shuffled in behind us. The jury foreman stood, and Judge Wells asked her, "Has the jury reached their verdict?"

"We have, Your Honour. We find the defendant guilty on the charges—" the uproar from Lady Prissy-Pants drowned out the rest of her words.

The accused shot up and screamed, "Ridiculous! You have no right to pass judgement upon me, you peons! You have no standing here! Can't you see this is a trick? Someone has contrived this evidence. The whole case has been concocted!"

The judge stood, towering over everyone from her dais, though I'm certain she stood no taller than I. "Madame! You will take your seat and moderate your tone!"

Lady Prissy-Pants grew shriller. "I will do no such thing!"

The judge pursed her lips and nodded to the guards. I noted with approval their bulk and unsmiling faces. "If you do not remain silent through the reading of the verdict, I shall find you in contempt of this court and have you bodily removed."

"And you! You are no proper judge. I refuse to—"

The guards chose this moment to grab each of her arms, which set her to squawking in a most undignified manner. She screeched and screamed, pulling in desperation on her captors. All dignity abandoned, she rocked and cried as they pulled her into a side door.

When the door slammed closed, the relief from both her body odour and her raucous cries sent a wave of sighs across the assembly.

Judge Wells nodded to the jury forewoman. "Please continue."

I didn't need to listen to the rest. The jury had convicted her on every single account. She'd be punished for her crimes and more, due to her outburst. I felt so vindicated, so joyful, I almost felt like Riverdancing.

Still, as she was led away, still protesting her innocence, a thought niggled at my conscience. What if she *had* been framed?

By mutual consent, we three escaped. While the stench had somewhat reduced when the guilty party left the room, it lingered and sank into our olfactory cavities with a disturbing effectiveness.

Damnit, now my thoughts had grown as convoluted as Sir Algernon's.

We returned to the shop, and each took a shower. I also threw our clothing into the shop wash. Until they finished decontamination, we wore bits of the less outlandish garb from our recent century racks. Mattea looked fantastic in full hippie tie-dye. Tarren had chosen something from nineteenth century San Francisco. My choice became more difficult due to my short stature but found a medieval Irish tunic that didn't drag too long on the floor.

When Pembley arrived, with a bottle of champagne of all things, he assessed each of us with concern. "Is there a fancy dress party invitation I didn't receive? Or have you each actually lost your collective minds?"

"We didn't wish to wear that stink one moment longer than necessary. I see you changed your own clothing. You had your uniform on in the courtroom."

"Ah, yes, well, that's true. I can sympathise. I have word from Sir Algernon, by the by. He'll finish his first stage of training soon."

I fetched mugs from the kitchenette cabinet. They weren't champagne flutes, but they'd do. "Oh? He finished rather quickly. Usually, it takes a full year."

He screwed his eyes shut as he tried to pop the cork. "Usually, we get rank amateurs. He'd already been a trained and well-experienced police detective before he applied. Many of the procedures were already familiar to him."

"Fair. Oh, did you ever find your mole?"

He shook his head, wiggling the cork when his first attempt failed. "Not yet. I want to find him but not let him realise I've found him. It could be useful to have a known mole."

I narrowed my eyes at the champagne bottle. "Mattea, will you help him with that? I don't want him shooting out a window."

She took the bottle from his strained grip, raised her eyebrows as she gently unscrewed the top. It gave a faint "pop" and the bottle outgassed before she poured us each a measure. "So, what's his next step?"

He looked pained, but that might relate to his inability to operate a champagne bottle, the fact that Mattea had just upstaged him in that area, or his coming words. "He needs to go on a training mission with an experienced agent."

Pembley stared at me with an unreadable expression as I digested his words around my sip of champagne. "Oh. Oh! Oh, no. Absolutely not. *Nope, never, nyet, nein, ní bheidh.*"

"He's already requested to work with you, Wilda. You understand his capabilities and his weaknesses. He—"

I put my mug down and Mattea filled it again, this time to the top. "I'd murder him in his sleep within three days, Pembley! Do you want an Agent, or a corpse? No."

He raised an eyebrow. "Didn't you say you'd always wanted to visit eastern France in the 1850s? Now's your chance."

I drank down the entire mug and slammed it onto the table. Mattea refilled it with a grin. "Eastern France? You're sending me to meet my great-great-grandfather?" For a moment, my heart leapt at the idea until practicalities overwhelmed the hope. "Wait, when did I even say I wanted to become a full Agent again? I don't remember ever saying such a thing to you."

"It's in Mattea's report."

I glared at my assistant, who grinned back in all innocence. I growled in response. "That was just hyperbole to derail our argument, and you know it."

Mattea laughed, throwing her head back. "Tell me it didn't have one kernel of truth. Tell me you didn't enjoy yourself, despite the privation, cold, weird food, and annoying strictures."

I pressed my lips together, unable to deny it. I shot an angry look at Pembley, Mattea, and for good measure, Tarren, though she'd been silently sipping her champagne through all this.

"What? I didn't say a thing! Though, to be fair, I think they're right. You never seemed so alive as when you returned from each mission."

I stood and paced around in angry circles. "What the Hell have I been doing for twenty years, shuffling around like a zombie? This is my life's work. *This* is my passion. *This* is my purpose. I'm a fifty-five bloody year-old female. What the Hell business do I have gallivanting around all of history on missions?"

Mattea's quiet words stopped me mid-stride. "You were happier in the past."

I turned on her. "What the Hell do you know about happiness? You're barely a grown woman yourself."

To my surprise, she fired back. "I know what happiness is. I know what love is. I know how much it hurts to know your love is long dead and buried. I understand why you refuse to let yourself love life again, but you can do it! I know you can.

"I always dreamt I'd love travelling to the past. I've learned otherwise. Unless there's a very strong reason for me to do so, I'll never do it again. But I *have* a reason, and that reason is Wula'mbes. Would you deny me my happiness?"

Taken aback, I took a step away from her onslaught. "Of course not. You know I've been working on your immigration paperwork. I want you to find your happiness."

Mattea stepped forward, not allowing me any space for comfort. "Then why would you deny yourself that same happiness?"

The silence grew heavy as I weighed her words. Did I deny myself happiness? I had my job, my friends, my flat, and my cat. What more could a retirement-age woman want in life? The flash of Sir Algernon's laughing face flickered in my mind, and I shook my head. Bloody ridiculous. I was no young woman, looking for romance and adventure. That had been me thirty-five years ago, not now. Never now.

I sat down and drank the once-again filled mug of champagne. How big had that bottle been? My head swam and my throat buzzed with bubbles.

Mattea didn't let me consider long. "You must promise me, Wilda, to consider Pembley's offer. Consider your direction in life, or you will live forever with regret. Whether or not I get my immigration, I will not stay here. I can't, not after all this. But you need to leave, too. You need to pursue a dream."

I didn't want to admit she might be right. I glanced at Tarren, who obviously agreed with Mattea. Pembley clutched his champagne mug as if it were a life vest.

"Fine. I'll consider it. Just consider it. No promises, mind you, but I'll do some research. Now, can we drop the subject?"

Pembley let out his breath while Tarren and Mattea shared a high-five. I glared at them for their premature celebration and gave one more order. "I'll tell you this, though. Whoever takes over this shop had best keep my quality up. I won't be sent on a mission in substandard garb."

Ah, crap. What would I do with Dinah?

Epilogue

I glared at the newly trained Agent with my arms crossed, waiting for him to answer my question. "Well?"

Sir Algernon, despite his height, looked sheepish. "I'm afraid you are absolutely correct. I did indeed make that suggestion to the authorities, my good lady."

"What on my ancestor's good green earth made you believe I would be amenable to being your training partner?"

He peeked up from under his brown-and-silver curls. "I rather thought since we'd already worked together so successfully, an additional mission with me would be to your advantage and pleasure, actually. Certainly, we'd already learned each other's quirks and preferences."

"I could do without the quirk of getting stuck in a bog."

He dropped his gaze again and didn't answer. Instead, he clasped his hands and sighed.

Damnit. He looked like a puppy who knew he'd done wrong to eviscerate my favorite couch, yet knew I'd forgive his adorable self. I refused to give in to such emotional blackmail. Still, I had my orders from Pembley.

"Very well. I will take you on one, and only one, training mission. However, there are rules."

He glanced up, eagerness apparent in his eyes.

"First, you will listen to my commands at all times. Despite your height and gender, I am the Agent in charge. I have far more experience than you in every way, and my judgement is far superior to yours. Despite being a trained police detective, you are not a full Agent. I am.

"Second, you are not to call me any diminutive, insulting, patriarchal, condescending nicknames, such as *my dear*, *my lady*, and certainly never *my girl*. I am not your anything. I am my own woman and will be until the day I die.

"Third, the first time you break either of these rules, we will immediately return to the present time, and you will be dismissed.

"Do you understand the rules in which we will be operating on this one and only Mission together, Sir Algernon?"

He nodded, his eyes once again on his feet. "I understand, my d… Agent Firestone."

I rolled my eyes. "Wilda. You may call me Wilda. Until you give me reason to revoke that particular privilege."

His answering grin was bright enough to illuminate the night.

* * *

Her mission to the past is in ruins. Her future's in deadly peril. Can this resourceful spitfire stop the present from going sideways?

Can Wilda fix this mess before it's off with her head?

Buy *Threads of Time* to unwind
a lethal conspiracy today!

books2read.com/Threads-Of-Time

Thank You!

Thank you so much for enjoying Time Tourist Outfitters, Ltd. If you've enjoyed the story, please consider **leaving a review** to help others discover Wilda's and Mattea's adventures!

If you would like to get updates, sneak previews, sales, and FREE STUFF, please sign up for my newsletter.
www.greendragonartist.com

Other Books by This Author

See all the books available through
Green Dragon Publishing at
http://www.greendragonartist.com/books

and fielded several of my questions, as did my husband. There are several tribes from the region, all under the Wabanaki group, such as the Maliseet, Mi'kmaq, Penobscot, and Passamaquoddy.

The indigenous people of these regions would typically have summer and winter homes, going where the most abundant sources were for food and game during the warm months, and sheltering in safer places during the cold ones. Many of the foods I listed, such as beaver tail, are considered a delicacy. They used birch bark for many projects, including cups, pouches, and canoes. Their homes were a variety of the tipi so iconic in many popular stereotypes, a conical structure built with branches and clad with fabric or hides.

Orkney:

The Orkney Isles of Scotland were under Norse occupation and rule since the late 8th century CE, and by the time Wilda and Mattea arrived, they were under the power of Earl Paul Haakonsson. He held the Orkney Earldom jointly with Harald Haakonsson. His sister, Frakkok, tried to murder him with a poisoned shirt, a la Medea, but she ended up killing Harald instead in 1127. Paul lost his spot when Rognvald Kali Kolsson invaded in the dark of the night.

The daily life of such places is not so different from any of the Nordic countries at that time. And they mistook Wilda for a völva, a seeress from Norse Mythology. She leans into this and uses her own knowledge of the immediate future to cement her status, to her detriment.

Historical Note

Dear Readers:

While the modern aspects of this story are based in Toronto, Ontario, Canada, and I used true geography and details as much as I could, the three historical periods visited by this story, as well as the flashback to China, are based on many historical facts.

Mali:

The court of Mansa Musa was during the early 14th century in the Mali Empire. The contemporary documentation of this place and time are limited, and mostly from traveler's accounts. The wealth of the kingdom was based on gold, so the ownership of said substance was restricted to the Musa. However, many things were paid for with cowrie shells or gold dust.

Local food, culture, and court etiquette had some basis in reality, and some created details where I could find no reference. However, if I named a food, it was part of the history. The game of Mancala is one such reference, which I found fascinating as I recall playing it as a child with my family. Mansa Musa did create his city as a center of learning, with the University of Sankore constructed during his reign.

Wolostiqi'ik:

I had a home-game advantage in researching the pre-Columbian cultures of Maine, as my husband's family is part of the Wolostiqi'ik people, also known as the Maliseet. My father-in-law, Jeffrey Nicholas, provided me with a lot of good information, some out-of-print books by local scholars,

About the Author

Christy Nicholas writes under several pen names, including Rowan Dillon, C.N. Jackson, and Emeline Rhys. She's an author, artist, and accountant. After she failed to become an airline pilot, she quit her ceaseless pursuit of careers that begin with the letter 'A' and decided to concentrate on her writing. Since she has Project Completion Compulsion, she is one of the few authors with no unfinished novels.

Christy has her hands in many crafts, including digital art, beaded jewelry, writing, and photography. In real life, she's a CPA, but having grown up with art all around her (her mother, grandmother, and great-grandmother are/were all artists), it sort of infected her, as it were.

She wants to expose the incredible beauty in this world, hidden beneath the everyday grime of familiarity and habit, and share it with others. She uses characters out of time and places infused with magic and myth, writing magical realism stories in both historical fantasy and time travel flavors.

Combine this love of beauty with a bit of financial sense and you get an art business. She does local art and craft shows, as well as sending her art to various science fiction conventions throughout the country and abroad.

Social Media Links:
Blog: www.GreenDragonArtist.net
Website: www.GreenDragonArtist.com
Facebook: www.facebook.com/greendragonauthor
Instagram: www.instagram.com/greendragonartist9
TikTok: www.tiktok.com/@greendragonauthor